THE FEAR
THAT DIVIDES US

THE DEVILS DUST
book three

Wendy -
love Baby ♡ M.N. FORGY

M.N. FORGY

This book is for all of those who have been tormented by pain.

Pain that keeps you from seeing a good thing

when it was standing right in front of you,

from seeking a path you so desperately want.

A pain that can come in many forms, both good and bad.

There is a playful spank, and there is one to mean harm.

There are words of laughter and some that are meant to judge

you. Don't let the worst keep you hostage from living.

Don't fear the pain; fear the message behind it.

six years earlier

essica

L OOKING IN THE MIRROR THIS MORNING, I WINCE AT THE ghastly sight of my face. The side of my cheek is completely black and blue, and my head hums with constant pain. A token for my lack of respect toward Travis last night. This is exactly why I can't go back to work anytime soon, no matter how much I miss being a doctor.

"I'm so stupid," I mutter, grabbing a pair of pants and shirt to slip on. My body aches, and my wrist screams with pain from being shackled. My core is raw. I was left bleeding from the relentless abuse Travis delivered last night. I am a wreck, a fucking wreck. He's going to kill me one day, physically and mentally, of that I am sure.

Travis came home last night, *drunk,* reeking of booze and expensive perfume. The hospital had another event and I am sure he had some nurse shacked up in the coat closet. But apparently, she couldn't satisfy him, who could with his sadistic desires. He ended up coming home to me for another round.

I was asleep in bed as he slid his hand into my hair, pulling it harshly to wake me up.

"Time to go down stairs," he breathed in to my hair, his teeth clenched in anger. That is where he always takes me to belittle me, the basement. His anger is nothing new, just my presence alone angers him. The look of disgust as he eye fucks me across the room when he's home from work is enough to make me shutter.

"Travis, I just got Addie to sleep, please not now," I whispered as he continued tugging my hair with a painfully strong grip. I knew it was stupid to resist, to defy him when he was in such a state; but for some reason last night, I just had enough of it. I live day-after-day in utter fear; scared I'm going to say or do the wrong thing in front of Travis.

"Who do you think you're talking to?" he gnashed, pulling my head back so hard it brought an instant headache. I knew I was going to pay for my outburst, but it felt good to defy him. It gave me a sense of hope, of control, which I wasn't allowed either. Hope was for those who were not owned, and control was for the strong. Travis had said those words to me countless times, each time breaking my soul into nothing but broken possibilities.

He stood up on his knees, pulling me along the bed by my hair as I tried not to scream. I didn't want to wake Addie, but I couldn't help it. Between the fear slamming against my chest, and the pain radiating from my head, I couldn't hold it in. I screamed and thrashed against the mattress as he pulled me off the bed like an old blanket, my feet striking the heated floors as I was pulled off completely.

"I think you need a reminder of who your master is!" he yelled, walking out of the room, still dragging me along behind him.

The back of my ankles thrashed against each step as he rushed down the stairs into the basement, the room slowly illuminating brightness as he turned on the lights.

He let go of my hair, relief flooding my scalp, but I couldn't gain balance quick enough, causing my palms to slam into the unforgiving concrete as I fell face first to the ground.

"Travis, please," I begged. I don't know why I begged; it did no good. In fact, it fueled the bastard on. My ounce of bravery was reckless. What was I thinking? I knew better.

I looked up, my vision blurry from the amount of tears rising in my eyes. I blinked them away, trying to stand, but before I could lift my leg, a hand drilled into the side of my head, causing me to fly backwards, making my head smack into the wall.

I cried out as my head rang, the sounds around me fading. With the collar being locked into place around my neck, my body instantly went into survival mode. Which was doing whatever Travis wanted from me without hassle. I was a slave in that collar, but at least I would live to see another day.

"Get in position," Travis demanded, his voice echoing in my head. I slowly stood, my legs wobbly as I walked over to the big bed covered in silver sheets. Sheets I had to wash with bleach plenty of times to remove the stench of despair and torture. Kneeling by the end of the bed, I waited for my next order, tears streaming down my face so fast my cheeks were raw.

Travis clutched my hair, pulling back harshly, making me look upward into his menacing blue eyes, blue eyes that had a sick way of penetrating what was left of my psyche. Which wasn't much. The only thing that was still there was fierce love for my daughter. I had to keep strong for her sake. It was my job to keep her safe and if I broke to the point of no return, she would be left for the wolves.

Many would call me crazy if I told them I loved this man not so long ago, was head over heels with him. We shared what every new couple felt, butterflies when we first met, the nights where we did nothing but lay in bed and talked about mindless crap, the feeding each other bullshit. It was all a façade though, leading to me being collared and slaved at the foot of an abusive husband. Like all crystal-clear skies, eventually a storm rolls through, darkening your perfect view of life. It's inevitable. With every hit of the whip, every grip to the throat, I wonder where I went wrong, but when the pain resides, and the air fills my lungs, I am reminded of where I messed up: I fell in love with a monster.

Travis leaned in and slid his tongue along my cheek, taking in my sorrow.

"Your sadness lets me know you know you're aware of your place. You are here to serve me, and deliver whatever I ask of you, my wife." He seethes the last part, making me clench my eyes shut. I tried to drown his words out, build a barrier.

"Do you understand?" he questioned. I nodded as a whimper spilled from my throat. "Say it," he gritted out, gripping my chin harshly, his fingers bruising the skin.

"Yes, Master," I spat, trying to pull from his hold. My tone takes me by surprise. I had no idea what had gotten into me.

"I see someone has attitude tonight. That's okay. I know just what you need." He grabbed me by the collar and lifted me, throwing me onto the bed face down. My legs twitched with the urge to run to the other side of the bed, but the collar, snug around my neck, reminded me of the punishment I would face for disobeying.

Straddling my body, slamming my wrists into the hard cuffs, pushing my head into the mattress hard enough to lock my collar into place, I was convinced I would suffocate. That finally the nightmare may truly end.

The bathroom door swings open, breaking my flashback of last night.

"You look like shit. Put some makeup on or something," Travis insults.

"I don't have any more makeup. I had to use what was left of it the last time you used me as a punching bag," I clip, slamming drawers shut. I wince from my outburst, knowing it won't go overlooked.

"What'd you say to me?" Travis grips my face harshly, making me instantly regret my choice of words. But why refrain from how I really feel about the bastard? Today won't be any worse than tomorrow; he'll still treat me like garbage.

"I said I fucking hate you," I snarl, and spit in his face. Travis closes his eyes as he wipes his face.

"You think you're something mighty, don't you?" He rears his hand back and slaps me in the mouth, busting my lip wide open.

I fall against the bathroom counter, my breathing becoming harsh from the amount of pain my body is suffering.

"Jessica, I can tell I have not been very attentive to you in the basement. I have been lacking on your punishment, in return making you suffer, causing you to act out. I will deliver the pain you so desperately crave tonight, and you can count on that, my darling *wife*," he grates out, pushing my head into the counter harshly. Tears fill my eyes. I'm exhausted, just plain fucking exhausted of this. I can't take any more of this shit.

"NO!" Addie yells, running into the bathroom. My heart stammers as I hear Addie, immediately scared for her safety, and terrified of her seeing me like this.

Addie attacks Travis's leg, yelling at him, scratching at him to let me go. I hear Travis exhale with anger as he pushes her off, making her stumble and fall to the floor.

Addie instantly starts crying.

"I don't have time for this shit. I have to go to work," Travis sneers, letting go of me and leaving the bathroom. I quickly fall to the floor and go to Addie, rocking her in my lap. I cup her cheeks and kiss all over her, noticing she landed on her face when she fell.

"Shit," I whisper, hugging her tightly to my chest.

I can't do this anymore. It was one thing when it was just me, but I can feel him becoming hostile toward Addie; it's getting worse. The way he sneers at her, eyes her with distaste from the corner of his eye when she's around him; it's a time bomb ready to detonate at any moment. I have to get out of here, but I have to be smart about it. Just thinking about running makes my heart accelerate at a dangerous rate. The last time I ran, he almost killed me. I shake my head; I can't think like that. I have to try. I have to try to get away. For my daughter. That means no calling my mother, no taking credit cards. I lift Addie up and go into the bedroom, open the safe, and take all the cash. Grabbing my purse from the counter, I run toward my car barefoot as quickly as I can, praying none of the house workers see us.

"Go bye bye?" Addie asks me.

"Yes, baby, we are going to go far, far away. Where daddy can't hurt us anymore, where we don't have to be afraid," I whisper, locking her into her car seat. Tears spill from my eyes as I think of taking Addie from her father, but he's not a father to her. He's not a husband either. He's just the warden to a fucked-up life that he's imprisoned us both in. I climb in behind the wheel, my hands shaking with adrenaline. What if he catches me again? What if he follows me? I shake my head; start the ignition, and just drive. Where? I have no idea, but I will keep driving, to the point we can't drive any further. Hopefully by then, I will have a plan.

Bobby

AS **I** TAKE A SIP OF WHAT'S LEFT OF MY BEER, MY EYES CATCH Babs coming through the kitchen over the top of the bottle. Her red hair is sticking to her face from the summer's heat, and she's mumbling about something. I set the empty bottle on the counter and watch her put up glasses and fill the ice bin. It's quiet here. Too quiet. Nights in the clubhouse are usually filled with easy women and drugs. Well, somewhat easy. Seeing as I'm still a prospect, I don't get near the amount of ass the patched-in brothers do, but I do all right. I peel the label from my beer and fold it in on itself out of boredom.

Old Guy crashes through the club's front doors, catching everyone's attention.

"Where's Bull?" Old Guy asks, his voice frantic.

I shrug, not sure.

"I think he's in his room. You want me to grab him?" Shadow asks, sitting next to me. I look over my shoulder at Shadow and grin. Ever since we became prospects, he's been kissing ass. I can't help but make fun of him, and I can get away with it because I knew him way before the club.

"Yeah. Hurry up," Old Guy demands. He runs his hands along the sides of his head, smoothing back the long hair that's escaped from its ponytail.

I slide off my bar stool and toss my bottle in the trash. I'm curious as to what has Old Guy in such a state. Bull comes out of his room, buckling his belt.

"This better be good, goddamn it," Bull mutters as he makes his way toward the front door.

Before we make it to the door, Old Guy comes in carrying a woman. She's curled up against his chest making it hard to see whether I know her or not. She has blonde hair, stained with blood in some spots, and clothes that look like they haven't been washed in days.

"What the fuck?" Shadow whispers with disbelief. My eyes widen, shocked at the state the woman is in.

"Who is she?" I ask.

"Not sure. She pulled up in a nice car and kept asking to talk to whoever was in charge about wanting to make a deal, before collapsing to the ground," Old Guy informs.

"A deal?" Bull asks. He walks up to the woman and brushes the hair from her face. "Someone did a number on her."

"There's more," Old Guy shifts his feet and looks downward. Movement catches my eyes. I look down to find a child clinging to Old Guy's legs.

"Fuck me," escapes from my mouth in shock. A little kid with long, blonde hair and red cheeks hugs onto Old Guy like her life depends on it. I notice her pink dress, and kneel to the little girl's height.

"Hi there, sweetie, is this your momma?" I ask, in a soft voice. I notice her left cheek is a little redder than her left, making me wonder if she fell down, or ran into something. Her face is stained from tears, and she has snot running down to her lips. She blinks her eyes a couple of times, as her bottom lip pouts. She looks at the woman in Old Guy's hands, and begins to wail. *Shit.*

"I don't think she can talk yet. She looks like she's only two," Old Guy says, shifting the unconscious woman in his arms. I shrug; I know nothing about kids.

"What do you want me to do, Prez?" Old Guy asks.

Bull nervously runs his hands through his black hair. "Shit, just take her to one of the rooms." Old Guy heads down the hall with the little girl clinging to his legs, crying.

"What are you thinking, Prez, taking in a stray?" Shadow asks, shaking his head.

"That woman obviously has nobody else. I'm not about to throw a child, with a passed out mother, onto the street," Bull says, his voice sharp and angry.

Shadow nods, knowing he overstepped his boundaries.

"What the fuck, man?" I ask Shadow. I know he has issues, but I'm surprised he has no compassion for the woman and child.

Shadow glares at me with those evil-as-shit blue eyes.

"I'll clean her up and take care of the child," Babs says, heading down the hall.

I follow her down the hall into one of the empty rooms. I notice the little girl still clinging to Old Guy's legs as Babs applies a wet cloth to the woman's face. I lean over Babs to get a better look at the woman who's lying on the unmade bed. She has a round face that's bruised on one side. Her pouty lips red with the top lip split. She has long, blonde hair, and a thicker figure than most girls around here. Her rack is nice, too, from what I can see of it pushing against her shirt. Her white top has blood and dirt smeared over it, and her jeans are just as bad. Her bare feet, mucked with mud catch my attention. She's not wearing any shoes. She must have been in a rush to leave without so much as grabbing her shoes. The woman's eyes flutter open, catching my attention. They're blue and bloodshot.

Instantly, the little girl clings to the blonde woman, the

contact making them both cry.

"What's your name, beautiful?" I ask the woman, as I sit on the bed.

Her eyes shoot to mine, her long lashes sticking together from what looks like her crying.

"My name's Jessica. Are you in charge?" she asks, her voice cracking. Her eyebrows crease and she waits for my answer.

"No. No, I'm not," I respond, with a kind smile. My heart thuds against my chest when her sad eyes catch mine, making me hold a sudden breath.

"This is Bobby. I'm Bull. I'd be the one in charge," Bull says, stepping up from behind me. "Who did that number on your face, darling?" Bull gestures toward her split eye.

"I need protection." Jessica looks over at her daughter. "*We* need protection."

"From who?" I ask.

She looks up from her daughter who is straddling her lap and her eyebrows furrow. Her lips part as tears cascade from her blue eyes, like what she's about to say is the hardest thing she's ever spoke.

"From my husband," she says softly.

She grabs her daughter's small frame and pulls her close, more tears escape her tired eyes.

"Who's your husband?" Bull asks, crossing his arms.

"His name is Doctor Travis Norwell, and he has connections everywhere, everyone is in his pocket," Jessica whispers into her daughter's hair, rocking the little girl back and forth.

"All right, let me talk to my boys, and we'll see what we can do," Bull says gravely, before leaving the room.

"Have you eaten?" I ask, surveying her and the child; they look like hell.

She sniffs and runs her hand along the bottom of her nose.

"No, I left with what cash I could grab. I ran out of money this morning, and we have been driving on fumes the last half hour."

"Where are you from?" Shadow asks, widening his stance.

"Nevada," she replies quickly.

"That's a hell of a drive. What made you come here?" Shadow interrogates.

"I was in town; saw the motorcycles going back and forth. I decided to try my luck and followed the bikes here, hoping for a trade in services," she says with a shaky voice, lifting her head to meet me with gorgeous blue orbs. Her eyes hide a vibrant light, an enigma to what state her appearance is in.

There is something about this woman. Besides her beautiful face and bravery, something about her has a hold on me and I can't figure out what it is. Her lips part as a tear rolls over the bridge of her nose and free falls, planting itself right on the top of her lip. Her eyes still staring at me, captivating me, I reach forward and brush the tear from her split lip. She winces, making me retrieve my hand quickly.

"If the club votes against your behalf, then you can come stay with me," I offer, the words taking me by surprise.

"What the fuck, man?" Shadow growls, hitting my foot with his boot. "You're a fucking prospect. You piss off Bull and you can kiss your ass goodbye."

I scowl at him.

The child stirs in her lap, catching Jessica's attention. She begins to rock the child again and hums. I can't look away. The damaged woman, who holds a beauty like no one I have seen before, intrigues me. Her vibrating hum reminds me of a hummingbird. The sound so sensual, so innocent. My mouth turns from a frown into a smirk.

"How old is she?" My question throws Jessica off guard, her

eyes pop open, and she stops humming.

"She just turned three," she says, brushing a strand of hair from the little girl's face.

"She's beautiful. What's her name?"

"Addie," she whispers. Addie moves her head slightly and looks at me, her innocent eyes staring into mine. A sudden feeling of protectiveness of Addie and her mother surges through me, taking me off guard, but I accept the idea of being protective of the pair sitting before me. They need saving and I'm the man to do it. I will make whoever did this to them suffer.

"Shadow, Bobby, bring Jessica to the chapel," Old Guy yells from down the hall.

Jessica stands on wobbly feet, the little girl clinging around her neck.

"Follow me," Shadow orders sternly, as he walks out of the room.

She looks at me with frightened eyes, her lips parted with terror.

"You'll be all right," I ensure, placing my hand on the small of her back.

After Jessica enters the chapel, I slide back onto the stool I was sitting on minutes ago, before Jessica showed up.

"You better get your shit together," Shadow scolds, his eyebrows raised in warning.

"Fuck you, Shadow. This club is that woman's last hope. Anyone can see that," I respond curtly.

Hawk staggers out of the chapel doors, his mustache shifting from grumbling under his breath, and makes his way out the front door hastily.

"Where the hell is he going?" Shadow asks, looking at the front door.

"Not a clue," I shrug.

Seconds later, Hawk enters the club carrying a big black purse under his arm, cursing under his breath some more. *That must be Jessica's purse.*

"Well, that explains that," I chuckle. Fifteen minutes later, Jessica leaves the chapel with tears streaming down her face. I immediately stand, nervous at what fate the club had given her.

"Just head back down the hall to the room you were in previously," Old Guy instructs, his hand pointing down the hall. Jessica looks my way, her face etched with sorrow and holding me in place, before heading down the dimly lit hall.

"Bobby, Shadow, Bull wants you two," Old Guy informs, before stepping back into the room.

"Shit," Shadow curses, sliding off the stool.

"We are taking Jessica's deal," Bull informs, his arms bending at the elbow as he rests his hands at the back of his head.

"Okay," I encourage him to continue, my forehead gathering sweat from the order.

"How are we taking care of the husband?" Shadow asks out of turn.

Bull snaps his gaze from the table to Shadow. "So glad you asked, son. It appears this guy is as dirty as they come. He will come looking for the woman and child, and when he does, I have no doubt he will make them suffer, possibly kill them," Bull says, his tone low with anger.

"He hits on the kid?" Shadow asks, his brows knitted together with shock.

Bull nods, his eyes closed.

The girl's cheek was red when she came in. I assumed being a child she fell, not that a grown man hit her.

"What's the plan?" I ask, anger flooding my bloodstream.

"Take him out," Bull says matter-of-factly, "and you and Shadow are going to be the ones to do it." Bull slides something across the table in Shadow's direction. I reach forward and grab it before Shadow has a chance to take hold of it, finding it to be a photograph.

"That's the husband," Bull informs. "Make sure you get the right one. Jessica said he has a brother who looks similar, but he's been MIA for the last month."

I study the photo. The guy has light-colored hair that is short, a little longer at the bangs. His eyes are blue, so light they look gray, and they hold a menacing edge to them. His cheeks are high and his jaw curves down to a point, his bright white smile blinding. He looks like one of the villains off a movie. My fingers curl around the photo, the urge to mangle him unbearable.

"Take him out, *now*," Bull demands, his tone threatening as he slams the gavel down.

◆ ◆ ◆

11 Hours Later

"This car smells," I sniff, looking around at the fast-food bags, and empty cups littering the floorboard.

"If you didn't have to stop every three hours to eat, it wouldn't smell like a dumpster," Shadow says flatly, staring out the windshield. I scoff; we only stopped twice.

"When was he supposed to be off work again?" I search the trash in the floorboard for the photograph Bull gave us to ID the husband.

Shadow looks at the digital clock on the dash. "Anytime now."

I stare up at the hospital. It's tall and white, with windows lining every floor. Jessica told Bull this hospital would be the best place to get to the husband, because their house would be loaded with security.

The sounds of a high-pitched squeal grab my attention. I look out the window to a guy twirling a dark-haired woman in pink scrubs, right in front of the hospital doors. He sets the skinny brunette on her feet, and gives her ass a hard slap making her laugh loudly. He shakes his head and walks toward the brightly lit parking lot as she heads inside the hospital. The streetlights cast a bright light across him as he passes us, but he seems oblivious anyone is in here. He looks up at the street-light as he passes, making the glow illuminate his features. His hair is lightly colored, matching the guy's in the photograph. His face is sharp, menacing, and vicious. He turns to look down the street, his eyes catching mine. I inhale sharply, my heart beating against my chest with vengeance.

"That's him," I say softly.

"Are you sure?" Shadow asks, grabbing the photo from my hand, his eyes squinting as he takes in the photo.

"I can't tell. It's too dark to get a clear identification," Shadow says, flicking the photograph with his finger.

A dark-colored Corvette tears out of the parking lot, catching Shadow's attention from the photo.

"What kind of car did Bull say he would be driving?" I ask, my eyes following the sports car out of the drive.

"Black Corvette, is what Jessica told him," Shadow says, sighing.

Shadow has a knack for this kind of thing, hunting people down and taking them out for the club. I have been with him on a couple of these outings. He takes in everything, analyzes every scenario possible; he's very thorough. I have seen him take days to gather information on a hit before going in. We don't have days. This guy is going to notice his wife and daughter missing, and is going to have a search party after her quickly. I start the SUV and slam it into gear.

"What the fuck are you doing, Bobby?" Shadow asks, his tone loud and angry.

"Taking him out." I press my foot on the accelerator to catch up to the Corvette, leaving the hospital parking lot.

"You don't know if that's him. You can't do this half ass!" Shadow yells, trying to grab the wheel.

"It's him! He is identical to the photo and drives the same colored car, Shadow. We don't have time for your ten-step program on how to kill a mark," I explain as we catch up to the speeding car.

"Fuck you, Bobby. My work isn't sloppy, and this is sloppy," Shadow insults, his finger pointing downward. I take my eyes off the road and lift my brow at Shadow's tone; he's pissing me off.

"I'm not doing a job like this, so you might as well turn this car around," Shadow informs. Angry, I pound my fist at the steering wheel. The rubber laced around it cuts into my knuckles. When we do a job like this, Shadow is the one who gets his hands dirty. Delivering the final blow to take the target out. He knows killing isn't my thing. That final look in some-one's eyes before you take their life causes me to hesitate. This guy I'm following though, I don't feel that hesitation. All I see is that little girl's red cheek and the blood smeared across Jessica's face. I grit my teeth and slam my foot on the accelerator again.

"Who says you're taking this dirt bag out?" I question hastily.

"What are you doing, Bobby?" Shadow asks, shaking his

head at me.

We round a sharp corner, our car feet away from the Corvette's bumper. I press my foot on the gas to urge us forward.

"Bobby," Shadow cautions, throwing me a look of concern, as our car inches near the bumper.

"Hold on," I warn, taking a large breath, and push the pedal to the metal.

Our SUV rears forward, barely clipping the side of the Corvette. Our vehicle swerves as the Corvette veers off the road and crashes into a tree.

I wrestle the steering wheel, trying to gain control, the tires screeching as we turn in a complete circle before coming to a stop.

I look over at Shadow, both of us breathing with excitement.

"You're fucking crazy," Shadow says out of breath.

I climb out of the SUV and grab the pistol out of my waistband, cocking it back to load a bullet into the chamber.

I hear Shadow's footsteps round up behind me, his gun clicking with noise as he loads it.

I come over the lip of the road and see the Corvette smashed against a thick tree trunk, smoke and hissing noises coming from the hood.

The driver door is pushed open and a man in blue scrubs falls out groaning, his head is bleeding, and there is blood smeared across the cracked windshield.

"I think I might be hurt," the guy grumbles.

"I'm sorry about that. Let me help you up," I sneer. I plow my boot into his stomach, making him lose his balance. He falls on his back, his eyes looking up at me. They are blue, making me think of the blonde goddess he mangled like a rag doll. I kick him in the ribs hard, making him roll over in pain. I dig my boot into his back, leaning down, and fishing out his wallet.

"Travis Norwell," I read loudly, confirming to Shadow that this is the scumbag we are looking for. Shadow scoffs, folding his arms in front of his chest.

"We don't have time for this shit, Bobby. We're in the open here. Do the job so we can get out of sight," Shadow scolds.

I toss the wallet at Shadow, and grab the back of Travis's hair, my boot still in his back, making him arch his neck back painfully.

"The things I would do to you if I had time. I would pull you limb from limb, burn the skin off your fucking dick. I would torture the hell out of you," I threaten, my teeth clenching, my body shaking with incorrigible rage.

"What do you want from me?" he sobs, his voiced strained from the awkward position his neck is in.

"Retribution," I whisper into his ear. I let go of his hair, letting his head thump against the ground hard. The impact making him clench his jaw, and groan in pain.

I close my eyes, trying to get a hold of myself, but all I see is the look of fear written on Jessica and her daughter's face. My nose flares, and my blood runs cold. I yell into the night air, slamming my boot into Travis's face as hard as I can. Bone cracks beneath my boot, the blood against my foot making the most disgruntled of noises as it spits across my foot. I slam my boot down again and again, my knee and ankle screaming from the impact.

"Bobby!" Shadow yells. I look down at Travis. His face is torn apart, his mouth whimpering with pain and fear.

"Fucking do it already," Shadow demands. I have seen Shadow kill. He never plays with his food; he does it clean and quick. So it's no wonder he is looking at me with concern.

I take in a ragged breath and point it at Jessica's husband's head. When he realizes my intentions, his eyes flare wide, what's left of them anyways. That look, the look of life fleeing a body when the reaper is breathing heavy on their neck, comes forth. I close my eyes and pull the trigger. Ending the suffering of Jessica and her daughter, allowing them to live in freedom and not in fear. My nostrils flare as a rush of relief escapes me. Travis will no longer be a danger to Jessica or her daughter anymore. I did that. I was the one who rid them of their burden. The feeling of finally doing something good and not completely fucking it up is deafening.

"You all right?" Shadow asks, stepping up beside me, taking me from that place of numbness.

I open my eyes and look at Shadow, the anger of the situation still pulsating through me. "I'm fine. Let's get this cleaned up." I side step Shadow and head to the SUV to get the plastic.

"We need to make sure we scrap this SUV," Shadow mutters, walking behind me. "There's evidence all over it."

"Yeah, but the job is done," I remind him.

◆ ◆ ◆

I enter the club in search of Jessica and her daughter, but I come up empty. I need to see the woman I killed for, the child I saved.

"What are you looking for?" Hawk asks, with a twisted face.

"Where is the woman and child?" I respond.

"I sent them back to Nevada," Bull interrupts, stepping out of the kitchen doors.

"What? Why, I thought we made a trade in services," I ask confused.

Bull tilts his head to the side; his eyes squinted with concern. "I needed her to play the grieving wife when her husband didn't return home the next day. She'll be back in a month or two, if not, you and Shadow will be retrieving her for me," Bull says, knocking his knuckles on the bar's counter.

I nod in understanding.

I walk back outside, rest my hands on my hips, tilt my head back, and breathe in the crisp air. What a fucking night. I close my eyes, the image of Jessica looking at me dancing behind my eyelids. I let out a breath and hang my head forward. There is something about that chick, the way she looked at me, the way she made me feel like... like the fucking world as I knew it had been upside down, and suddenly went right side up when she walked in. I lift my head and open my eyes. I gotta get a hold of myself. She'll be back, and when she does, I'll be waiting for her.

1
Bobby

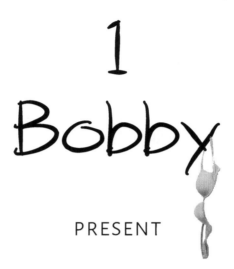

PRESENT

MY EYES CRACK OPEN FROM THE UNFILTERED SUNLIGHT SPLIT-ting through the room landing right on my face, blinding me. I groan and sit up, my body aching from the abuse of the night before. I rub the sleep from my eyes and feel something gently press into my leg. Out of reflex, my head snaps to the side, causing my head to pound instantly. I find a young blonde sleeping soundly, a pink blanket wrapped snugly around her naked frame. Fuck, not again. I throw my head back and sigh, running my hand over my face. I hate when I wake up in unknown places, which happens often.

I look around the room and notice an abundance of pink. The curtains frilly and pink, the walls covered in pink shit, and shelves full of useless fucking pink crap. It looks like a Barbie threw up in here. I slowly push my way off the bed trying to be quiet, praying not to wake.... Trina, Sara, hell , I have no clue what her name is. I grab my clothes off the floor and head to the door, making sure to open and close it as quietly as possible.

I step into a hall and immediately feel thick blue carpet squish between my toes. I look up and down the hall and find doors lined on both sides, girly shit hanging from them. I pull my jeans on, and dress myself quickly. I have no clue where I am. I really have to take it easy on the drugs and booze. I take a chance and go left, coming to a flight of white marble stairs. Looking over the banister, I notice a grand piano sitting below with glass windows lined along the wall. I hurry downstairs, taking two at a time as I shrug my cut on. Nearly tripping on the last step, I stop to tie my boot.

"Hi."

I slowly take my gaze from my old boot to the voice. My heart slowly increasing its beat as my gaze rakes over a bunch of half-naked girls sitting around a breakfast bar and kitchen table. Catching a couple of the shirts they are wearing, displaying a weird A and O on it, I realize where I am. I'm at a sorority. *Shit*. There are blondes, brunettes, and redheads. A buffet of beautiful, young women. I let the breath I was holding out, my shoulders sagging with relief. I was not sure what I was going to see when I looked over, a pissed-off dad holding a shotgun maybe? *Wouldn't be the first time.*

I wave my hand and give a light smirk. "Hey, ladies," I respond, standing up.

I pull my phone out looking at the time. Damn, I have to get to the club, no time to play. I'm the road captain of the Devil's Dust MC, but even with the freedom of living by our own laws inside the club, my president, Bull, will not hesitate to kick my ass if I'm late for our meetings, also known as Church. I grin at the sexy girls and head toward the double doors directly in front of me, hoping it leads outside.

I see my bike parked right out front, and a pink heel laying in the gravel right next to it. I climb on and can't help but laugh as I kick the heel away from the tire.

I take the back way toward the club, wanting to avoid the freeway as much as possible at this hour. Even though I can weave through vehicles on my bike, rush-hour traffic in the morning is a nightmare.

When I arrive at the clubhouse, I park my bike next to Shadow's. Shadow and I go way back. He was my first real friend when I was a kid, and I'm pretty sure I was his. Growing up, I didn't make friends easily, at least not true friends. According to the guys beating the shit out of me, I was a nerd. That's what they called me. That alone resulted in me being bullied a lot; add in the glasses and being smart, it's easy to see why I was targeted. I thought I fucking rocked though, still do actually. I was just fascinated by how things worked, how pieces were put together to make a bigger picture. That was why I was intrigued by Shadow when I first met him. He was different from other kids. He didn't want to make friends; couldn't care less about what everyone was into, and he fucking sucked at anything educational. When I talked to him for the first time, I realized we did have one thing in common: getting into trouble. He was a puzzle I wanted to put together. In doing so, he showed me loyalty and became my family. He was all I had after my mother and father passed away, killed by a drunk driver. I would put my life on the line for Shadow, have actually, and he would do the same for me. Over the years, he has showed me the depths of true friendship. There is only one other person in this world who has thrown me for a loop. The bigger picture I can't seem to piece together. That is Jessica, Doc, as she is known around the club. I gave her my number shortly after she arrived back at the club years back, helping us out as repayment for her protection. She ended up feeding me the same line I fed girls I have no intention of calling back.

"Yeah, okay," she said hesitantly, avoiding eye contact and stuffed the paper containing my number in her back pocket.

I have slept with her off and on through the years; which isn't a lot. After the times we slept together, I would wake up to try and slip away, not wanting to complicate things, to find she beat me to it. Gone.

She comes around the club for a couple of parties here and there, and then she'll split for weeks at a time, distancing herself. I've tried to crack what goes on in that beautiful mind of hers, but it just makes her push herself away from me more. Which is probably a good thing. I like the way things are going for me. I'm carefree, and without limitations. Knowing Jessica more will throw me over the line of freedom and into something complicated. I have seen firsthand what that does to a man. Look at Shadow and Dani. They became careless after they got too close, and it cost me two bullets!

I enter the clubhouse and walk right past everyone at the bar, going into the kitchen needing something to wet my dry mouth. I must have smoked a lot of pot last night. Shit always gives me cottonmouth something bad.

Grabbing the orange juice from the fridge, I drink directly from the jug. Replacing the container back where I found it, I wipe my mouth with the back of my hand, and then close the refrigerator before heading out of the kitchen.

It's quiet, too quiet. I stride back into the common area and notice everyone huddled over the bar looking at the flat screen TV hanging on the wall.

"What's everyone—"

"Shhhh!" Shorty snaps at me, her brown hair flinging over her shoulder from whipping her head in my direction. The intensity of her brown eyes as she scowls makes me grin. Shorty was brought in by the ol' ladies several months after Babs passed away. Babs was the mother of the MC, and could never be replaced, but it's nice having Shorty clean up around here. She's short and cute as hell. I'm not entirely sure what her story is. I heard some shit about her dad abusing her, but I'm not sure if it's true. She helps behind the bar, and though her food tastes like shit, she tries to cook.

I turn my gaze back to the TV and see a reporter frantically trying to get past a crowd of gawking people.

"Really big wreck on the freeway," Shadow whispers, watching the TV intently, his arms crossed in front of his chest while he stares at it.

"Damn, glad I took the back way then," I respond.

"Back way? Where did you come from?" Shadow questions, his tone curious.

I raise my eyebrows and smile. "A sorority."

Shadow smirks, shaking his head.

Jessica

I WAKE TO A LOUD BUZZING, CAUSING ME TO ROLL OVER AND slam my hand down on the alarm clock.

"No, not yet," I mumble into the pillow. The loud buzzing continues, making me lift my head from the pillow to inspect the alarm. The alarm isn't going off; it's my cellphone. *Shit, I'm on call at the hospital.* I hurry out of bed and grab my phone from the charger.

"Dr. Wren," I answer, my voice cracking from speaking so quickly, and not fully awake.

"We need you to head over to where the 10 intersects the 405," my boss instructs.

"Why?" I don't usually get a call to go to a scene. Actually, it has never happened.

"There has been a multiple car pileup and we need you there now. There are several casualties and not enough ambulances or EMTs to assist." Her voice shaky as if she is overwhelmed.

"Yeah, okay, I'll be there as soon as I can," I yawn into the phone.

I end the call and groan. This always happens having the job I do. I plan things, but get called in making me reschedule. Today was supposed to be mine and Addie's day and I don't even get to take her to school. I pull on my white robe and head down the hall to the apartment directly across from mine. Looks like Bree will have to take her. Bree is Addie's babysitter. Luckily, she lives right across the hall, and adores my daughter. She is great with Addie, helping her with schoolwork, and even letting Addie stay the night when I'm on call or on graveyard shift.

I rasp my knuckles against the door, and lean against the doorframe.

The door swings open and a smiling Bree hands me a cup of coffee. Her dark hair is pulled up into a messy bun, and her glasses are sitting on the bridge of her nose, causing a slight red indent creasing it. Her eyes are bloodshot; she must have been up studying all night for her college exams. I met Bree when I moved in. She locked herself outside her apartment, so I offered for her to stay at my place until the landlord called her back. I found she was going to school for nursing, taking online classes, and evening classes when she could afford the tuition. I gave her tips for studying, and advice on the exams she'd be taking. Next thing I knew, she was over every other day, asking questions she couldn't figure out on her homework, and on breaks, she'd play with Addie.

"I saw the news. I figured they would call you in," she says, pointing over her shoulder to a reporter on the TV.

"More like calling me to the scene. I'm guessing it's pretty bad. I need to get there quickly. Can you get Addie up and take her to school?" I ask, taking a sip of the coffee.

"Sure thing," she says, closing the door behind her, following me to my apartment.

◆ ◆ ◆

Driving to the scene of the accident, I can tell it's going to be total chaos. There are fire trucks flying past me, and ambulances every which way, and miles ahead, smoke is rising above. I mentally prepare myself for the carnage that will take place as I pull onto the shoulder, passing the stopped traffic. I get as close as I can to the scene and park. Getting out, I pull my supply bag from the back seat. I reach in and grab my gloves, placing them on my hands for protection. It's then that I hear it. The distraught screaming from the wounded; doctors yelling orders, and sirens from emergency vehicles sounding in the background. I close my eyes, take a deep breath, and head toward it all.

When I round the yellow tape surrounding the large scene, my heart stops. There are cars turned over with mangled bodies hanging halfway out. Trucks are piled on top of trucks with blood staining the pavement.

I look down at my bag and realize I need more supplies, a lot more. I turn on the heel of my foot and all but sprint back to my Jeep. I dig in the glove box and find more gauze and antibacterial wipes. I grab anything I can find, including pens. They can be a great tool when you are left with nothing else. I throw it all in my bag and jog back to the scene as quickly as I can. I'm suddenly pulled back by dainty little fingers just feet from the yellow tape, causing me to nearly trip on debris scattering the ground.

"Ma'am, can you tell us what you are seeing on the other side of the wrecked cars? How many injuries do you suspect? How many fatalities? Can you tell us anything?" a reporter quizzes frantically, waving a camera in my face. I turn trying to hide my face, not wanting the exposure.

"Dr. Wren, over here!" Is yelled at me from the other side of the tape. I yank my arm free from the reporter and make my way toward Doctor Meldon who is standing above someone trapped under a car. Doctor Shane Meldon recently transferred from a hospital in New York. We seem to be on the same shift together often. He is all right, but is persistent in asking me out on a date. I just tell him I don't date those who I work with. But in all honesty, he has *Stage Five Clinger* written all over him.

Bobby

I WATCH THE REPORTER FRANTICALLY GOING ON ABOUT HOW A truck driver caused the accident during rush-hour traffic.

I start picking at the bar's loose wood grain, listening to the reporter ramble on about how it's the worst wreck this state has seen in years.

"Ma'am, can you tell us what you are seeing on the other side of the wrecked cars? How many injuries do you suspect? How many fatalities? Can you tell us anything?"

I look up after nothing but silence follows the reporter's sudden questions, and I find a stunned Jessica. Her round cheeks flush, and her pink lips part as she stares at the camera. God, she is beautiful. I haven't seen her in weeks. She's avoiding me; avoiding is what she does best. My chest tightens as I stare at the scared look on Jessica's face, my fist clenching with the urge to protect her.

A loud crash sounds from outside the club, grabbing everyone's attention from the TV to the front door.

"What the fuck was that?" I question, standing up from the bar.

"I'm not sure," Bull drawls, eyeing the door.

I head to the entry and see Tom Cat on the ground, his bike laid over, knocking a couple bikes over in a domino effect.

"Oh, shit!" I curse, running out to him.

He is mumbling in pain, and his body is trembling.

"What the hell happened?" I question, squatting next to him.

He rolls his body just slightly, his leg standing out, resembling raw ground-up meat. His pants leg is ripped and tattered up to his thigh, with grooves and chunks slicing through his leg. Little hues of pink dot the top of the knee, deepening into red further down his leg. The red is so dark; it looks black in the fattier part rounding the calf. It's road rash. I've gotten it before after taking a corner too fast and dropping my bike. I know what that shit looks, and feels like.

"Fuck," I mutter, eyeing his torn-up leg.

"What happened?" Shadow asks, slipping his arm under Tom's arms to lift him from the ground. I didn't even notice Shadow followed me; I was so focused on Tom's leg. I move around Shadow and wrap my arm around Tom's waist to help carry him into the club. Tom was patched in a few months ago. Now Shadow has been dubbed Vice President, Tom is busy learning the reins of Sergeant At Arms, Shadow's old position.

"Fucking wreck on the freeway," Tom grits, his body wracking from the pain. We get him in the club and lay him on the couch.

"What did you do? Wreck and decide to drive here?" I question with a hint of humor.

"I wasn't fucking staying around all that. People were screaming." He pauses, swallowing hard. "It was like nothing I've ever seen before."

"Damn, brother," Bull says, eyeing Tom's leg. "I'll call Doc, but she might be a minute from the looks of the TV."

Tom growls in pain, closes his eyes, and leans his head back on the armrest. It sucks that he is in so much pain, but I can't help but be a little excited to see Jessica.

2

Jessica

I ENTER THE DEVIL'S DUST CLUBHOUSE AND AM MET WITH THOSE defining blue eyes of Bobby's. Fuck, I was hoping he wouldn't be here. My eyes travel to his plump lips standing out against the blond scruff growing into stubble on his tanned cheeks. I pause in my step, holding the door as I walk in. His hungry eyes rake me in from head to toe unforgivingly, causing a warmth to blossom between my legs.

He is fucking gorgeous and hard to stay away from, when that's all I need to do; stay away from him. Every time I see him, his presence is a challenge; he lays on his charm, and seductive ways. I can usually resist, but every so often, I find myself become weak and give in. Only to wake the next day scared and regretful. Bobby is known for his playboyish ways. He is no doubt a heartbreaker. It would be stupid on my part to let anything between us escalate. Not to mention his lifestyle. That danger he drinks in so vigorously along with the laws of the club, claiming women as their property, not letting them go, is exactly what I escaped from years ago. I have to think of my daughter and her safety, and keep away from Bobby and his brothers. It's the hardest thing I have ever had to do in my life, and I am faced with it every time I see Bobby. I want to be with him, but I have seen the dangers this club circles around. *Safe*, is not the word I would use to describe it. Yet confusingly, Bobby makes me feel safe. Makes me want him to be mine every time he sweet-talks his way into my pants.

Bobby smirks, putting those dimples to work. Lust filters through my body causing my cheeks to warm, and me to quickly look away. He climbs my wall of defense every time I see him, pushing past every thought of staying away from him. But who am I trying to kid? Bobby's charm is relentless and I'm weak resisting it.

"Bull, when you said someone had a rash, I thought you were talking about Bobby. I even brought some penicillin for whatever critters he might be carrying," I tease as I make my way into the club, breaking eye contact from Bobby. I walk to the bar and risk a look in Bobby's direction. He laughs at my humor as the rest of the boys chuckle at his expense.

I hear a deep, strangled moan and look behind me, noticing Tom on the couch and his leg covered in road rash.

"He was in that wreck that's all over the news," Bull informs, standing next to him. I walk over to Tom and kneel down.

"Why didn't you stay at the scene?" I ask Tom, my tone dour as I inspect his leg.

"You were there. You saw it. I couldn't handle those screams, the cries of people suffering. I couldn't do anything to help them. I could barely ride my bike back to the club," Tom replies gravely, his eyes closed and jaw ticking from the amount of pain he's in.

I nod. I understand what he means. It was terrible. I came across four deceased, and two died on me when I was trying to stop horrendous amounts of bleeding. I ran out of supplies quickly, having to use what I could find in cars that were overturned, and napkins from fast food bags that had fallen from the back of trucks. The feeling of not being able to do everything you can is hard to bear.

"Okay, well, I need to clean it and it's going to hurt. I'm going to have to stitch the bigger gash on your calf too, and you could probably use a tetanus shot," I inform, placing on some latex gloves. Tom lays his head back on the side of the couch and silently nods, preparing himself for the pain to follow.

An hour and a half later, I finally finish on Tom's leg. He's passed out from the drugs I gave him, which is for the better, considering the way he was wincing when I was cleaning it. The entire time I worked on Tom, a blaze of desire raced along my skin from Bobby's eyes burning into my back. Pulling my bloody gloves inside out, I toss them in the trash, and go to wash my hands in the kitchen.

"Why don't you stay awhile?"

I turn around and see Bobby leaning up against a counter with his legs crossed in front of him. His black shirt fitting snuggly against his torso, outlining the curves of his muscles beautifully. I bite my lip and turn back to my hand washing.

"Can't. I gotta get to the hospital and check on my patients," I tell him. It's not a lie. The amount of people admitted to the emergency room, I know they need me. I grab some paper towels and dry my hands.

"What about after?" Bobby suggests. I know what he is doing; he's laying on the relentless charm.

I toss the towel in the trash and turn to face him. He has the smirk, the one that makes my whole body thirst for him. His tattooed hands are barely inside his jean pockets, and his eyes are at half-mast as he devours me with his eyes. I close my eyes and turn my head to the side, hoping when I open them, they will be looking at something other than Bobby.

"Can't." I push off the counter, and walk past him. I've gotta get out of here. I grab my bag off the floor next to Tom and head toward my Jeep.

"Can't or won't?" Bobby asks, jogging out of the club, following me.

I stop and sigh, wishing he'd stop pursuing me.

I turn my head slightly but continue to walk forward. "Bobby, you can have any girl you want who's a lot easier to get than me. Leave me alone," I quip dryly, the words hard to spit out. You would think after as many times as I have said them over the years, they would get easier to say, but they don't, and he never listens.

"I'm just having a conversation. Who says I'm after you? A little presumptuous, aren't we?" he mocks. I bite the inside of my lip to keep from smiling as I continue to walk forward.

"I have to go," I reply softly, grabbing the door handle to my Jeep.

Bobby nods, and looks out over the courtyard. "Yeah. Okay," he responds, while tucking his hands into his pockets. I give him one last look. That blond hair, blue eyes, and his tattoos make me inhale sharply, before I climb in my Jeep and drive away.

Bobby

I WALK BACK INTO THE CLUB AND ALL THE GUYS HEAD INTO THE

chapel, ready for a meeting.

Bull and Shadow sit at the head of the table, while I take my usual spot in the middle. I'm still not used to seeing Shadow sit next to Bull. When Locks, our Vice President, was killed, Bull made Shadow his new VP. Shadow deserves it. He'd do anything for this club.

"So, it seems we have been making bank on some of our investments, as you all are well aware of with the payout you have been receiving lately," Bull states, sitting back in his chair. Shining from the light above, his black hair illuminates some gray slicing through it. I'm sure his daughter Dani had something to do with some of that gray. When she and Shadow got together, it was the biggest shit-storm this club has had to stampede through.

"Can't complain about getting money," Tom Cat slurs, a little dazed from the drugs Jessica gave him. We have been paid pretty well lately. I can't deny that. Got me a nice little blue Chevy heading my way from a man in the Midwest; I'm itching to break her in.

"We need to find a front, a legal business that we can exaggerate costs coming in," Bull says, lighting a cigarette. "Lip brought it to my attention his uncle was opening a titty bar up the way and he thought we might be interested in the business." Bull motions toward Lip sitting next to me.

"Who let one of the girls in here?" I tease, looking around the table. We used to have a girl run through here who slept with all the brothers. Her name was Lips; she had big blowjob lips that could suck start a Harley. Our man, Phillip, who goes by Lip for short, was in the joint doing time when she had arrived, and she left right before he got out. I like to give him hell for his nickname though. It's what I do best around here.

I turn in my seat and grin at Lip, his brownish copper-colored hair all spiked up like he just rolled out of bed and didn't even take the time to swipe his hands through it, and that damn lip ring sticking out of his lip glaring against the light. He narrows his brown eyes at me, interlocks his fingers sitting on the table, sitting up straighter.

"It's fucking Phillip," he clips angrily.

Everyone at the table laughs, pissing Lip off more.

"You got news for me or not?" Bull asks around his laughter.

"Yes, my Uncle Warner is opening a bar a few miles away—"

"That one just built?" Shadow cuts in, his voice sounding just a little too animated for the guy who married the president of the club's daughter.

"Wicked Birds?" Old Guy questions anxiously, his eyes lined with wrinkles from age, as they rise in excitement.

"Yeah," Lip answers shortly. "They are hiring girls for the floor today, I believe," he informs, the tip of his tongue playing with his lip ring.

"I think we should go over there and acquaint ourselves with the potential employees," I suggest with a smirk.

"You just want some pussy. I saw Doc turn you down out there," Hawk says, laughing from the back of the table, before hurling into a fitful cough. Nobody here believes I've slept with Jessica, and she does nothing to prove she has slept with me. The boys often think I am telling stories when I speak of being with Jessica. It irritates me that she does nothing to admit to being with me at all either, but what am I supposed to say? She made it clear from day one that we were not together.

"She didn't turn me down, and what would you know about pussy? You haven't seen any since you came out of one." Hawk and I don't see eye to eye on anything. Ever since I was a prospect, he has been giving me hell. But I know he would have my back in the line of fire; he told me when he was drunk and all sappy one night.

Hawk stands up angry, his face scowling, making his lips come up to his eyes because he doesn't have any fucking teeth.

"All right, boys," Bull warns. I take my gaze from Hawk and look at Bull, who is eyeing me grimly. I shrug. I live to piss Hawk off.

◆ ◆ ◆

We pull up to the Wicked Birds and see pink etching around the top of the building and around the black double doors. It's nothing but black brick, and is windowless. There's a small pink awning poking out from the building sheltering the doors.

I climb off my bike and follow the rest of the brothers to the door where two men in black jeans and black shirts stand guard. Their arms crossed at the chest, their faces are humorless. There is pink velvet carpet lined outside the doorway, with tall hedges in planting pots on either side of the entry.

"Not open," one of the guards says dismissively, his face directed at the parking lot instead of our direction as he speaks. They are both bald and pale, their arms bigger than the width of my head.

"It's okay. They are here to meet my uncle, beefcake," Lip insults, pushing past them. The guy on the right who is a fraction slimmer than the other guard, pulls his black sunglasses down the bridge of his crooked nose and looks Lip up and down before stepping away from the doors, replacing his sunglasses over his beady eyes.

Walking into the club, I'm hit with the overwhelming scent of perfume and beer, mixed with a hint of fresh paint. The lights implanted in the ceiling display three stages with chrome dance poles along with one that holds a cage around it. The carpet is black and the walls are painted a dark, sultry purple.

"My favorite nephew!"

I look over my shoulder and see a tall, bald man standing behind a bar, with a wooden case in his hands. Looking above the bar, I notice a black leather swing hanging above him. *Is that a sex swing? I have never played in a sex swing, but looking at that black leather contraption displayed above the bar, the idea of having a woman naked in it makes me want to go buy one.*

"Uncle Warner, it's good to see you. You said you were interested in doing some business with my crew. That offer still standing?" Lip asks, walking toward the bar.

"Of course. I have been waiting for you to bring them by so they can see what I have to offer!" Warner chuckles, radiating his cockiness. He steps around the bar, holding his hand out to shake. Bull steps forward to reciprocate the greeting.

Warner has a white dress shirt elegantly tucked into his expensive-looking jeans, giving off the image of professionalism, but by the look of his huge gold chain hanging from his neck and shaven head, I know better. His eyes are dark and beady, giving a presence of danger, like he's been through some shit. That alone tells me he's a 'take no shit' kind of guy.

"You got a nice place here," Bull says, eyeing the joint.

"Of course it is." Warner crosses his muscular arms across his chest, his comment full of arrogance. "It's mine, and if you work with me, you will benefit from it nicely," Warner smiles, revealing a gold tooth.

"Shall we talk business elsewhere?" Warner asks, his smile suddenly fading. I turn away from the guys checking the place over.

"Too Fat. Too Fake. Stay away from the tanning bed and maybe…" A bitchy tone sounds from behind the stage behind us. I walk toward the sound, ever curious, and see a woman with a clipboard hurling insults at a line of half-naked women.

"Maybe one of them will pity you enough to fuck you," Shadow says, his voice serious. I look over my shoulder and see him smiling wolfishly, glancing at the women.

"What's that supposed to mean?" I ask, eyeing him intently. He folds his left arm across his chest while the right one rubs at his chin as if he is thinking of a clever comeback.

"Doc turning you down in front of everyone at the club," he recalls.

"Yeah, but you know how she is," I reply. He knows mine and Jessica's game; knows how she's hot and cold because he's seen Jessica and I together before, making him nosey as a fucking female, so of course I spilled. Relieved someone knew I wasn't making up stories.

Shadow chuckles. "Yeah, but maybe if you tell one of the strippers, they'll feel sorry for you and shit. They look to be up to your standards. They're breathing," he jokes, making me smirk.

"Hey, Bobby needs love too," I reply, eyeing the beautiful women standing in a perfectly straight line.

A voice interrupts my ogling. "Aw, yes. These are the final ladies. Very talented but I can't keep them all, unfortunately."

I look over and see Warner standing beside me with the rest of the brothers in tow.

I look the line over again seeing a bunch of sexy women.

"Glad I don't have your job," Bull laughs.

To cut any of these women would be a tough job, they're all beautiful, and look like they belong in a porno.

The lady hurling insults steps back as Warner walks the line of girls, staring them up and down. The women stand straight, some twirling their hair and flashing slutty glances at him. They know who is in charge, and not afraid to play the game to get what they want. I love women like that.

I walk behind him, taking the girls in. A blonde with an eyebrow ring blows me a kiss and pushes her breasts up, making me groan in excitement.

"I wouldn't say talented, Warner," the bitchy woman spits.

Warner takes his gaze from the gorgeous talent in front of him and looks at the dark headed woman who is staring down at the women, her face twisted in disgust.

"Birds, how about we give the Devils a show? Show them just how good my girls are," Warner suggests, his arms held out to his sides, looking at the girls with a smile.

The girls start cheering and bouncing up and down, causing more boobs to pop out than being at a rock concert. I glance over at Bull curious at what he thinks about Warner's attempt to sell us partnership. Bull leans back and hooks his thumbs in his belt loops, a smirk fitting his face, apparently enjoying the pitch.

"I am still in the middle of clearing out the duds," the woman snaps, throwing her clipboard to the ground. Her black hair is down, framing her sharp cheekbones. She has on a black bra, outlined in gold sparkly shit, black shorts, and black stockings that climb up her legs. Her ribs are protruding out, and her collarbone is poking out from her body. Definitely not my type of woman, I need a little more to grab on to.

"Can it, Sasha," Warner snaps, his tone angry and threatening. So the bitch has a name, Sasha.

I look the girls over again, a short girl with dark hair, and honey colored eyes catches my attention. She looks Mexican, and is fucking hot. She has on a black corset with red lace peeking out from her ample breasts. I groan uncontrollably, I need to get out of here before I embarrassingly bust a nut in my jeans.

I see Warner look at me from the corner of my eye. He follows my gaze, looking at the girl I'm eye fucking. He snaps his fingers at her. "You, come here." The girl I'm eyeing walks out from the line, her eyes holding a seductive energy as she bats her lashes making me ready to bend her over the stage and fuck her.

"Name?" Warner asks curtly.

"Diamond," she responds, her voice like silk.

"Dance," he demands harshly, ordering her as if she were cattle.

Her tongue snakes out and licks her red plump lips as she nods in agreement.

"Klines, spin something," Warner orders, pointing up at the DJ booth behind us.

Diamond strides up the steps leading to one of the stages, her black fuck-me heels clicking against the stage floor.

The club is suddenly filled with Snoop Dogg's "I wanna Fuck You", and Diamond immediately grinds against the pole, her body instinctively knowing how to work it. Her fingers play with the black ribbon tying up her corset. As the ribbon loosens, more of that red lacy bra comes into view, making my dick swell. She slides her tanned leg around the pole and does a basic swing around it as the music picks up. She slowly walks around the pole, my eyes trailing up her legs before catching her eyes pinning me down. Her plump ass comes into sight as she prances around the chrome, and I bite my lower lip, but what I want is to bite that ass.

She is sexy as hell. A fucking tease, but hot. She flings

around the pole as if she was made for it, every move making my dick that much harder.

As the song finishes, she grabs onto the chrome with one hand and swings herself halfway around it. Her knees bend as she finally makes her way around the pole before landing on the floor.

"Congrats, dear, you are now a Wicked Bird," Warner cheers loudly, clapping his hands.

"Now, let's talk details. Shall we?" Warner questions, pointing down a hall with dim lighting. Diamond walks off the stage, winking at me before stepping back in line.

I shake my head at her flirting, and head down the hall. I can't help but wonder what Jessica would look like naked and sliding up against a pole seductively. The thought makes a growl escape my throat and look into buying a stripper pole for my room back at the club. I walk into the office and sit on a black velvet couch as Warner makes his way behind a big wooden desk with a computer sitting on it.

"So what kind of deal are you offering?" Warner asks, cutting to the chase.

"Depends. What are you looking for?" Bull asks, leaning against the closed door.

Warner relaxes back in his chair, his hands poised in a steeple in front of him. "What are you looking for?" Warner quips, his eyes squinted as he observes Bull.

"I need partnership in the business. That's it," Bull says it like it is—no bullshit.

Warner nods slowly, thinking it over. "You send me some of your crew on the weekends for when things get rowdy; let me dip my fingers into your drugs when I want. Give me fifty percent of the cost of what you're running under the table and I'll make you a partner," Warner says calmly. My lips twitch with amusement. He has lost his mind if he thinks he is getting all that.

Bull laughs. "Fuck no."

"To what exactly?" Warner asks, eyes furrowed in confusion.

"To the fifty percent," Shadow declares in disbelief. I nod in agreement. That is a shitty offer.

"Okay, what would be reasonable?" Warner asks, shrugging.

A knock comes at the door, interrupting Bull before he has a chance to counter offer.

"What?" Warner hollers, his tone edging on frustration.

Sasha walks in, her red lips pierced with irritation. "One of the girls is not taking rejection very well and has locked herself in the cage," she states, exasperated.

"Damn it," Warner curses, standing up from his desk. "I'll be right back," he mutters, leaving the room, shutting the door behind him as he goes.

"What do you think?" Bull questions to no one in particular.

"I think nothing more than twenty-five percent," I suggest, shrugging.

"Why's that?" Bull asks, looking my way.

"He's a cover up. A way to hide what we are making under the table. A trade of services would do us better than throwing cash his way. I have seen strip clubs come and go, not to say anything bad about your Uncle Lip, but who's to say this one won't close in a month leaving us back where we are but with less money to entice a new partner?" I reply.

"Think he will take twenty percent?" Shadow questions. By the looks of Lip's uncle, favors and drugs wouldn't be a problem.

"He's a fucking convict, of course he will," I scuff.

"He is?" Old Guy asks, looking at Lip for the answer.

"How did you know that?" Lip questions, his eyes furrowed.

"Just the looks of him. I can tell," I reply bluntly.

Warner comes back into the room, nearly slamming Shadow against the wall with the door. "What the fuck, man?" Shadow snaps, pushing the door away.

"Sorry about that, and for the interruption. Now, where were we?" Warner asks, sitting behind the desk.

"Percentages," Bull reminds him.

"Right, so what are we thinking?" Warner questions.

"Twenty percent, drugs, and a few of my men on the weekends," Bull offers. Warner rests his elbows on the desk as his eyes furrow in concentration. Just as I think he is going to reject the offer, he smiles, revealing his gold tooth.

"Deal." Warner stands, his arm held out straight to shake Bull's.

"Deal," Bull repeats, shaking his hand in return.

3

Jessica

I GRAB MY CLIPBOARD FROM THE COUNTER LOOKING AT THE patients still in the emergency room from the wreck. My vision's doubling from the exhaustion the day has held.

"Been a madhouse in here today," Doctor Meldon says, stepping up beside me.

"Hey, Doctor Meldon," I reply. He's been here all day from the looks of it.

"Would you stop calling me that? Call me Shane," he demands, his head tilted to the side, annoyed.

"Fine. Where is my resident? These cannot be right," I state, flipping through patient files that are half-ass filled out.

"We've got Debra," Shane answers hesitantly. I look up and see his brown eyes shine as they meet mine. His dirty blond hair is combed over, and his defined cheeks hold a five o'clock shadow. I can't help but look him down. His arms are toned, but not muscular, and with his blue shirt tucked into his scrub bottoms, my hands twitch to untie them. My cheeks stain from the thoughts drifting in my head.

"Did someone say my name?" Debra asks, walking up to me. Her face is flushed red and she has stray hairs everywhere. She is the most disorganized resident I have and a giant pain in my ass. Last week, she almost killed a patient because she failed to read their allergy chart. Which is something you learn to do as a ritual with a patient on day one. So her ass is on probation and doing my paperwork, for now.

"Fix these," I snap, piling the folders in her arms.

"I will," she replies with a shaky voice as she walks away.

"So, you wanna go grab a bite?" Shane asks, leaning against the counter. He is almost as relentless as Bobby, but I have no problem telling Shane no, unlike I do with Bobby. Shane is a good-looking guy and has a lot going for him, but I don't want a relationship. Judging by the behavior of Shane since he has been here, he wants something serious, and I'm not the kind of girl who wants serious. I don't want love, or the heartbreak that accompanies it.

"Nope, I don't," I reply flatly, looking over discharge papers the nurse just gave me.

"Come on, Jessica. You can't turn me down forever," Shane chuckles, tapping his knuckles on the counter.

"Oh, but I can." I look up from the papers and smile wolfishly at him.

"Dr. Wren, I'm sorry to do this, but you were put on call for the night," a nurse informs me. I look over the desk with disbelief, my eyes burning a hole through her. I was supposed to have tonight off. I know for a fact I'll be called in five minutes after leaving this place.

"What?" I all but shout.

"Don't kill the messenger," she replies meekly, walking away.

"Shit. I was supposed to take Addie to pick out movies tonight," I mutter, sliding my hands through my hair in anger. My job has impossible hours, making the time I have with Addie limited. She is going to be livid when I tell her. I've canceled movie night three times already because of having to work extra hours unexpectedly.

"You go on a date with me and I'll take your shift. You can go home to your daughter with no interruptions," Shane show-tunes, focusing on his clipboard and feigning nonchalance.

I throw my head back and growl in frustration. The only dates I do are one-night stands. No strings attached. No complications. But I don't want to skip on movies again with Addie. What harm could one date with Shane possibly do? We'll go eat and then I'll head home. Maybe he'll see I am not who he is looking for in the end and leave me alone.

"Or I can settle for a quickie in the supply closet," Shane suggests. My head snaps over and looks at him, trying to read if he is joking or not. His head tilted to the side, and his brown eyes are staring at me intently.

"Oh, my God, you would," Shane whispers, his eyebrows lifted. My hesitation making him think I would be as easy to give a quick rump in the closet.

"What? No, I—"

"Date it is. See you this weekend," Shane chuckles, walking away.

◆ ◆ ◆

A guy rushing into the ER who had stapled his thumb to a board at the end of my shift means I'm home late. Surprisingly, we get a lot of those cases. I love the ER, the adrenaline that pumps through my veins when someone rushes in after a chaotic experience, depending on you for their wellbeing. However, it's not that thrilling when it happens right before you're about to clock out.

I go to key in the code to the security gate at my apartment and the gate pushes open before I even have a chance to press a button. I scowl and try to shut the gate, curious as to why it's not locked. It's not shutting at all. *It's broken.*

"What the hell?" I yell, flinging the gate open.

Damn slumlord is letting this place go to shit. Some kid in his early twenties who just likes to sit around and get high inherited the place after his dad passed away. It has been a 'fix it yourself' ever since. I head up the stairs to my apartment and find a note taped to my door saying Addie is staying with Bree, since her niece came over for the night. Addie loves playing with Bree's niece so it doesn't surprise me she wants to stay over.

I look over at Bree's door contemplating knocking so I can see Addie. The security gate not working is going to have me up all night worried. I know it's late though and she's probably asleep. I open my door and slam it shut with my foot, dropping my groceries to the floor. I fish out the bottle of wine and head to the kitchen to remove the cork. I don't even bother with a glass; I just drink from the bottle. I'm classy like that.

I drink alcohol more than I should. It helps forget the pain, the memories, and the fear. That and what single mother doesn't need wine occasionally? I don't have a problem with it though. I never drink when I am on call, or around my daughter. Heading into my bedroom, taking a big swig from the bottle I stop in the doorway and inspect the drawers of my dresser all pulled out. My clothes sprung from one end of the room to the other. Looks like Addie played dress up again. My shirts are mostly strung out, along with all my lipsticks scattered along the top of the dresser. I swear she's nine going on sixteen. I'm going to have my hands full with her. Maybe I should start buying gothic lipstick, leaving it in her reach, then she can run around looking like a member from KISS; it would be better than the bright pink or red she obviously was wearing.

I fall on my bed landing on my back, my hand holding the bottle of wine dangling over the bed as I look up at the ceiling. I wonder what Bobby is doing. I wince at my internal thought, and close my eyes tightly.

"This is your fault," I whisper to the bottle of wine in my hand. The wine helps with a long day, but often brings me to thinking about Bobby. I hate how he makes me want him; has me thinking about him all the time. Not to mention, Bobby's a rock star in the sack, making it that much harder to stay away. I'm usually so high on desire from his skilled fingers and the affection he shows my body, that I don't realize what I'm doing until it's over. He's not the one afraid of taking what we have and complicating it. Bobby has made it clear, as I have, that he has no desire to take things further. That's not what I necessarily want, but absolutely need. What we have works: no attachment, no broken hearts.

I groan and sit up, taking another big swig, the fruity goodness numbing my senses. My phone vibrates in my back pocket making me jump and spill wine all over myself.

"Shit!" I yell, licking my fingertips to get every drop.

I slide my finger across the screen bringing my phone to life, cursing it at the same time. There's a message from Bobby.

Bobby: Naked?

I should tell him I am wearing tan granny panties, and a

nightgown my grandmother gave me. See if that gets him all hot and bothered. But knowing Bobby, it probably would turn him on.

Me: Hardly.

Bobby: I can help with that!

Me: Going to bed.

Bobby: Think of me, Hummingbird.

I sigh. I hate it when he calls me that. He says I hum a lot, reminding him of a hummingbird.

I toss my phone on the floor, and take another big gulp of wine, letting it slide down my throat, praying it helps numb this feeling of grief in my soul. I ran to the club a few years back, my last resort in saving my daughter and me from Travis, my deceased husband. I never thought I would trade a life of danger for the temptation of another hell.

I roll over and see my closet lit up, my eyes catching my forbidden shoebox at the top.

"Don't do it, Jessica," I whisper to myself. I know nothing in that box will help with what I'm feeling. The box that keeps little snippets from my past. I don't know why I keep it. Actually, I do. It reminds me why I'm doing all of this. Living carefully and loveless. I'm caged by fear and tormented by recollection, making my life pretty monotonous.

I take another big gulp, my head lightening from the wine's effect as I stand from the bed, and make my way to the closet. My fingers brush against the brown box. As a tear slowly escapes my tired eyes, the scars across my back blaze from terrifying memories.

"Your life as you know it will be mine. It's up to you how long that life is to be endured and how. You will learn your role as my wife, and your happiness will depend on that," Travis whispered, *his voice calm and solemn against my ear. My body raised in fear when I heard the slight noise of something trailing along the floor as he paced behind me.*

Wine splashes my feet, along with a loud crack, waking me from my dreadful memory. I look down and notice the wine bottle has slipped from my grip, landing next to my feet. I remember that night more than most. I went out with my girlfriend, Heather, and we got a little crazy and drank too much. A police officer drove us home so we didn't have to drive. Travis was furious when the officer dropped me off. As soon as the door closed behind us, he grabbed me by my hair, and pulled me down to the basement.

Bobby

I AM BLOWING ON MY CUP OF COFFEE WHEN JESSICA WALKS INTO the clubhouse. Her pink scrubs snug against her body and her blonde hair pulled up into a tight hair tie immediately draws my attention. Her vivid blue eyes spot me on my stool and she smiles. Her smile is contagious, holding me hostage for a moment before I manage a smile in return. Her face is round in the sexiest way. The hint of neutral red on her defined cheeks speak of the summers she stayed outside as a kid, staining her cheeks with a permanent glow. I swear every time I see her, my chest cramps and my dick swells painfully.

"I'm here to dress Tom's leg," she explains, holding up her black bag. She has been here every day for the last few days since the wreck happened. I've been here every time, and I've tried every day to get her to stay afterwards, go for coffee, anything. My efforts have been turned down, as usual. But when I do finally break her wall, she's worth every painful stab to the chest caused from the countless rejections. I know she's afraid, terrified of giving her heart to someone she trusts only to have it violently ripped from her chest. She needs to be pushed past her threshold of security to know I'd never hurt her. However, I'm terrified too. I fear pushing her to the breaking point and her never returning back to me. So I tell her what she wants to hear... that we're just friends and nothing else. No complications.

"I'll go get him," I reply, getting up from my stool, giving her a wink.

I walk down the hall and open the door to Tom's room without knocking. Tom is passed out, hanging halfway off the bed, naked. I lift my boot and kick the side of the bed.

"Get up. Jessica is here to replace your bandage."

He groans and rolls over, his bright-colored tattoos running up his arm catching my eye. I swear he gets the color in those touched up every few months.

"I'm up," he groans, running his hand through his long, tangled hair.

I make my way back to the bar finding Jessica drinking my coffee. Her slightly pink lips curve over the rim of the cup, taking a small sip.

"Help yourself," I clip.

"I did, and it tastes like crap." She twists her face in disgust.

"Made it myself," I reply proudly.

"I figured," she says, laughing, before turning and grinning.

"Club is having a party tonight. You should stop by," I suggest, brushing my finger against her cheek.

She blushes and her back stiffens from my touch.

"Can't," she answers flatly. Her rejection feels like a horse kicked me in the fucking chest.

"Can't or won't?" I ask. She looks at me, setting the coffee cup down.

"Can't," she replies softly, with a weak smile.

I smirk and nod. Guess I'll call Diamond from Wicked Birds. Looks like I ain't breaking Jessica's resistance this time. Before me and the boys left the club the other day, Diamond grabbed me by the arm and wrote her number on my palm with a magic marker. She kissed me on the cheek before walking away, swaying that fine ass of hers.

Jessica knows I sleep around. Jessica and I are nothing but late night booty calls to one another. We're not serious and don't have a label on what we are. But, even so, I still find myself coming back to her, always thinking of her. I can't for the life of me fucking figure out why. I've slept with a bunch of girls; I can hardly remember any of them, and for damn sure, I forget their names. But I've never forgotten mine and Jessica's first time, or any other time after that.

It was at the club about six months after she came back from playing the grieving wife. She seemed reluctant to my advances, as if she wore a repellent to my charm. That night the club had some random party and she actually stayed. I finally broke through her defenses.

"It's so loud in here!" Jessica yelled, her forehead creased with little wrinkles as she looked around at the club. She was sexy as hell, wearing a tight black long shirt, some cut-off shorts, and sneakers. Every time she bent over, my eyes darted between her cleavage and her ass like a Ping-Pong ball.

"You wanna get out of here?" I yelled back, leaning into her so she could hear me. She nodded, causing her blonde hair to fall in front of her face, her cute nose scrunched up. I grabbed her hand, pulling her through the crowd of people before she changed her mind.

As soon as we got outside, it was near silent. The only thing you could hear were crickets chirping within the depths of the darkness the street lamps glow didn't reach. There was nobody around; everyone was in the club, leaving just Jessica and me standing out front of the building.

"You wanna go for a ride?" I asked her, nodding toward my bike. She looked over at my ride, her eyes widened, and lips parted as she took in my motorcycle.

"I don't know," she sputtered, looking up at me under her thick eyelashes.

"Come on, just a short one," I encouraged, my chin raised and eyes at half-mast as I persuaded her.

She laughed, her mouth turning into the cutest fucking smile I had ever seen on a woman. She tossed her hair over her shoulder and looked at me. Adorable little dimples forming below her cheeks.

"Just a short one," she breathed heavily, biting her bottom lip as she hooked her thumbs into the waist of her cut-off shorts. God fucking help me. This woman was going to bring me to my knees.

I smirked and grabbed her hand.

"I'll give you one hell of a ride," I remarked, my smirk turning into a wolfish grin.

"Oh, I have no doubt that you will." She dragged me toward my bike.

Heading toward the ocean, her arms wrapped around my waist and her fingers trailed along my abs as she took in the *passing buildings. I couldn't help the fucking smirk that slipped across my face, the feeling of her on my bike and her arms around me was thrilling. Jessica was different. The way she drove me wild, I couldn't help but feel on cloud fucking nine at that moment that she was finally giving into me. I pulled back on the throttle a little, a cocky smile taking over my smirk. I knew she'd give in eventually.*

I rode us under a wooden bridge with the beach and ocean feet away. Throwing my jacket down on the sand, I turned toward her. Taking me by surprise, she jumped in my arms and clung to me.

Pulling away briefly, she leaned in and kissed me, her soft mouth taking mine with a passion I had yet to experience. I had made love to girls, at least I thought I had, but never had that unspoken connection like I did with Jessica. Until that kiss, I never really knew what I was missing. Kissing a woman before was nothing compared to the way Jessica's mouth and mine connected. Her lips fitted against mine perfectly. The way my gut fluttered with excitement when her tongue tasted mine was an experience I wanted to experience over and over again. She consumed me.

She pulled from our kiss leaving me breathless, and walked a few feet away. Mesmerized, I watched on as she pulled her top above her head, revealing her naked tits. Knowing she hadn't been wearing a bra made my mouth instantly go dry, thirsty for her. She looked down at herself, and then peered up at me nervously. Her hands slid over her abdomen reaching the buttons on her shorts, unbuttoning them, and lowering them down her long legs.

Unable to resist any longer, I leaned in and tucked my hand behind her neck pulling her toward me.

"You are so fucking gorgeous," I whispered, looking her body

over.

She released a soft laugh, causing me to smirk. I lowered my hand, feeling her warmth behind my palm. The soft touch making my dick swell with eagerness. My hand slid further down her shoulders onto her back, feeling rough grooves. I frowned, and looked over her shoulder finding her beautiful body marred with scars.

"What the fuck?" I questioned, trying to turn her so I could get a better look.

"It's nothing." She shrugged my hand off her, and crossed her arms, trying to hide her body. She reached down and grabbed her top, pushing her arms through its sleeves. I felt my chest seize as she tried to hide, to end what we just started.

"Whoa, whoa." I grabbed her shirt and pulled it from her.

"I don't want to talk about it, Bobby," she huffed.

"We don't have to talk about it," I agreed. I slid my hand under her chin lifting her face up to look at me.

"You are fucking beautiful. Don't ever feel ashamed of your body. Ever."

I pulled her arms away from her body and caressed her breasts. Hissing between my teeth at their firmness. Her body instantly reacted to my touch, causing her to wrap her arms around me, whispering my name. I lowered her onto my jacket slowly, pulling my shirt above my head as she made herself comfortable. When our eyes met, I knew I was done for. She looked at me with such reliance, like I was her world. Everything around us was black and white, and standing still. Nothing mattered but us.

She taught me the emotional side of being with someone intimately. The way she touched me with such care, and her body igniting from the simplest of touches, I was taken into another realm while having sex with her and I responded by *drowning her in pleasure. Making her feel admired and wanted... because she was.*

I made love to her that night. It was incredible and mind altering. I didn't know what to take away from it; she brought a side out of me I never knew existed. She didn't show up at the club for four weeks after that. I thought I had my heart broke as a kid, but having Jessica not return my calls, and acting as if nothing had happened; it was fucking brutal. When she did finally come back to the club, it was to tell me we could only be friends; that she couldn't be anything more even if she wanted to. I have complied since then. I'd rather have what I can of her, than nothing at all.

4

Jessica

I WAIT OUTSIDE OF MY APARTMENT FOR SHANE TO COLLECT ME. The night, thick with humidity, causes sweat to bead along my legs. It's only spring but summer is making an early appearance.

"This is stupid," I whisper, looking at my phone for the time. I don't do dates, yet this is a date. Shane is a nice guy, but I don't want to give him the wrong impression. Dates lead to feelings, which lead to love and ending in heartache. I look down at my black dress and black heels. What was I thinking, dressing up like this? I should have dressed in sweat pants or something unattractive. This is going to give him the wrong idea for sure.

Just as I'm about to turn around and head back into the building, Shane pulls up in a red convertible. I wonder if he's trying to compensate for the size of his penis with such a flashy car. I bite my lip trying to stifle the laughter rippling up my throat at the internal thought.

"Sorry, I'm late," he says. I step up to the car and slip into the passenger seat before he has the chance to get out. I don't want him to open my door for me, or have the idea this is anything other than two colleagues going out for dinner. That's it.

"Where would you like to go?" Shane asks, shutting his door, twisting in his seat to look at me. As usual, his blond hair is combed back and he is wearing a white dress shirt with the sleeves rolled up, and what looks like khakis. I can't really tell in the dark car.

"Me? You're asking me?" I asked surprised, pointing to myself.

"Yes. I had to bribe you into coming on this date in the first place, so where can I wine and dine you? Where will you feel most comfortable?" Shane questions, a smile crossing his face. "Hopefully not a supply closet," Shane teases, making me laugh.

I give him the address and he drives off. He'll be pissed when he sees where I am taking us, but the place won't give off a romantic vibe, or the idea I'm going to call him for a second date.

◆ ◆ ◆

"A coffee shop?" Shane questions, as he looks out the car window.

"Hey, you said anywhere," I laugh.

"You really want to get rid of me, and quick," he laughs, taking his gaze from the shop to me. His forehead creased in worry lines.

"Come on, you can get a donut," I tease, climbing out of the car.

"Oh, can I?" Shane mocks.

"You owe me another date, a real one where I pick," he demands, his voice serious as he opens the door to the coffee shop.

"No, the deal was a date. We're on a date. No second dates were in this deal," I remind him.

"This is not a date. This is out for coffee, which we do in the break room. Therefore, you owe me a date," Shane explains, smiling big.

Well, this plan backfired.

I sit on the soft tan couch in the back of the coffee shop as Shane grabs us some coffee. He knows how I like it, straight with two sugars. Actually, I'll drink any kind of coffee, any which way; I love the stuff. I'm addicted and I could use help for the things I would do for a cup of coffee.

"Just how you like it." Shane sets the coffee down as he sits next to me on the couch, crossing his legs as he leans back.

"So, Jessica, I have been working with you for a couple months and know hardly anything about you. Tell me about yourself." He turns his head just slightly, pinning me with his brown eyes. I shift uncomfortably.

Maybe the coffee shop wasn't a good idea. I should have picked somewhere that allowed no talking, like a movie.

"Not much to tell. I work and when I'm not working, I'm with my daughter," I respond quickly, avoiding eye contact.

"Hmm, I see," Shane says, taking a sip of his coffee. "Where are you from?" he continues to question.

I sigh and set my coffee down on the wicker table next to me. "Nevada."

"I see you're not much for talking," he says with a chuckle.

"I just—"

"It's fine, Jessica. I know you're not one to dive into your personal life. I know you better than you think though," he says with a smile, lifting his right eyebrow.

"You think so? And what do you know?" I ask, shrugging. He sets his coffee down on the table, taking a deep breath. This ought to be good, 'cause I don't even know myself.

"I know you love sports," he responds, looking at me, his brown eyes glistening with brightness that he thinks he has me figured out. "I know you love the color pink, and you hate company get-togethers," he continues, his eyes never leaving mine.

"How do you know all that?" I ask.

He leans in close, too close, his lips brushing against my ear. "I have seen you sneak into the lounge to see the score of a football game," he replies softly. "You are always wearing pink scrubs, and I never see you at company functions."

I pull my face from his, my cheeks flushing from the amount of blood pumping through my body from how close he is, but he's wrong. I wear pink scrubs because they are the only ones that were in my size when I last went shopping. And I hate sports with a passion. That day I was in the break room, when he is referring to me sneaking off, I had heard they found a dead body in Nevada; it was all over the news in the surrounding states. I was scared to death of who that corpse may belong to, so I watched the news every chance I got that day. I live in constant fear that Travis's body will be found. Fear of my past, fear that it may come forward and repeat itself. It turned out to be some judge who had gone missing due to Alzheimers. How they haven't found a body that belongs to my ex-husband is beyond me. I guess the Devil's Dust is that good, which is frightening.

I give a weak smile at Shane and look across the coffee shop. A young couple, both with blond hair are snuggled closely together. The young, handsome guy's whispering into the woman's ear. Her face down, there's a glow staining her cheeks. I notice her hand sliding up his leg under the table, sneaking a feel. They look so lost in one another, completely oblivious to the rest of the world. I look away, thumbing the top to my coffee. I don't want love. It starts out like something out of a fairy tale sure, but it ends like a horror movie. I glance back up, watching the couple. I would be lying if I said I didn't miss those days of having butterflies and laughing over nothing from being so stupidly in love. The sudden thought of love consumes me, ravishing my mind. Sometimes, I wonder if I am in love with Bobby. The way he makes me feel when I am with him and how our bodies speak to one another when we have sex always stays with me. But then I remember what it feels like when your world is turned upside down; how it felt to run as the sun was rising, terrified. I quickly realize love is not a good thing, nor something I want to pursue with anyone.

"I need to get home. I work tomorrow," I state, standing up. My thoughts taking a turn for the worse, I suddenly feel uncomfortable.

Shane smirks, and stands with me. "Right, well let's get you home then. But I'm serious; you owe me a date."

Walking out of the coffee shop, a bright flash glares in my face making me wince and cover my eyes.

"Get back!" Shane hollers in the direction of the blinding flashes, grabbing my hand, and yanking me forward. I look past the flashing and see a man with a camera, who's frowning at Shane's harsh tone.

Shane opens the door to his car and shoves me in, before racing around, and getting in on the other side.

"What was all that about?" I ask, my hands shaking from the excitement.

"Who knows. Let's get you home," he replies, his body stiff and unfriendly. For the first time since I met Shane, he is not looking at me when he is talking to me, and his eyebrows are pinched together in frustration. He is lying. I can tell.

I sigh. I just need to get home. This whole date was a big mistake. My nerves are on end, and I may throw up. My mind instantly coming to Bobby, wanting to seek comfort in something familiar.

As soon as Shane drops me off at my apartment, I tell him goodbye and head toward the building. Not giving him the chance to ask to come up, or the 'should we kiss' awkwardness that might follow after going out with someone. I go inside and dig for another wine bottle in my cabinets, needing the comforting numbness it brings. I sigh and lower the bottle. Deep down, I know I could just go find Bobby and he'd stifle the overwhelming loneliness that's eating away at my conscience, but I know I shouldn't.

Bobby

SMALL HANDS SLIDE UP MY LEGS, WAKING ME FROM MY SLEEP.
The familiar scent of coffee and perfume greet me: Jessica. I sit straight up, only to be knocked back onto my bed when Jessica plows herself into me. Her hands grasp the side of my face as her plump lips kiss mine feverishly. I wrap my hands around her back, and pull her onto me, my dick tightening knowing what's to come. Jessica's body does something to me, makes my dick crave for more. When Jessica and I are together, the rest of the world doesn't exist. Nothing from

today or yesterday matters. It's just us, delivering what the other needs... each other. Sliding her hands into my hair, she pushes herself closer. Her tongue darts into my mouth, deepening the kiss.

This is Jessica 101: her sleeping with me has to be on her terms. I lay the charm on thick, yet she denies me on the spot. She does eventually come around, usually in the middle of the night.

She pulls her body away from me, her hands cupping my cheeks.

"Bobby." She rests her forehead against mine, the smell of coffee and alcohol slipping from her breath.

"Yeah," I reply.

"What do you know about me?" she asks, her voice giving off a sense of vulnerability.

"What's wrong, babe?" I ask, sensing something is off. I sit up, with her still in my lap. The light from the hallway skids underneath my door providing just enough glow to see her flushed face. Her eyebrows are furrowed and her eyes hold a sense of grief.

"Just, tell me what you know about me," she demands, her tone soft but stern. I rub my face and think about it, trying to make sure I don't say the wrong thing.

"I know you love coffee. You care about your daughter more than anything. You're strong and take no shit." I pause, trying to think about something personal, like a hobby. "I know you love to surf, love cherry cheesecake—"

"Stop!" she demands, running her hand through my hair.

"How do you know those things?" she asks, leaning into me, her lips brushing against mine. I close my eyes, and try to calm my anxious breathing.

"You are always stealing my coffee; plus, you smell of it. You go to great lengths to keep your daughter safe, and I have seen the shit you have gone through to do it. I have had you in my bed with sun-kissed cheeks and the smell of salt lingering on your body, bruises etching your knees from when you have surfed that day, not to mention your surfboard is attached to your Jeep to confirm it. And when we have family parties, you always go straight for the cheesecake," I explain, pulling her face to look at me. "I know you, Jessica Wren," I mutter. I know most things about her, just not her darkest secrets. That's what kills me. I want to know everything about her.

She smashes her pouty lips against mine, her tongue greedy as it assaults my own. My hands slip from her waist to her thighs finding bare skin. I slowly slide my hands up and under her dress, my fingers teasing the hem of her panties. My cock throbs painfully, begging to be inside of her.

I know I am not a good man. I have done plenty of things that would justify that. But the feeling I have with Jessica, the way her scent surrounds me and the comforting high I get from her warm skin against mine while we are together, makes everything seem as though I am finally in the right place; doing what I was meant to be doing. There's no guns blazing, transactions of the club to be dealt with, or blood being shed. It's raw emotion; Jessica bringing a side out of me I don't get to experience near enough.

She pulls her lips away, and her head lolls back as a seductive moan escapes her parted mouth.

"Damn," I growl. That sexy-ass mewl that escapes her mouth when she's turned on does something to me. It unhinges me and any morsel of self-control I have. My only mission is to have her, be inside of her, and make her mine for the night.

I dig my fingers into her thighs, rocking her clit against my hard cock. The only thing keeping me from being inside of her are my boxers and her dainty underwear.

I slip my finger and thumb under the elastic of her panties, and tear them from her excited body. Our heavy breaths and the tear of the fabric echo through the dark room. The friction feels fucking amazing, causing me to clench my teeth.

Her pussy parts, ready for me to take her, as it crosses the material of my boxers, sliding over my dick that's sticking up under the thin fabric. She's wet, the damp heat slipping through my boxers as she firmly rocks against me. My rough hands edge up her back, reaching for a way to remove her dress. I'm ready to take her.

"It's a zipper," she tells me, her voice breathy and nearly incoherent.

I find the zipper and pull it down, my hands sliding along her curves as the material loosens. I want to take my time, savor every second we have together, because I know hours from now, she'll be gone. But it's nearly impossible to take my time and go slow when all I want is to feel her body wrapped around mine as she whispers my name while she comes.

She slips the straps of her dress off her shoulders, making it fall to her waist. I cup the back of her neck and lean my head down grazing the swell of her breast with my teeth, causing her breath to catch in her throat. My hands skim from her neck downward, before they glide across rough grooves; the scars that mar her perfect body. Her body stiffens, and she pushes herself off me. She pulls on my arm, hinting she is ready to be on the bottom.

It's the position Jessica usually demands when we have sex; she has to be on the bottom. She has these rules, or rituals, when we fuck. No lights, nothing but missionary so she is always on her back, and no asking why. Sex is still excellent with her; it's the best actually.

She pulls on my arm again, trying to get me to let her go so she can roll over. I stiffen my arms and look at her, wanting her to ride me, to let loose.

"Bobby, I can't, you know that," she whispers. I trail my tongue along my upper lip, and nod.

Whatever it is that keeps her from doing anything more adventurous than missionary, she won't tell me. I've tried to get her to talk about it, but pushing her to discuss her scars, or try anything more than what she is comfortable with, causes bad memories. The pain that flashes across her face and the way her eyes take on that look of terror, it kills me, and that's why I don't push her. I am pretty sure it goes back to her husband, though.

I flip Jessica on her back, my body hovering over hers. Her blonde hair spreads across the pillow as she looks up at me with heavy eyes. I grip the dress tangling around her waist and pull it down her legs. She leans up, grabs the elastic of my boxers hugging my hips, and pulls them down to my knees. I push her legs open with my hands and slide myself between them, resting my elbows on either side of her head. My dick finds her pussy quickly, and slides in with welcomed arousal. She's the only chick I'll let ride my dick without a condom. She's the only girl I trust to be clean and she's told me before that she's on birth control. Her back arches off the bed and a sexy growl sounds from her chest. I lean down and pull her nipple into my mouth, the sweet taste of her skin gliding along my tongue.

I thrust my hips hard, causing the bed to bang against the wall, and her to moan into the night air. She pushes her head back into the pillow and thrusts her hips up, eagerly wanting more.

"Say it, Jessica," I demand.

"Say what?" she questions, as she pants for air.

"Say you want more," I reply.

"I want more," she drawls out, thrusting her hips again.

I slam my dick into her hard. Her hands fly into my hair and tangle themselves, her legs wrapping around my waist as I begin to pound into her relentlessly. Her panting transforms into little moans as her body rocks with each of my thrusts. An electric pulse builds in my balls as my release rises. Her moans grow louder and animalistic as her legs squeeze my hips like a vise. She clamps her mouth closed trying to stifle the noise, and moans through her nose, giving off a humming sound.

I sit up, putting all my weight on my knees, and grab one of her breasts, fondling it. Her pussy grips my cock, her body thrashing around the bed, and her controlled moans are lost into a fitful of pleasurable cries. My balls squeeze tightly as pressure rips up my cock and spills out, making all the muscles in my body stiffen, causing me to growl while I come violently. My teeth grit as I pump into her a few more times, not wanting it to end. Her screams quiet as she falls against the mattress, breathing heavily, and I am following right behind her.

I lay beside her and listen to her harsh breathing. Her blonde hair tangled along the pillow, and the smell of sex filling the air. My chest aches trying to catch my breath, my eyes heavy as they want to sleep, but I try and fight it. I hate how fucked up I get over Jessica, and hate it even more when I wake and she's gone. Sometimes I wish she never came into the clubhouse looking to be saved. I wouldn't know what I was missing if she never introduced me to the feeling of wanting someone so badly only not to have them fully. I look over at the girl who dumbfounds me, tucking a stray hair behind her ear as she drifts off to sleep. Yet, I am fucking thrilled she picked my club to save her. One day, she'll give into me.

◆ ◆ ◆

I wake up to the sun just beginning to rise, producing barely enough light to see around the room. I sit up and look beside me finding an empty bed. Only the creased sheets greet me, reminding me of the incredible sex we had. She's gone. I fall back against the pillow and sigh, before closing my eyes and falling back to sleep.

I finally wake up around noon and grab some jeans and a t-shirt to get dressed. Sliding my hands through my hair as an act of combing before entering the hall, I walk up to the bar, blinking my eyes rapidly trying to wake up.

"You slept in late," Hawk observes, his eyes squinted as he glares. His once peppered-colored hair and beard are starting to turn a vigorous white, a staining of old age. He's fucking old as hell. I don't even know how old. He is our treasurer, been here way before I came into the club.

"Had company," I declare, glaring right back.

Hawk chuckles.

"You aren't going to say Doc visited you again, are you?" he questions, his tone disbelieving. His beard twitches back and forth over his mouth as if he's chewing on something, but I don't see any food around him. He does it a lot, and it's fucking irritating. I look at him, curious as to why he would ask if Doc visited me last night, he hardly talks to me.

"Why, you wouldn't be jealous would you?" I ask, shifting on my feet, leaning against the counter.

Hawk tosses a newspaper my way and chuckles. I raise an eyebrow at him and grab it, shaking it to smooth out the wrinkles.

Front page is Jessica and some guy walking out of a coffee shop. Headlines, in big black letters reading

HOLLYWOOD'S FINEST OFF THE MARKET.

My eyes bulge as I pull the paper close, reading the fine print. It says Doctor Shane Meldon has been said to be engaged to Doctor Jessica Wren. Resources say, he bought a ring yesterday before the date.

I grip the sides of the paper angrily. My nose flaring from rage, a burning building in my chest. What the fuck? She went on a date, got engaged, then came and laid in my bed? Let me fuck her, all the while wearing a fucking engagement ring?

◆ ◆ ◆

Me: We need to talk, now!

Jessica: I'm working.

Me: Either you come out to the parking lot, or I'm coming in.

I lean against Jessica's blue Jeep. Anger searing through my body, and a million thoughts swimming through my mind. I'll give her two minutes to get her ass out here to explain, and then I'm going into that hospital and confronting her. I know Jessica and I are not exclusive, but I thought I meant something to her to where she would tell me if she was in a serious relationship, *before fucking me.*

I push off the Jeep; her time is up. I can't wait here for two fucking minutes. I take a few steps and find Jessica walking out of the hospital.

"What the hell, Bobby?" Jessica questions, her arms held out on each side as she walks toward me. I pull the rolled up newspaper from the back of my jeans pocket and throw it at her.

She huffs, leans over, and picks it up.

Her eyes widen, and she brings the paper closer, wrinkles forming in the corner of her eyes as she squints at the paper puzzled. I tilt my head to the side, confused at her reaction.

She shakes her head back and forth, her lips pursed. "It's not true," she states, still looking at the paper.

I snort. "So you're saying you didn't get engaged. The paper is lying?" I question, my tone disbelieving.

"Not that it's any of your business, but yes, it's all bullshit," she replies, her forehead creasing with irritation. Nothing is any of my business, a line I hear from her more often than not.

I walk up to her, and get right in her face. My vision blurring from the fury running through my veins.

"It is my fucking business when you crawl in my bed with a fucking engagement ring on your hand, and come on my cock!" I yell, my face inches from hers.

"I'm not engaged to anybody!" she screams back at me, showing me her hand.

Relief floods my system, my head that was once pounding from the rush of blood flowing through me dissipating. I take a deep breath, and back away from Jessica.

"Who is this guy?" I ask, nodding toward the paper in her hands. He has to be someone important for cameras to be following him around taking his picture.

She looks back at the paper, and shakes her head. "Just some guy I work with," she remarks. I turn looking at the parking lot, and inhale sharply. I'm angry, more than I have ever been. The idea of Jessica being engaged, or dating someone so serious has my entire world at an end. But still, why did she come to my bed last night if she had a date with that guy? Does she do this often?

"Was he why you came to my bed last night?" Her head snaps up from the paper, her eyes pinning me down as her eyebrows furrow inward. She looks around her, and walks closer.

"What? Is that another one of your hard limits? We're not supposed to talk about *us*?" I question, my tone harsh. She opens her mouth to reply, but I cut her off. "You can't be seen with the likes of an outlaw is what this is all about, what it's ever been about," I announce, damn near shouting.

"Why are you acting like this?" Jessica tilts her head to the side, her eyes scanning my puffed-out chest, and curled fists. I have never behaved like this before; my emotions have me acting like an idiot.

"Do you talk to him? Do you tell him things you won't tell me?" I stalk toward her, and lean in close, lifting her chin with my finger. I want her to look me in the eyes when she answers me.

"This is enough. I need to get back to work," Jessica states, jerking her chin from my hold, and handing me the newspaper. I scoff. Typical Jessica. If I start asking any questions, she bails. When is enough, enough?

I inhale deeply, trying to calm myself. "All I have ever wanted was to protect you, and all I ever asked in return was for you to be open with me," I mutter.

She has never opened up to me. Not ever. Last night when she asked if I knew her, I was shocked. Her tone was sentimental yet desperate. It wasn't like Jessica, not at all. She took my dick like it was her lifeline last night.

"Bobby, you and I both know what we were getting into

when we started sleeping with each other. There is nothing between us and never will be. There can't be," she replies softly, her words angering me.

I always thought we were just denying that we wanted nothing more than to be friends, saving ourselves from the reality of what could happen if we didn't work out. But hearing her say those words without so much as a blink of an eye, feels like a bullet to the fucking chest, releasing the reality that I am nothing to Jessica and never will be.

I look back at her, her arms crossed in front of her, her blonde hair blowing with the breeze. I glance back at myself, all puffed out and angry. I've lost control. I've fucking snapped. I can't do this anymore.

"We are done," I mutter.

"What?" she asks frazzled, her eyes widening at my statement.

"You don't want anything from your life to be my business. Don't want to tell me anything about your past, even though it was me who got you away from your past!" I shout. "Let me make it easy for you. We. Are. Done," I snap, my jaw ticking.

"Bobby," Jessica cries out, her tone distraught. I throw my hand up dismissing her, walking back to my bike.

I slam my helmet on my head, looking at Jessica's pleading eyes as I start my bike. My heart is hammering against my chest and my body is sweating with my impulsive outburst. I don't want to walk away from Jessica. I don't want us to be over. But she has clearly made her mind up about me; that I am nothing more than a good fuck. I'm done taking the attention she throws my way. I need more from her. Me ending us will either have her step outside her comfort zone and give me more of her, or it will end us indefinitely. My chest tightens with that last thought, my hand itching to pull my helmet off and go cradle Jessica in her distressed state. All I have ever wanted was to keep her safe, make her happy. But how can I when she won't let me in at all? It doesn't have anything to do with crossing the line and complicating things. It's about trust. I blow out a breath, look away from her, and drive from my parking spot.

5

Jessica

IS HE SERIOUS? IS HE WALKING AWAY FROM ME AND LEAVING ME? My chest burns and my throat constricts from the emotions bubbling up inside of me, demanding to be released. He just threw me to the side in the middle of a parking lot. I grab the newspaper and stomp inside the hospital searching for Shane. I want to know why I had my fucking picture taken with him, why I'm supposedly engaged to him, and why anyone would care enough to put it in the paper.

Just as I enter the hospital doors, I find him coming out of a patient's room. I grab him by the shirt, and drag him into the lounge. Tripping over his feet as he tries to keep up with me, I pull him along.

"What the hell is this?" I snap angrily, slapping the newspaper to his chest once we are alone.

He looks at me confused, shock laced in his raised eyebrows from my angry tone as he grabs the paper.

"Shit," he mutters, looking at the paper, his hands running

through his perfectly combed hair.

"What the hell, Shane?" I ask.

"I'm sorry about this, Jessica," he replies, looking the paper over.

"Why does the paper care if you are engaged? Who are you?" I demand, questions flying from my mouth quickly.

Shane sighs, dropping his head, his fingers pinching the bridge of his nose.

"My father," Shane remarks, like that just answered everything. "He is a retired actor. Reece Meldon," he elaborates.

My eyes widen. I know exactly who that is. He was in some big action movies years back. "Ever since I was a kid, I have had people follow me around shoving cameras in my face. All hoping one day I would follow in my father's footsteps," he continues, setting the paper down on a nearby table. "I went to the jewelry store yesterday to get my watch fixed. It must have caught some wind. People get paid for stories and the paper just prints them, whether they are true or not," he adds.

This is what he was hiding last night, when that guy took a picture of us outside the coffee shop. He could have easily fixed this problem then. He could have taken the camera, beat the guy up, anything. I close my eyes and sigh. Listen to me, 'beat the guy up'. Bobby has rubbed off on me; the club has tainted my mind. Bobby, his look of anger and disappointment when he threw the paper at me flashes in my mind. He just walked away from me because of this shit. Leaving me feeling emptier than I have ever felt.

"This caused me a lot of problems," I remark, pointing to the newspaper. Tears threatening to spill from my eyes.

"It won't happen again," Shane states, nodding and looking at the paper now resting on the table.

◆ ◆ ◆

I drive to Addie's school, park in the circle parking lot, and wait for her to come out. I notice all the married couples picking up their children, laughing, smiling; they're picture perfect. I snarl at them, disgusted by their happiness. The way they make it look so easy to find a soul mate, appear to be so flawlessly in love without a care in the world angers me. I clench my jaw, my eyes narrowing. I stare at my fingers deep in thought. I have been on a path of fury since this morning. Bobby declaring us over is all my fault. See why love is a disaster waiting to happen – at least for me it is. I want to be open with Bobby. I want to tell him everything that has ever happened to me, but what good would it do? When I'm with Bobby, when we are together, I am free from every burden. I'm in another dimension, another world. The only thing on my mind, the only thoughts in my head, is the pleasure between him and me. I didn't want to complicate that with explaining my fucked-up past. Now, I don't have Bobby at all, which is worse.

"Hey, Mom!"

I look behind me finding Addie climbing in the back seat. She looks so beautiful today, her blonde hair in pigtails, and her cute little red dress, with black leggings on. I had just missed Bree taking her to school this morning.

"Hey, baby, how was your day?" I question, smiling. It doesn't matter what kind of day I've had, or what terrible feeling I am experiencing, Addie with her innocence and bright personality always makes those dark moments vanish. Being a single mother is hard, but I wouldn't trade it for anything in the world. Every memory from her throwing up on me in the middle of the night, to losing her first tooth is a memory I cherish.

"Eh, it was school. Do we get to pick up movies tonight?" she asks, pulling her seatbelt across her lap.

"Yes, we can," I reply, pulling from the circular drive. Since she stayed at Bree's the other night, we didn't get to have our movie night that I had previously promised.

I look in the rearview mirror, and notice Addie is smiling like a goofball out the window as we pull out onto the main road.

"What are you so chipper about today?" I laugh, looking back in the mirror. Addie takes her gaze from the window to me, her little braces gleaming with the sunlight as her soft round cheeks take a hue of pink.

"I think a boy likes me," she squeals, her cheeks going from pink to red. My face falls, and my heart plummets.

"What?" I turn around, taking my eyes off the road, making a car honk its horn in passing.

"Shit," I curse, pulling on the steering wheel to get back in my lane.

I look in the rearview mirror at Addie, her smiley red face gone and now frowning. I shake my head, silently cursing myself for my outburst. But my little girl is only nine, boys already?

"That's great," I try to muster, putting on a fake smile. Her face beams as her braces come back into full view with a big grin.

"He is *so* cute, Mom. His name is Anthony, and he is *so* good at basketball," she rambles, her voice giddy and happy. "You don't have to worry. He's not one of the bad kids in class or anything. He's really smart," she comforts, trying to ease my mind. I give a tight-lipped smile and pull into the movie rental's parking lot. I'm not worried about him being a bad kid, not at the age of nine. I am worried about him breaking my daughter's heart. All boys are heartbreakers, wearing what's left of a girl's heart they broke on their sleeve.

◆ ◆ ◆

I love my daughter, but the movies she's picked for tonight have me wanting to pull my eyeballs out.

Armageddon, Never Been Kissed, and *A Walk To Remember.* Someone shoot me.

"How about we watch mine first?" I suggest, tossing the DVDs on the coffee table. Addie turns from the sounds of popcorn popping, and her face twists as her nose turns up.

"*Chuckie?*" Addie asks, her voice laced with disapproval at my movie selection. What can I say? I love scary movies.

"No thanks, Mom," she replies, pulling the bag of popcorn out of the microwave. I sigh and plop down on the couch. Sappy love stories it is then.

Addie doesn't even make it through all of her movies. She passed out thirty minutes ago, leaving me to a pillow clutched against my chest, and tears running down my face as I watch the ending of *A Walk To Remember*. I shake my head, wipe away the tears, and silently curse Addie and her puppy love. I place a blanket on Addie, not wanting to wake her and turn the TV and lights off. I walk into my room, pulling my sweats off, and releasing my hair from its ponytail.

My eyes land on my phone next to my table as I climb into bed. I want to call Bobby. I don't want us to end. I don't know what *we* even are to one another, but when he walked away today, the earth fell from under my feet. He is the only security I have in this world. I can't lose him.

Do I fight my fear? Triumph the terror wracking my mind

and soul and gamble on the chance that Bobby can reset it all, make me forget my past and actually restart and build a life without being afraid? Or do I do what I know best, resisting, and run home behind my door with the security of three deadbolts and wonder what if?

I have tried therapy, tried stupid medications to overcome what scares me every day, hoping one day, I can find a great guy and extend our little family, but none of it ever works. I have nothing because of the terror that lives within me, and I have no idea how to get rid of it. But Bobby, he wants to help me. He wants to make me better. But how? How can he make it better when nobody else can? He doesn't even know why I am the way I am. I sigh, close my eyes, and feel the loneliness creep into my soul.

Bobby

I ROLL A JOINT, TRYING TO ESCAPE THE THOUGHTS OF JESSICA plaguing my mind. I reach for my lighter as my cell phone rings, stopping me. I fish out my phone instead of the lighter, and answer it.

"What do you want to know?" Jessica asks, her voice soft and shaky. I drop my joint to the floor, my mouth parting in shock. Did I hear her right? I have tried to get information about Jessica's past for years, and here she is asking me what I want to know, like an open book. I run my hands through my hair and sit up straight in my chair. Why is she wanting to tell me now? Is my walking away a big deal for her, too?

"Why are you willing to tell me now after all these years?" I question. I have to know. I need to know what's different.

I hear her inhale through the phone as she prepares for her reply.

"Because, you're the only person who might be able to free me from my past, from the fear that plans my daily agenda. I trust you," she replies. I nod, knowing exactly what she means. Even with me not knowing a lot about Jessica, she is always safe with me. I could never fully walk away from her, even if I really wanted to, and it really pisses me off sometimes.

"I want to know where the marks on your back came from. Why they are there. I want to know why you sleep with me in only one position and with the lights off. I want to know why you are so afraid of living." The questions that have played through my mind every time I see Jessica spill from my mouth uncontrollably.

I hear her choke as a sniffle sounds through the speaker. I hear her breaking, making me second-guess this whole thing. Jessica is a strong woman. I haven't heard her this wrecked since the day she showed up at the club, it guts me.

"Why, why do you want to know those things so badly, Bobby?" she whispers painfully.

"I killed a man for a woman I knew nothing about; still don't. But with killing him, I thought I would save you, set you free, Jessica, but I didn't. Something still haunts you," I answer grimly.

She sniffles through the phone, her breathing trembling in short spurts.

"Let's start out small. How did you meet your ex-husband?" I ask, trying to ease her into the difficult memories. The line is quiet, making me wonder if she hung up.

"Travis wasn't always a monster. I loved him at one point," she laughs bitterly. "That's what makes it so difficult. You really think you know someone, only to discover you were so fucking wrong."

I have come across a few people like that inside the club before, so I know where she is coming from.

"I understand that, believe me," I mutter.

"My father was an ambitious man, wanted what was best for the family. I was to walk in his footsteps joining only the best of the medical practices in the state. But that all took flight when my father met Travis Norwell." Her words grit with anger as she says her ex-husband's name. "*Travis* was my father's golden ticket to the board of the most prestigious hospital in the state. Gone with what was best for his daughter and family. The only thing that mattered was what was better for him. He told me I would marry Travis, and do my family the honor of taking on the Norwell name. When I met Travis, he was strikingly good looking, smart, and very kind. I could do a lot worse, so I didn't resist. Things became serious between us over the summer. I was very inexperienced, where he wasn't. We grew hot and heavy for one another quickly. After some short months of puppy love, we decided to get married," she replies, her tone a little less strained. Travis sounds like a fucking Ken doll. Where did it all go wrong?

"Where did the marks on your back come from?" I question, jumping forward. Maybe I'm wrong. Maybe the marks aren't from the husband.

"The marks on my..." she trails off, her voice cracking. She clears her throat as if she is trying to get a hold of herself.

"The marks on my back are from Travis," she starts, her tone emotionless; it's as if she is reading a book aloud. "After several months, my new husband told me he was bored with our sex life. That he needed more excitement in the bedroom. I agreed. What could it hurt, ya know?" she remarks. I shrug even though she can't see me. "Things were spectacular as we went to spanking, and sex toys. I loved it. He wanted more in-depth BDSM, and I agreed," she explains, her tone excited, but taking an edge of grief. My dick jumps at the thought of spanking Jessica, making me rub my crotch to ease the tension.

"One night he brought home whips and handcuffs. I was down for it, excited really. When we—" she stops, the sound of her breathing through the phone making my body shutter and my dick go limp. I literally hear the pain in just her breathing. I want to tell her to stop, not to bring on the hurtful memories, but I'm selfish. I have to know. I *need* to know if I have any chance at helping Jessica move forward from her past.

"He got really rough," she continues softly. "Left whelps all over my body and face from the cheap whip and my wrist broke in the handcuffs, from being placed too tightly. I kept screaming for him to ease up, that he was hurting me, but it was as if he fed off my cries of pain," she continues, her tone laced with misery. My jaw ticks and I close my eyes. Bashing that fucker's head in with my boot and shooting him was too easy of an out for him.

"He told me the next day he was sorry, that he didn't know what had come over him, that he would be more gentle next time," she snorts. "The next time he wasn't any better. When he was done with me, I was bleeding from the nose and down—" she stops, and I swallow heavily. I'm not sure I can handle much more of this knowing what he did to her, and I can't bring him back from the dead to kill him all over again.

"After a few more weeks, I healed, and he wanted to go back into the whips and cuffs. I refused. I told him he became a monster when I gave him that kind of control." She inhales a big breath. "He dragged me into our basement, slapped me around, and made me submit to him. Months of this occurred.

He had upgraded to all kinds of sexual devices to use on me by then. I was not allowed to work anymore. I couldn't with all the marks on me. I was to ask permission for pretty much everything, and call him Master. If I didn't comply, I suffered the consequences."

"Jesus," I whisper, pinching the bridge of my nose. I never knew it was that bad. I knew her husband was a monster, but even monsters have more remorse than her ex-husband.

"I found out I was pregnant and I tried to run one day. What any normal person would do. I couldn't have my child around that kind of abuse, but Travis had men waiting for me at the airport. They grabbed me and threw me in the back of a car. When they brought me back to the house, Travis pulled me out of the car by my hair, dragged me to the front porch, and handcuffed me to a large pillar. Ripping my dress off my back, he plucked a whip from the willow tree out front and thrashed it against my back so hard, it made everything I had endured before seem like a walk in the park. He made me scream that I would obey him, never leave him again, that he was my master. He would make me yell that I loved him, and in return, tell me I was unlovable, that I was incapable of having another's love. If I refused or objected, he would lash the whip at me again," she sobs into the phone. "That's where the scars on my back came from," she whispers solemnly.

"Damn, Jessica," I mumble into the phone, images of her cuffed to a porch and being whipped flashing in my mind's eye.

"And that Bobby, is why I am, the way I am. I see his face all the time, feel the burn of the scars on my back when I am doing something he would not have allowed," she continues, her tone a fraction stronger than before.

"He can't hurt you anymore, babe," I reassure, trying to comfort her.

I have more questions, but after all that, I can't stomach anymore. My gut twists with empathy for Jessica. She went through a life of hell with that son of a bitch, and even dead, he still haunts her.

"I didn't tell you all this for pity. I told you so you would understand," she explains, doing so with confidence.

"I want to help you, Jessica." I run my hand over my face, stressed.

"How?" Her voice trembles, giving away she does want me, needs me, even if she doesn't realize it.

"I don't know, but I'll figure it out," I respond truthfully. I will figure it out, and I will help her. I took on the position when she came into the club years ago, accepting to kill her husband so she and her daughter didn't have to live in fear, but the job isn't finished.

◆ ◆ ◆

I have no idea how to help Jessica. Not a fucking clue. But I banged this therapist a few times some months back and she would go on and on about the people she was treating before we fucked. I even gagged her at one time to shut her up. Maybe she can give me some insight into what I am dealing with and how to go about it.

I dial Hilary's number, hoping it's not too late for her to answer.

"Bobby, ready for another therapeutic session, baby?" she coos, her voice smooth and seductive. I smirk; this girl could use some therapy herself.

"I need some advice on how to go about something," I reply, ignoring her advances.

"Like what, hun?" she asks sweetly, her sultry tone gone.

"There's this girl. She has been through an abusive relationship; just an overall shitty past. She was married to a man who sounds like a sadistic fucker. He made her a sex slave basically, abusing her if she disobeyed. She's haunted by it and can't escape the memories of what she had been through," I explain.

"Sounds like Post Traumatic Stress Disorder," she answers quickly. I lower my head, running my hands through my hair. Shit, I am out of my league here.

"Okay, how do I help her?" I question. I have heard of the term but know nothing about it.

"Therapy is an option. Medication can help," she rambles as if she is in therapist mode. I know Jessica and she either has already tried those, or is too stubborn to ask for help.

"What else ya got?"

"Hmm. You could try exposure therapy. I have had a bit of luck with that one. Plus, you would love the benefits of it," she giggles, her tone back to slutty.

"What the fuck is it?" I ask, dumbfounded.

"You will expose her to what she is fearing. Replace her bad memories with good memories. For example, if you're scared of the dark, you send the patient into the dark. In a safe setting of course. You wouldn't throw them in the middle of an alley at night and tell them good luck. You would start in a bedroom with you guiding them, comforting them along the way," she explains further. "So in your circumstance, you will introduce her to a sexual setting outside of her comfort, teaching her how to make it comfortable and pleasurable again. But I'm warning you, I have seen patients become very agitated, and physically violent with this type of therapy," she warns.

"Shit," I mutter.

"If she rejects the treatment, it could do more harm than good, and if this woman means anything to you, you could lose

her permanently," she mutters, her tone stern and professional.

"Thanks for the information, Hilary," I reply.

"Good luck, babe. If you need me give me a shout," she adds
before hanging up.

"Fuck," I whisper to myself. I'm scared shitless. I'm not
going to lie. There is a big possibility that I will do more
damage than good, and become the Devil Jessica thinks I am.

Jessica

I WAKE UP FEELING A LITTLE LIGHTER THAN USUAL THIS
morning. Maybe it's because I told Bobby some of my past;
things I have tried to forget about but don't seem to be
vanishing. Like they say, the truth will set you free. I smirk,
and roll out of bed. Shit, today I meet my mother for lunch.
Despite the things that have happened with my father and
Travis in my past, I still speak to my mother. When I would
show up at my parents' house years ago wearing long sleeves
in the summer, or sunglasses in the dimly lit house, my father
always acted as if it was normal behavior and turned a blind
eye. My mother always looked at me warily, but never said
anything.

I had thought she was just as cruel and greedy as my father,
until the night I returned home from coming to the Devil's
Dust for help. My mother was at my house when I returned in
the wee hours of the morning, concerned about where I had
gone. I didn't tell her of course. After ignoring her and tucking
Addie into bed, she insisted she stay the night to make sure
Addie and I were okay. The police showed up on my doorstep

hours later, not giving me the chance to report my husband not returning home from work.

They asked me a million questions, but the person who saved my ass was my mother. She gave me an alibi. Said I was with her scrapbooking. She even got the housekeeper to confirm it. How? I don't know. I never told her what happened with the club and Travis, but I think she knows I had something to do with Travis's disappearance. I see her twice a month here in California for lunch, catching up on a few things and giving her time to see Addie.

I walk into the living room and find Addie watching cartoons on TV. Her hair is a blonde mess and she is still wearing pajamas, a bowl containing some leftover cereal and milk sitting on the coffee table.

"Hey, I am going to see Grandma Wren today. You want to come, hun?" I ask, getting my coffee fix. I can't get enough of coffee, without it, there is no way I would have survived Addie's baby years, or the difficult hours of my job.

"No thank you," she replies, not taking her eyes from the screen.

"How come?" I question, grabbing a mug from the cabinet.

"Just don't feel like it today," she responds. I shrug. I am not going to force her to see my mom. I know she can be a little too excited when she sees Addie, coming off crazy with her high screams and arms held out wide.

I get dressed in a white shirt and blue jeans, throw on my flats, and head across the hall to Bree's apartment.

I knock on it sipping my warm coffee. Hopefully, she won't be taking any exams today and can keep an eye on Addie, otherwise Addie will have to come with me.

"Hey, what's up?" Bree asks, opening the door. Her dark hair is pulled into messy pigtails, and she is still wearing her pajamas.

"Have you been to bed yet?" I laugh, looking at her bloodshot eyes.

"Yeah, I got a couple hours of sleep. I have a paper due and waited 'til the last minute," she yawns, pushing her glasses up.

"Can you watch Addie for me today? I am going to go see my mom and Addie isn't up for it."

"Yeah, sure, babe, let me grab my books," she replies, twirling her left pigtail.

"Awesome, make yourself at home. I have plenty of groceries if you get hungry," I add, walking back into my apartment to grab my purse and phone. I lean over the overstuffed couch and give Addie's head a big kiss, her smell of bubble gum shampoo wafting around me. I'll never get tired of that smell. It's a smell of comfort and a reminder of how blessed I am to have her. If Travis and I did anything right in our relationship, it was creating her.

"Be good, baby. Call me if you need me," I mumble into her hair.

She nods, while keeping her eyes glued to the TV.

◆ ◆ ◆

I drive to the country club that is over two hours away. My mother has my back with Travis's disappearance, but I can't take any chances. I wish I could see her more, but to put Addie and me so close to Travis's side of the family in Nevada is too risky. Nobody asked questions when I said I was moving after Travis's disappearance luckily, making it easy to get away from any suggestion that I had something to do with him being missing. I simply said I couldn't be in our house anymore; that it brought too many memories. Everyone took it to be endearing, but in reality, I meant it in a traumatic way.

I pull up to the white marbled building, a huge bright green golf course surrounding the estate, with a red barn filled with top-bred horses sitting off in the distance. It's a country club for the wealthy; it's the only place my mother ever wants to meet.

I drive onto the circular drive, parking under the canopy where a valet stands professionally with his arms crossed behind his back. Wearing a black hat and a maroon vest, his cheeks are shaved clean and his brown eyes greet me brightly.

His eyes form a scowl as he eyes my Jeep. My car is not something he is used to seeing at such an establishment I'm sure.

I climb out and toss him the keys, causing him to eye me like I've lost my mind. I wink and walk inside, heading to the restaurant in the club. The carpet is soft under the soles of my flats, and the smell of expensive cigars and perfume invite me as I walk in.

Looking over the sea of white-clothed tables, I spot my mother right away. Her blonde hair is flawless, skirting down her shoulders, a poufy hat on her head, and she is wearing some hideous peach-colored dress. She hands a fork to a waiter with a disgusted look on her face, before her eyes catch mine. She immediately stands, her eyes sparking with excitement. I smirk and head over to her.

"Jessica, my dear," my mother greets, taking me into a big hug. Her perfume is strong; I can't even make out what it smells like aside from alcohol. It makes my head swim from the fumes.

"Where is Addie?" my mother asks, looking behind me as if Addie will magically appear.

"She wasn't feeling up to it today," I reply, sitting on the stylish chair across from her.

"I see," she replies, disappointed as she takes her seat. "I wish she would have come. I hardly get to see her as it is," she continues, her tone calculating and stern.

I give a tight-lipped smile and pick the menu up. My mother may seem like an over-the-top priss but she really isn't. I have seen her when she's not in the public's eyes, or around my father. She is awesome and actually kind of cool. But she would gasp in horror if she heard me refer to her as cool.

"Are you going to give me any more grand babies, Jessica?" she asks casually, gazing over her menu. "Have you met anyone yet?" she continues to question after I chose to ignore her. I sigh heavily; we have this conversation every time we see each other.

"I'm going to give you the same answer as last time; no," I answer just as casually, looking over my menu.

My mother collapses her arms on her menu and groans. Her face doesn't scowl or frown from all the Botox, but I can tell she is displeased.

"You are free, Jessica. You can be with anyone now. Why are you doing this to yourself?" she nags, shaking her head.

My mother doesn't know about my fear, or that I have night terrors of Travis. She had no idea that I was terrified of falling in love with someone. I keep everyone at bay to keep that from happening in fact. I loved Travis. I fell for him hard after he took my virginity when we were younger. I was one of those girls, yes. After he literally beat me into not loving him, preaching in my ear that I was unlovable, the last thing I want to do is get cozy with any man.

My mother knows nothing of that. She refers to me being free and being able to be with anyone I want, and has done so since I was a teenager, or more specifically, from the first time

I rebelled against my father. We were at one of our usual stuck-up family gatherings. My mother was showing her new furniture off while my father was handing out expensive cigars, and I was outside on the patio away from it all. I didn't even know everyone. My family gatherings consisted of a handful of actual family members and high-profile couples my parents knew. If my father or mother saw me, they would call me over and brag about how well I was doing in my educational courses. How I had colleges already interested. It was humiliating. I loved medicine, don't get me wrong. But sometimes, I just wanted to run with the wind to see where it took me.

I was sitting outside in some over-the-top black dress my mother insisted I wear in the heat of the summer, bored out of my mind when I met Vincent. I had seen him from parties my parents had before. He would stare at me from afar, an alluring smirk across his face as his eyes devoured me. He made me feel taboo. The unknowing in the ripe ages of my teen years.

The day I actually talked to Vincent, he was wearing black dress pants, and a button up shirt that was partially unbuttoned at the neck, and he had the sleeves rolled to his elbows. He wasn't that attractive really, but was different from most of the people I came across.

"Why are you sulking? Did princess not get her way?" Vincent ridiculed as I sat on the fluffy patio chair.

"Excuse me?" I questioned, holding my arm up to shield my eyes from the blazing sun. He smirked and looked out over the pool, running his hands through his short sandy-colored hair. He pulled a cigarette from behind his ear and lit it. He slid his gaze from the pool and looked at me, his vibrant eyes looking me up and down as he blew smoke out of his nose into the summer heat.

"So why are you so sad?" he asked, taking a drag from his cigarette.

"I'm not sad. I'm just bored," I replied, wrapping my arms around myself. I had never had anyone talk to me in such a manner before.

"Bored?" he scoffed, sliding his tongue over his bottom lip that looked like it was healing from being split open. "What do you do for fun?" he questioned, humor lacing his words, implying I wouldn't know what fun was.

"I don't know, stuff," I responded, tucking a stray hair behind my ear.

"Stuff?" he snorted. "Like being nose deep into some medical book?" he asked condescendingly, tilting his head to the side as he placed the cigarette between his teeth. I couldn't stop looking at him. He was bad, so very bad, but beautifully bad.

"Everyone around here has heard how Jessica Wren is destined for great things. Hell, my father won't shut up about how great Dr. Wren's daughter is," he huffed, pacing around me. I shook my head and gritted my teeth. I hated how my father showboated; I was nothing special. The only reason I did so well in my academics was because he drilled my head into medical book after medical book. I was homeschooled by the best.

I stood up and grabbed his cigarette from his mouth, placing the butt of it between my glossed lips.

"I have a lot of fun; I'll have you know," I responded, taking a drag. Its metal taste burned my throat, urging me to cough, but I held it back. He smirked, his grayish eyes looking at me with interest.

"So, then what are you waiting for?" he asked, his smile daring and scandalous as he took the cigarette from between my fingers.

"What?" I questioned, my eyes widening in panic.

"Let's go. Show me what you do for fun," he continued smoothly, grabbing my hand. *My heart pounded faster than it ever had as he ran toward a bright red barn near the property line, my hand in his sweaty palm.*

My father found us behind the barn making out a couple hours later. Vincent was my first kiss. I felt things I never had before. He made me laugh, made me feel like an actual woman in only a couple of hours. I kicked my heels off and climbed a tree that day, caught my first frog by hand at the pond behind the barn. He also managed to get to second base. I felt free from accusing eyes, not worried if it was lady like or well mannered.

I remember my father's trusty sidekicks dragging Vincent under his arms into a shed on the property that was always locked after they had found us. I never saw Vincent again. I yelled that I was running away and that I hated my father; that I was a prisoner in his household. My father told me Vincent was the kind of scum who would use me. That Vincent left without hesitation when my father asked him to stay away. That if Vincent truly wanted to be with me, he would show back up. I waited at our security gate for three days, but he never showed up again.

"Jessica!" My head jolts upward from looking at the white tablecloth, lost in my memories of early childhood lust.

"Yeah?" I question, my voice cracking my suddenly dry mouth.

"I don't know a lot of what happened between you and Travis," she mutters. She holds her hands up and pins me with her eyes, "and I don't want to know, but I would think you are lucky getting the second chance at life after escaping such a dreadful marriage. Don't waste it."

I give a tightlipped smile and look back at my menu while

thoughts of Vincent still swim in my head.

"What ever happened to Vincent?" I blurt out.

My mother's cheeks turn red as she licks her lips slowly.

I stare at her intently, waiting.

"Your father told him to never come near you again," she responded quickly, looking at her menu.

"Did he? Did Vincent ever come back?" I ask. My mother sighs and sets her menu back down.

"Yes, but he was no good for you, just like your father said. You were so young, capable of so much. Vincent was a wild child. He would have taken everything you worked so hard for and ran with it before you even had the chance to discover what you truly wanted in life. I don't know what his kind was doing at our party," she continues, shaking her head. I slam my menu down angry. This is not my mother talking; this is the woman my father has sculpted.

"Stop the act," I snap harshly. She jumps and looks at me with wide eyes.

My mother nods, taking a deep breath.

"Why didn't you stand up for Vincent, for me?" I interrogate further. Maybe if she had, I would have never ended up with Travis.

"Your father had his eyes sat on Travis at that point, Jessica. There was no interfering with that," she answers softly, pursing her lips. "If I thought it would have helped, I would have stepped in," she continues. "After your father met Travis, all he could see was making it on the board of the hospital and you working in that hospital; it was his dream." I try not to roll my eyes. My mother loves my father. She will never speak ill of him. To her, my father ignoring my bruises and black eyes was him reaching *his* dream.

"How is that working out for him, being on the board?" I

interrupt, done talking about me. She shakes her head and looks out over the tables.

"Ever since Travis went missing years back, things went downhill quickly with Travis's family. Your father has pretty much taken over everything at the hospital. Travis's father became a drunk, and was taken off the board soon after Travis's disappearance. Last I heard, they were bankrupt and living in the worst part of town," she continues. I close my eyes, hating to hear Travis's family is suffering. I assumed they would move on from the loss of their son, and continue ruling the medicine industry. But why would I know that? I don't talk to them and my mother usually knows not to talk about them around me.

I nod, and raise my hand ready to order. Ready to eat and leave.

Over the rest of our meal, we talk about my mother wanting to repaint a room in her house, and celebrity gossip. I give her a big hug and kiss, and nearly sprint to my Jeep, ready to get away from memories that always seem to swim forward when I'm around my mom.

I lean over and turn the stereo on, Usher's "His Mistakes" is playing. Travis, Vincent, and Bobby all come to my mind at once. Making my body tense. I'm more than aware that Vincent and Bobby have more than a few similarities. Why did I run to Vincent but run from Bobby? I take a deep breath and roll my window down. I run because of Travis, the middleman between it all.

6
Bobby

Parking my bike in front of Jessica's apartment, I head to her gate. As I go to punch in the numbers, the gate swings open. It's not locked.

"What the hell?" I push the gate the rest of the way open, and head toward Jessica's apartment.

I notice stains on the carpet as I walk in, and the hallway has a musky smell to it. I haven't been here in a few months, but the last time I was here, it was an upscale place, and if I remember right, Jessica said the rent wasn't cheap.

I knock on Jessica's door, hoping she wasn't called in to work.

The door whips open and Jessica is standing in a white tank top, white panties, and an untied blue robe. The cool draft coming from the hall causes her nipples to peek through the thin material of her top. I can't look away, my mouth watering to have them in my mouth.

"Shit, I thought you were Bree," Jessica shrieks, trying to cover herself with her hands. "What are you doing here?" she asks harshly, wrapping the robe around her half-naked body. She doesn't like it when I come to her house, but I do it anyway.

"I made sure to wait until Addie was at school, chill," I reply, stepping around her, making my way into her place.

She sighs and shuts the door behind me. Her apartment is clean and smells of coffee. The overstuffed tan couch sits in front of an entertainment center, and there's a desk in the corner with a large computer. Looking to my right, a small kitchen with a wooden top island sits, complete with white bar stools, and stainless steel appliances lining the back wall. She moved a few things around since I was here last, but it's mostly the same.

"We need to talk," I inform her, sitting on one of the stools. Her eyes peek above her coffee mug as she takes a sip, looking at me with a concerned glare. My eyes travel down her body, the tops of her breasts swelling above her top, and a sliver of her belly showing between her shirt and panties. I turn my head and adjust my semi-hard dick. Jessica is the most stunning woman I know. If I keep eye fucking her, I'll never get out what I came here to say.

"I think I can help you," I start, biting my bottom lip in nervousness.

Jessica's body stiffens and she looks away from me. "How?" she whispers, instinctively knowing what I am talking about. I interlock my fingers sitting on top of the island, and swallow.

"I think you have Post Traumatic Stress Disorder," I inform softly, waiting for her to bite my head off and argue. I wouldn't have said it if I didn't believe it though. I looked up PTSD all day yesterday, and I'm certain that is what Jessica has.

"No, I don't," Jessica snaps offended, her blue eyes stabbing me angrily, and her fingers digging into her mug.

"Yes, you do, Jessica. You live in fear of your ex-husband. He's conditioned your mind, trained you to behave a certain way. You can't do things you used to do because he is still in your mind, haunting you severely," I bark, pointing to my head to emphasis my point.

Jessica leans against her counter, scowling, and shaking her head at me.

"I have a friend who is a therapist. I briefly told her what was going on and she said it was PTSD," I answer, my tone more gentle than before.

Jessica closes her eyes and huffs. I can tell she is not happy I told someone else about what she told me, but I was out of my league and I needed advice.

"Medicine doesn't work. Therapy doesn't work, so whether or not I have PTSD is pointless. Nothing helps," she clips, shrugging.

"I have a different medicine," I smirk. Her scowl turns into a look of curiosity.

"What?" she questions, her blue eyes looking at me like I'm her last hope.

I also searched exposure therapy all day yesterday. It has a high rate in effectiveness, making me more eager to try it. I worry my lips between my teeth and take a deep breath. I'm a little nervous at how she is going to react.

"Sex," I respond.

Jessica laughs, setting her cup on the counter. She's not taking me seriously. I knew she wouldn't.

"Okay, time for you to go," she remarks, still laughing.

"I'm serious, Jessica," I interrupt. "It's called exposure

therapy. From what you told me, most of your abuse was when your husband made you submit to him sexually, abusing you in the bedroom," I say seriously, standing from the stool. Jessica's face stills, her smile from laughing fading into a frown. She runs her hand through her long, blonde hair, the ends curling around her fingers. Her chest rises as she breathes harshly from my confrontation.

"So I should just go have as much sex as I can? I've tried that. It doesn't work. It just..." She stops, taking a deep breath. I close my eyes, not really caring to hear about her sleeping around to help overcome her tormented life.

"Not with just anyone, but with me," I grit. "I will take those situations, the condition he programmed into your head and redo them in a setting that makes you safe, replace the bad memories with good, with pleasure rather than pain." I walk around the counter and grasp her by the hips, making her look at me. Her blue eyes glossy with tears, her cheeks flushed.

"How are you any different than sex with anyone else?" she asks, a tear slipping over her lips.

I reach up and rub the tear off her bottom lip with my thumb.

"Because you trust me, and you're safe with me," I comfort honestly. She smirks, licking the rest of the tear from her lips.

"What if it doesn't work?" she questions, shrugging.

"What do you have to lose?" I state, running my nose along her cheek.

Jessica runs her hand under her nose trying to get a hold of herself.

"I don't know. This sounds silly. What do you get out of this?" she implores, grabbing her mug off the counter, breaking from my grip.

I snort and smirk. "Seriously?" I laugh. "I get laid." I am not going to lie. I am pretty good at sex; it's one of the few things I am awesome at. I know for a fact I can fill Jessica with pleasure easily. It will be getting past those memories that will be the hardest.

She laughs, and takes a sip of her coffee.

"I also get to help a friend," I respond truthfully, my joking set aside.

"I don't think this is going to work," she says softly.

I nod and brush the hair behind her ear. "I've done a lot of research on this. It will work if you let it work," I inform. Her eyes widen, and she turns her head to the side, looking at me quizzically.

"You researched it?" she questions, her eyes looking me over longingly. She fucking loves it when I use my intelligence; the way her eyes get heavy and she looks at me hungrily. I eat that shit up. I can be smart when I want to be. But that's it; I have to be interested in learning it.

"You have to trust me, Jessica," I mumble, running my hand down her soft cheek.

Jessica's eyes look up at me, my frame towering over her in her small kitchen.

"I think we need some rules, Bobby," she whispers, pushing me back a step. I take a deep breath and back up. Rules. I hate that word. Everyone has them and I'm a pro at breaking them.

"Like what?" I ask, exasperated, walking back to my stool on the other side of the counter.

"I don't know. I just feel like this is going to turn out badly," she says, leaning over the island, giving me a clear shot of her breasts. I groan as my dick pulses from the teasing glimpse I have of them.

"I don't want this around my daughter," she says sternly, her eyebrow raised to indicate her point. I cock my head to the side and cross my arms. I have seen Addie only a handful of times since the night Jessica and Addie came to the club for help.

"What do you have against me so badly I can't be around Addie?"

She shrugs and lifts from the counter, taking my view of her tits away, causing me to regret my question.

"The club is dangerous. I don't need some thug using my daughter as leverage to get back at you guys," she continues. I want to argue, but she has a point.

"Okay," I reply, clearly defeated. "Is that the only rule?"

"And," she pauses, setting her coffee down. She looks up, and brushes her hair behind her ear.

"You can't fall in love with me. We can't let this get emotional," she mutters, her eyes peeking up from under her thick lashes.

My eyebrows narrow. "Why is that?" Am I that bad to fall in love with?

"I have seen the men in the club when they love a woman. I was already trapped in one relationship. I won't be an ol' lady," she continues, her jaw clenched. I swallow the lump in my throat and nod.

"Well, I'm not looking for anything serious, so you won't have to worry about that," I respond, nodding. I look down at my hands, avoiding eye contact.

"I think this is just a way for you to get in my pants when you want, but at this point, I am desperate to try anything," she informs with a chuckle.

I laugh and stand. Placing my hands on the counter, I lower my head, and gaze at her longingly.

"I'm going to fuck you mindlessly, Jessica. Giving you that exhilarating feeling of your body going numb, and your toes curling from the overwhelming high from my dick hitting you in places you never knew it could." I lean over the counter, brushing aside a hair that fell in front of her eyes. "When I'm done with you, you'll never want to walk away from me, Jessica," I whisper, my tone deep and arrogant.

"And now that I mention it." I walk around the counter, my boots thudding against her tiled floors. Her eyes look at me lazily, her lips parting.

I grasp her by the hips, pull her toward me roughly, and lean into her. I brush my lips against the shell of her ear, causing her body to rise with a sudden breath.

"Yeah?" she whispers, her tone dripping with lust.

"During this whole process, you are only to be mine," I whisper, nipping her earlobe. I'm not going to share Jessica. Not if I don't have to.

"I don't know if that's a good idea," she breathes heavily, turning her head, inviting me into her neck. My dick jumps with the invitation, excited she's giving in.

"You're mine right now," I inform, scraping my teeth against her neck, just enough to make her whimper.

I grab her under the thighs and lift her on top of the counter, her hands clawing under my shirt, feeling my abs.

I press my lips to her neck, the smell of apples and lilies coming off her skin. My hands squeeze her ass cheeks as my lips make their way up her neck and across her jaw, finding their way to her ample lips.

Her tongue slides into my mouth hungrily, devouring me with one swipe. I grab the sides of her robe and pull it down her shoulders. She wiggles her body trying to help get the robe off completely.

"Fuck," I growl, grabbing the bottom of her top and lifting it above her head. Her perfect heavy breasts fall out of her tank, her pink nipples hard and perky. I wrap my arm around her back and lean down, taking a nipple between my teeth. Her legs fly up and wrap around me and her hands tangle into my hair as she gasps.

"Say you're only mine, Jessica," I whisper against the warm skin between her tits.

Her hands pull on my shirt as her body ignites around me.

"I'm only yours," she mumbles softly, making it hard to hear her.

My hands glide down her torso as my mouth sucks along the peaks of her tits, making their way into the valley of them. My fingers sweep underneath her panties, finding their way between her wet heat. I slip two fingers in with ease, her pussy clenching around them as they enter. I slide my fingers in and out slowly, my thumb swirling her clit. She pants, her back arched inward as I finger her relentlessly. Her eyes pin me as her mouth parts in pleasure. Desire emanates off her bowed frame as I fuck her with my fingers.

My dick throbs with a slight pain, so hard it hurts. I pump my fingers one more time, before pulling them out, and sliding them into my mouth, tasting her sweetness. I grab the sides of her panties and pull them down her legs as she grabs my belt to unbuckle it, pulling it from the loops of my jeans, and dropping it to the floor. The belt buckle makes a clanking noise as it hits the tile. Her feet grab the sides of my jeans and push them down my legs, making my dick spring free instantly, grazing the side of the counter.

"No underwear?" she pants, eyeing my dick like dessert.

"Not today, baby," I respond with a smile. I grab her by her bare ass and walk us toward her room, my jeans wrapped around my ankles and boots making it hard to walk.

I toss her onto her perfectly made bed, her naked frame

bouncing on the mattress as she lands. I kick my boots and pants off, and pull my shirt and leather cut over my head with one tug.

Jessica's hand clutches my dick, her hand pumping my cock while the other plays with my balls. My shaft tightens, wanting so much more of her. I'd blow my load if she wrapped that mouth of hers around my cock. She's never given me head. Yet.

She lets go of my dick and uses her elbows to crawl backwards on the mattress, getting into her normal missionary position. Her knees slowly pull apart, revealing her sweet, pink pussy. My balls throb just looking at it, thinking about her tight wetness milking my cock.

I grab her by the foot and pull her to the edge of the bed, making her squeal. I lean down and pick her up, causing her to wrap her legs around my waist. My dick skirts along her heat, causing my head to bud a bead of excitement. I smash my lips to hers, biting her bottom lip as I turn us and fall on my back on the bed. She pulls from me, the look of fear on her face as she realizes I am not letting her on the bottom.

"Ride me," I mutter, my voice rough with the urge to come.

"I-I—" she stutters, her body tensing. Her head falls downward, her eyes closed. I already want to give in; I don't want to see her in pain, scared.

"Take control," I encourage softly. She bites her lip and glances over at the dresser. Her face brightens with a devilish smirk and she climbs off me, scampering over to the dresser and picking up two headbands.

"Get on the pillows," she demands, pointing toward the headboard.

I smirk and climb to the head of the bed.

Jessica being demanding is fucking hot.

She crawls on the bed seductively and climbs on top of me,

her breasts brushing across my body as she grabs one of my wrists and places it against one of the bedposts. She wraps a black headband around my wrist and ties it to the distressed-white post. She climbs across me, her wet pussy gliding across my pecs as she ties up the other hand.

My heart skips a beat as I eye her pink, shaven pussy with eagerness, so badly wanting to watch her ride me, and in daylight nonetheless. I am about to blow my load just thinking about it.

She sits back eyeing her handiwork. She closes her eyes, and runs both of her hands through her hair anxiously. She lowers her head, her wary eyes looking at me, captivating me.

"I'm not going anywhere. Trust me," I mutter, admiring her vixen stance. Her hair is falling over her flushed face, kneeling with her legs spread.

She takes a deep breath, looks up at the ceiling, and exhales. After battling her demons, she straddles my hips, her ass cheeks resting just above my dick. I test the restraints finding they're weak. I could easily break out of them, but I won't. I need her to feel safe. I need her to release me from them.

She closes her eyes and takes another deep breath. I can see she is still nervous being on top. Her breathing is labored and she keeps fidgeting with her hands.

"It's just us, Jessica," I encourage.

She pulls herself up, grips the head of my cock, and positions it under her pussy, the warmth coming from her radiating onto my shaft. She slowly slides down on my cock, her mouth parting as I fill her; my cock stretching her. She rests her hands on my chest as she lifts herself with her knees, sliding herself up and down on my dick.

I close my eyes and hiss, wanting this to last forever, but the way my balls are squeezing, it won't.

Jessica's knees tremble on my sides as she whimpers from pleasure. I reach forward wanting to feel her tits, but am stopped short from the headbands restraining me.

"Untie me," I whisper, pushing my hips upward, meeting her thrust.

"No, I can't," she replies, her head falling back as she rides me greedily, her mouth vibrating a low hum. I smirk, pleased with the pleasure I am giving her.

"Untie me, Hummingbird," I mutter, calling her the nickname I gave her.

"No!" she moans loudly, her nails digging into my chest as she rides my dick feverishly. I pull my hips back, making the head of my dick miss her G-spot. Her head snaps forward and she scowls. She twirls her hips trying to regain her rhythm, but I pull the opposite direction.

"Untie me, Hummingbird," I demand huskily.

She eyes my restrained wrists, still pumping her hips up and down, desperately trying to regain that build of pleasure.

I thrust my hips just right, hitting her sweet spot, giving her a taste of bliss.

"Do it," I whisper, watching the spark of desire ignite in her eyes.

She eyes me warily, her hair falling around her sweaty face. Her hands planted firmly on my chest, anchoring her on my cock.

"Come on, untie me," I persuade.

"I can't, Bobby. I'm not ready for that," she pants, stopping all movement. I still, panic thudding against my chest as the pleasure running through my dick dissipates.

"What's wrong? Why'd you stop?"

"I can't do this. I thought maybe I—" she pauses, her voice cracking with pain, her eyes squeezing tightly shut.

"You can trust me," I whisper, thrusting my hips. Her eyes flutter open, pinning me. "You can do this," I encourage, swirling my hips to hit that sensitive spot deep inside her.

Her head falls back as her pleasure races back through her body.

"Oh, God," she moans, pushing off the mattress with her knees to meet my thrusts.

"There you go, baby," I pant, my dick warming with over-whelming pressure.

Her head falls forward, eyeing my wrists. I can tell she wants to untie me but she's haunted by her traumatized past.

"Just untie one," I groan, my dick vibrating with pleasure.

She nods, her silky hair flinging back and forth as she does so.

She leans over and unties my right hand, her pussy not leaving my cock. As soon as she unties my right hand, I dig my heels into the mattress and push myself upright, wrapping my free arm around her waist tightly. I drill my dick in and out of her, hitting repeatedly that spot that makes her go weak. She wraps her arms around my neck, bringing her breasts right to my face. I lick and then bite the top of her right breast as I continue to fuck her, her legs strangling my hips. My shoulder, from the wrist tied to the post, cramps, but the tightness surrounding my dick overrides the pain. I swirl my hips, making her entire body clench around me, an animalistic growl leaving her lips as her head falls backward. My dick instantly pulses, spilling warm cum into her. My shaft ignites with waves as an electric bolt shoots through my limbs.

I lie back on the bed, her naked, sweaty body on mine, and slide my free hand up her back, my fingers coming across her scars. Jessica tenses under my touch, making her roll from my grip onto her back.

"How did you do that?" she whispers, staring at the ceiling.

"What?" I ask.

"I was certain I wouldn't untie you. Knowing you couldn't touch me and I being in control made me feel being on top was okay, but I still untied you," she answers softly, confused by her actions.

My skills in the sack make me smile arrogantly. Having sex with Jessica has always been an ultimate high, but today was an eternal mindfuck.

"Are you going to untie me?" I question, quirking an eyebrow at her as my hand pulls on the last restraint.

"No," she responds flatly.

My face falls flat, my shoulder blazing with tension in the ungodly angle it's in, and my eyes widen. She looks over at me and giggles, completely amused with herself and climbs on top of me.

"You're not as cute as you think you are," I laugh, as she unties me.

"Yes, I am," she quips.

My arm falls to the bed weightless, my entire limb burning as the blood regains flow. I feel Jessica's finger slide across my scar indenting my side as she lays across me. I was shot taking a bullet for Shadow a couple of years ago. I died a few times on the way to the hospital, but it was worth saving my best friend. I couldn't let a sleazy kingpin named Augustus take him out.

Jessica's phone rings from the nightstand, making her whip her hand from my stomach to answer it.

"Dr. Wren," she answers professionally. I take a deep breath and roll out of the bed in search of my clothes. I grab my pants and boots, putting them on while Jessica talks on her phone. I feel like I should leave. I'm not sure why. Usually when Jessica and I have sex, it's in the middle of the night and she is the one leaving. However, to keep things less complicated, easy for her, I should bolt.

Jessica continues to talk on the phone quietly, her eyes peeking over her shoulder as I head for the bedroom door.

"I'm going to go," I whisper. She nods in understanding and turns, dismissing me.

I walk out of her apartment, the scent of her and tones of coffee lingering on my skin. My phone buzzes in my pocket, making me dig inside my jeans for it.

Not paying attention, I bump into someone, causing me to drop my phone.

"Watch it!" a man's voice snaps. I grab my phone off the floor and look at the person I bumped into. His hair is dark and cut into a mullet. His white shirt's splattered with mustard stains and his jeans are cut-off at the knees.

"You watch it," I bark, standing up straight. He is almost two feet smaller than me, making him cower under me.

"Oh, sorry, man," he replies as I glare down at him, my lip curled in disgust. "I'm Dudley, the landlord," he continues, his tone friendly as he wipes crumbs from his beer gut.

I cross my arms and widen my stance.

"The landlord, huh?" I question. "So you're the reason this place has gone to shit," I state.

His mouth falls open with a gasp. "It's not as easy as it looks, man. This place is a dump," he defends, snapping his gaping mouth shut, and pursing his lips.

I jab my finger into his chest hard, my face scowling at his response. "I know for a fact this place is not cheap on rent, and was in a lot better shape before. You better get it back that way before I come back here again. You can start with that security gate outside," I growl, jabbing him in the chest once more. His eyes widen in fear from my aggressive tone as he nods.

"Yeah. Yeah, I will," he answers, running his hand through his greasy hair. I scoff and walk around him. He clearly has been taking the tenants of this building's money and pocketing it, letting everything fall to shit.

◆ ◆ ◆

Arriving back at the club, I see Cherry leaning against her car. She has on those cute-as-hell short shorts that fray at the bottom, and a white top so tight, it's causing her nipples to slightly pebble against the material. She's cute as hell, but can be a pain in the ass.

I head into the garage, curious if my Chevy truck has arrived yet, when Cherry yells my name.

"Shit," I mumble, trying to act as if I didn't hear her.

"Bobby!" Cherry yells again.

"Yeah?" I reply, walking into the garage. My eyes light up; my truck arrived! *Fuck yeah!* I run my hand over the blue hood, eyeing the detail of the paint. It's vintage and overall completely badass. I head to the driver's side, excited to hear her purr when I start the engine.

"Do you know how to weld?" Cherry questions, leaning against the truck as I climb behind the wheel. Emanating a comforting smell, the leather of the seats wafts around me as I gawk at the craftsmanship. I take my gaze from the gray dashboard and raise my eyebrow at Cherry. "Why?" I ask, my hand on the keys, waiting for her to spit out what she wants so I can start the truck.

"I need some help with something," she responds vaguely, looking the other way. I groan and drop my hand from the ignition. She is not going to make this easy.

"What do you want?" I respond exasperated.

"There is this playground that has a metal jungle gym, and a piece of it has come apart cutting the kids. I was wondering if you could fix it," she finally says, tucking her strawberry hair behind her ear, her grayish eyes brightening with hope.

"Why do you care?" I interrogate further. Why the hell would she would be at a playground?

"I just do. Can you do it or not?" she snaps, her eyebrows furrowing inward.

"Where is this jungle gym?" I ask, leaning my head back against the seat.

She licks her bottom lip, taking a deep breath. "The south side, over at Gold Trailer Park," her grayish eyes leave mine as she turns, looking off into the distance.

I shake my head, my eyes widening with disbelief.

"What the hell are you doing over at that side of town, Cherry?" I nearly yell. Lip wouldn't let her over there surely. It isn't safe; that's where more crimes in the entire city occur. Where people on probation, or running from the law live.

"Does Lip know you were over there?" I continue, my hand testing the steering wheel as I wait for her to answer.

"I just care about the neighborhood. I grew up there. Can you help me or not?" she sasses, throwing her hand on her hip.

I shake my head, scoffing. I flick my gaze from my truck's gauges to her, holding more of a sincere look than annoyed. She grew up there? I couldn't imagine what kind of life she had growing up in such a place. I don't know a lot about Cherry, a lot of people don't. Phillip knew Cherry briefly before he was taken to prison. He made Cherry an ol' lady so that we would have to take care of her while he was locked up. Everyone knows that.

"No, I can't. I am not getting in the middle of whatever you and Lip got going on," I reply as nicely as I can. I want to help her, but the last thing I need is to go against a brother.

Cherry scoffs, and rolls her eyes.

"Fine," she mumbles, turning. She stops in front of a toolbox, grabbing a roll of duct tape. "I'll fix it my fucking self," she snaps, walking out of the garage.

What a pain in the ass. I grab the key in the ignition and turn it. The truck starts with a loud roar echoing throughout the garage. I grin wide, the smell of exhaust bellowing from the back of the truck. I press my foot on the accelerator, causing her to rumble. Fucking A.

Jessica

I SIT ON THE BED, LOOKING AT THE PHONE IN MY HAND. MR. Lanks had just called me; he's the club's lawyer. He's dirty basically, but trustworthy. The club hired him for me after everything that had happened with Travis, making sure I didn't say or do anything that would raise suspicion. I found out that Travis's will was astronomical after his disappearance. From the house and land Travis was given from his grandfather, the lethal amount of money his grandfather gave him in his passing, along with the insurance money, Travis turned out to be worth more dead than alive. Everything was to go to me and Addie, but we haven't seen a dime of it. Which is fine; I don't need it. But it would be nice to put it in savings for Addie, for college. We haven't seen anything of the will because it takes seven years for a court to sign off on a death certificate after someone goes missing if there is no evidence or signs of an immediate death. From what Mr. Lanks and the police told me back then, all they found was Travis's car rammed into a tree, with the car door open, and some splatters of blood on the ground. No fingerprints or body parts. I was just told by Mr. Lanks that Travis has officially been declared dead though. The court signed off on his death certificate today.

My hand sweats as I palm my phone, my chest beading sweat from the overwhelming anxiety running through me. I run my hands through my hair, and graze my fingers over my cell phone's screen. Addie's picture smiles back at me. Maybe Mr. Lanks is a sign that today is a day for a new beginning. As crazy as Bobby sounded earlier today, maybe he can help me. Maybe I can get a hold of myself and create the life I always wanted. Finding a loving man, maybe give Addie a brother or sister. With the money coming my way, I can slow down at work and spend more time with Addie even.

I climb off the bed, still naked and walk over to the closet, eyeing the box that haunts me. I take a deep breath and grab it, sliding it from its place on the shelf. I walk over to the bed and sit smack dab in the middle, crossing my legs as I contemplate opening it. I run my hands over the lid, my heart picking up as I look at it. I haven't opened this in over two years. Biting my lip, I pull the lid off, the box filled with pictures, a collar, and my wedding rings stare back at me. My finger runs over the white leathered collar, the one Travis would put around my neck when he wanted me to obey him. I push it aside and grab the first photo I see. A picture of Travis's family, along with Addie in Travis's hands. I smile. Addie was so small; it's crazy how she has grown.

My finger runs over Travis's face, his chiseled jaw, and piercing eyes. He was handsome, but held a severe presence to him. Being on top with Bobby today was scary on so many levels. I wasn't allowed on top with my husband much; it gave a sense of control which I wasn't allowed. When Travis did allow me on top, he made sure I knew who was in control, and it wasn't pleasurable. The acts with Bobby today caused memories from being with Travis to form behind my eyelids. Travis's voice would sound in my ear, his hands gripping me painfully, causing me to have a panic attack. I never let go, never felt anything other than fear. Not 'til today. After I tied Bobby up, and had the warmth of combusting from the depths Bobby was hitting, I forgot all about Travis, until afterwards. *What was so different?*

I slide my finger over a picture of Travis's brother, Grant, who looks identical to him. I never saw much of Grant; he was always away, hardly ever at family gatherings. What Travis said about Grant led me to believe he was the problem child of the family. From what I gathered, it was because Grant didn't want to follow the family's footsteps into medicine, but I had no idea what the truth was. I look the box over, images of being dragged into that basement and screaming for remorse fire in my mind like a collage. My heart races, making me inhale sharply. I grab the lid and slam it back on the box, walk back over to the closet, and push it in its spot.

"Shit, what time is it?" I mutter, looking at the clock on my phone. I notice I have been sitting in the same spot for hours. It's already three in the afternoon and is time to pick up Addie.

7
Bobby

I'M SITTING AT THE CLUB, WATCHING THE NEWS AND DRINKING A beer, thoughts of Jessica reeling through my mind. The way she opened up and took charge was beyond my expectations. The display of her riding me is an image I swear I'll never forget. The look of her flushed face, the stray hairs hanging over her face, and her parted mouth as she rode my dick, makes my cock ripple with eagerness just thinking about it. I close my eyes, and shake my head to clear the image, taking a sip of my beer.

Hearing giggles, I glance over my shoulder, seeing Juliet, a tattooed redhead pull Tom Cat down the hall. Looks like someone is getting lucky tonight. I pull my phone out and lay it on the table, contemplating calling Jessica. I want to call her, but after the boundaries we crossed today, I'm not so sure if that's a good idea. She might want space and shit.

"What's up with you?" Lip asks dryly, sliding onto a stool next to me.

"Nothing." I bring the tip of the beer bottle to my lips. "Where's Cherry?" I question, keeping my eyes on the TV.

"Dunno. She's not at the house, and I can't get a hold of her. Seems to be a trend with her since I got out of the joint," he grumbles, running his hands through his hair. I bite my lip, wondering if I should bring up her wanting me to go to that shitty trailer park. I think better of it and decide not to. I don't know if Cherry is cheating, or what is going on, but I know I don't want to be in the middle of it.

My phone vibrates, catching my attention. Reading the name on the screen has my eyes widening.

Cora.

I haven't heard from her in years. She only calls when she needs me to boost a car. My tongue darts and licks along my bottom lip at the thought of a little action, making me answer it.

"Cora," I greet casually.

"Bobby, baby, how are you?" Cora answers, her voice holding a sense of authority and class. Which is exactly what she is; she's just an educated, classy outlaw.

I met Cora when I was around sixteen. I saw a Corvette sitting in an empty parking lot, located right next to some docks, and decided to take it for a joy ride. Twenty minutes later, Cora, her father, and their men pulled me from the car violently. Apparently, they had just stolen the car and were in the process of loading it on a shipping container before I took it. She was impressed with how I hotwired the car, no damage to the ignition. She threw me a wad of cash and became my mentor for years.

"Good, what's up?" I ask, getting to the point.

"I need you for a boost. You're the only one I trust for the job," she breathes into the phone.

"When do you need it by?"

"Tonight," she clips quickly. I sigh. This is why she is calling me. She needs someone quick, and efficient. That would be me. I can boost a car and get it where it needs to be without a scratch and in a blink of an eye. Been practicing since I was a kid.

"Text me the details of the car's location and all," I request, taking a sip of my beer.

"The location is wherever you can find me a black Lamborghini," she informs, her tone giving off a hint of sass.

"A motherfucking Lambo?" I shriek, wondering if I heard her right.

"Is that a problem?" she asks, her voice silky as she speaks through the receiver.

"No, I'll find one," I answer, hanging up. I haven't stolen a car in a while. I'd be lying through my teeth if I said stealing cars was not one of the biggest rushes of my life. The feeling of being caught at any moment, and the luxury your ass is sitting in when you're going 100 mph. My heart is slamming against my chest in excitement just thinking about it.

I look over and see Lip staring at me with a huge grin on his face.

"What?"

"I want in brother," Lip remarks, nodding.

"No," I laugh, shaking my head. "I work alone," I inform, watching my phone.

"I know where to find a Lamborghini," he show tunes, reaching over the counter, and swiping my beer.

"You and Cherry are perfect for each other. You're both a pain in the ass," I sneer, making Lip laugh. "Fine," I reply exasperated, grabbing my beer from his hands.

"The Ivory Gentlemen's Club is full of those arrogant fuckers driving nice ass cars, with fly-ass women hanging off them. Not sure how you are going to get the car being as busy as it is though," Lip informs, shrugging. I smile and take a sip of my beer.

"I'll figure out a way. I always do," I smile wolfishly.

◆ ◆ ◆

Lip parks his car in a garage around the back and follows me. I head toward the back of the gentlemen's club, smiling at everyone who walks past.

"What the fuck is the plan, man?" Lip whispers, jogging to keep up with me.

"Shut up and follow me," I whisper back.

We make our way through the kitchen, nobody even noticing we are in the damn place, even after Lip steals a fry off someone's tray in passing. We travel to the back of the club until we come across the employee lounge. I slowly step in, making sure it's empty before continuing in. I notice a TV in the corner and gray lockers along a wall, stickers slapped on a few of them. I start opening lockers and searching through the coat racks.

"What are you looking for?" Lip asks, opening a locker beside me.

"A valet jacket," I mutter, opening another locker.

"Like this?" Lip asks, holding out a red velvet jacket.

"Perfect," I whisper, grabbing it from his hands.

"There's two in here," he mutters, grabbing the other one.

I slide the velvet jacket onto my shoulders, the fit very snug.

"You look ridiculous," Lip laughs.

"It'll work," I state, pulling at the fabric bunching tightly around my biceps.

Lip pulls on his jacket, and shuts the locker. "Now what?" he asks, adjusting the collar.

"We find us a Lambo and hope it's black," I mutter, heading out of the lounge.

"Hey, Mike is going on break," a guy in a matching red jacket says, entering the room, mistaking us for working here.

"Yeah, we're on it," Lip responds, not missing a beat.

We head down the hall, finding a steel door with a sign reading Valet.

"Could they make it any easier," Lip chuckles, opening the door.

We walk out, finding a tall brown-headed kid standing behind a podium.

"We'll take over, Mike," I inform, slapping him on the shoulder.

"Thank God, I gotta piss," he groans, running toward the door.

"Go find me a Lambo," I instruct Lip, as I open the box on the wall full of keys.

"We got a little problem," Lip sputters, his voice high pitched. I close the box and eye him quizzically.

"Cameras," Lip remarks, pointing to a camera in the corner of the garage.

"Fuck," I whisper, eyeing the beady camera pointing in the opposite direction of us, a small golf cart sitting under it. I shrug the valet jacket off, and stride toward it. I climb on top of the golf cart, ducking my head so the camera doesn't catch a glimpse of my face, and throw the jacket over it.

"You better find us a car fast; they are going to notice this pretty fucking quick," I inform, jumping off the cart. With that,

Lip sprints down the garage, and I head back to the keys.

A few seconds later, Lip is running back toward me.

"I found one, and it's black or at least it looks black," Lip yells, huffing out of breath.

"Lot number!" I yell, knowing our time is running out.

"Lot 41A," he pants. My hands grab the keys and run. I follow Lip, passing some high-end cars along the way, before he stops right in front of a sleek black Lambo.

"Fuck, she's beautiful," I whisper, trailing my hand along her body.

"Holy shit," Lip mutters, eyeing the detail.

"I have a hard-on," I laugh, unlocking the car.

"Me too. Me too, brother," Lip chuckles.

I slide into the seat; its luxury overwhelming me. The seats are black with red stitched in the middle, and the dashboard and console lined in chrome.

Lip slides in with me, his eyes devouring the beauty of the craftsmanship .

"What now?" Lip asks, looking at me for direction.

I take my eyes away from the buttons and knobs, and look at Lip with a wolfish grin across my face.

"We joyride."

I put my foot on the brake, and press a button on the console, causing the Lambo to start with an intoxicating purr. The car reverberates with power as I put it into gear.

"I love it when she talks dirty to me," I laugh, referring to the glorious roar of the motor.

I put the car in reverse and back out. I put her into first gear, her mechanisms switching flawlessly and slowly pull out of the garage. As soon as we are out of the garage, I throw her into the next gear, and let her loose.

Lip grabs onto the door as we are thrown into our seats

from the horsepower.

"I think the plan is not to draw attention to ourselves," Lip bitches, making me roll my eyes.

I turn the wheel, my foot pushing on the accelerator as we slide around a corner as if we were on ice.

"What fun is that?" I chuckle.

We race past a cop sitting in an alleyway. Looking in my rearview mirror, I notice him pulling out, turning his lights on, but by the time his car is straightened out to take the chase, we are long gone.

"Woooo!" Lip yells as we fly onto the freeway toward Cora's drop location.

"How long have you been doing this?" Lip questions.

"I've been stealing cars since I was a kid," I inform, looking in the rearview mirror for any boys in blue, but there is nothing.

"Ever get caught?" he asks, running his hand over the console.

"Couple times when I was younger, got thrown in juvie, but all that did was teach me how to get better at stealing cars," I laugh, pulling onto a side road.

I pull up to the dock, with a huge boat parked next to it, and get out.

"I knew you wouldn't disappoint. You never do," Cora chimes, climbing out of a black BMW, buttoning up her suit jacket. Her hair, short and curly, flutters with the wind. Her porcelain skin illuminates in the night as she walks toward us, her heels clicking against the broken asphalt.

"Who's this?" she questions, tilting her pointed chin toward Lip.

"This is Lip," I inform, shutting the door to the Lambo.

"Here's your cut," she states. One of the guys standing

behind her tosses me a yellow envelope.

I open it eyeing a large sum of cash.

"One of my men botched this boost, and is sitting in jail, the car wrecked. I owe you one for your eager participation on such a short notice, Bobby," she remarks, her voice strong and sure.

I nod, dipping my hand into the envelope pulling out half the cash.

"Yeah, I haven't heard from you in a while," I state, walking around the car toward Lip.

"I only use my good resources when I have to. My other men are not as good at getting the job done, but cheaper," she answers, crossing her arms. I hand Lip half the cash, and close the envelope.

The guy with his hair braided down his back whispers in Cora's ear, making her nod.

"I have to go, but I'll be in touch, Bobby," Cora warns, her lips quirking into a smirk.

"So, how do we get home?" Lip asks, looking around him.

"You can take one of the junkers off the lot," the bodyguard with the long hair suggests, pointing toward a broken down Neon, the paint nothing but primer.

"It ain't no Lambo," Lip chuckles.

We make our way toward the car as I stuff the envelope in my back pocket.

"Please tell me you banged that broad," Lip laughs.

"Once. She's just as uptight in the sack as she seems outside of it," I inform, getting into the passenger side of the car.

"Gee, thanks for letting me drive something tonight," Lip laughs, climbing behind the wheel.

"What can I say, I'm a generous kind of guy," I shrug, sliding into the ripped passenger seat.

8

Jessica

It's been three days since I last saw Bobby. I usually don't count the days in between seeing him, but every day since, I have thought about him, about the sex we had in my room. When I go to bed at night, I smell him, his manliness lingering on my blankets. I'm glad he is giving me space, letting me cope with the progress I've made. Being on top was scary on so many levels. Just thinking about it makes my body tingle and my head dizzy. I close my eyes, trying to steady myself.

"Do you hear me talking to you, Jessica?" Travis hissed from beneath me. I gritted my teeth in anger, my neck aching painfully as he gripped my neck.

"I am in control. Not you," he grunted, taking his hands from my throat to my thighs, pinching incredibly hard. I yelped, trying to grab at his hands to stop the piercing pain riddling up my thighs, only to find my wrists jolted against the handcuffs. I looked down at Travis, my eyes welling up with tears at how broken I was.

"Don't look at me. Look at the wall," Travis ordered, *replacing his hands around my throat as he drilled into me hard.*

I peel my eyes open and gasp as the hard memories vanish. Sometimes they're hard to snap out of they feel so real.

I don't know how I did it; how I just let go. Losing control with Bobby frightens me more than anything.

I walk into the main lobby of my apartment building and notice a man shampooing the carpets, and the smell of lavender masking the smell of musk. I lift an eyebrow, a little shocked someone is actually cleaning this place. I head up to my apartment door, playing with the keys in my hand when my phone buzzes in my purse. I fish it out, unlocking the door at the same time.

Bobby: I think you need therapy ;)

I smirk.

"Mom, can I stay over at Izzy's?" Addie asks, walking into the apartment from Bree's.

"Why? I thought we were going to have a mani-pedi night?" I ask, setting my purse and phone on the counter.

"Mom," Addie says dryly, her eyes looking up at me under her lashes.

"Fine, but they have to come get you and you need to be back by tomorrow morning," I reply, grabbing a water from the fridge.

"Yay!" she yells, running off to her room.

My phone buzzes sitting on the counter.

Bobby: You don't want to ignore me.

I shake my head and do just that.

125

After Addie has left with her friend, I opt for a big bubble bath in my porcelain claw tub. I walk in my room and inhale the sweetness from my soap in the hot bath, inviting me. I turn on the stereo, and head toward the tub. I put my foot in, testing the water before slipping myself all the way in.

The hot water makes my skin sensitive, causing it to turn red. I breathe in deeply, taking in the scent of honey as I lather the water and bubbles up my chest. The feel of my hands along my skin makes me think of Bobby. I slide my hand lower down my abdomen, and my core clenches with tension. I'm horny. I should have just told Bobby to come over, but I want to make sure we have distance between us. I don't need anything more between him and I, and having sex constantly will complicate that. I may have sold my soul to a Devil, but I won't fall in love with one.

I spread myself with my fingertips, running my hand back and forth over my sex. My mouth parts as my body begins to spark with recognition causing my breathing to hitch. Bobby's skilled fingers play in my mind as I glide my free hand up my chest, tweaking my nipple, causing desire to tremble down my body and making my knees bend involuntarily so I can fully reach my clit with my other hand. I thumb my clit, causing my head to fall back on the side of the tub, and my eyes close as I swirl the sensitive bundle of nerves.

"You could have just invited me over you know."

My hands fly from my clit and nipple and quickly grasp the sides of the tub, pulling myself upward. My body heaves as I eye Bobby standing in my doorway, a sly smirk playing across his face.

"What the fuck are you doing in here?" I shriek, lowering my body under the bubbles for cover. He runs his hand through his shaggy blond hair, and stares me down without remorse. His eyes look at me with hidden promise; warmth igniting behind them as he devours my wet body covered in a mass of bubbles.

"I told you not to ignore me," he retorts coolly, looping his fingers into his jeans pockets, an evident bulge protruding through the fabric.

"I ignored you for a reason. Now get out!" I yell, pointing at the door. My cheeks warming from embarrassment that he caught me during such a private moment.

"No," he replies.

"No?" I question, frustration rising through me.

"Your classic routine is to bang me, then not talk to me for weeks at a time. Not happening anymore," he answers, shaking his head.

I scoff and turn my head toward the spout. "How did you even get in here?" I ask, not looking at him.

"Your door wasn't locked."

I shake my head at his response. I must have forgotten to lock it after Addie left.

Bobby's boots thud against the tiled floor as he makes his way toward me. I turn my gaze from the faucet to him, his hand holding a white towel.

"Bobby, get out of here," I mutter, staring at the towel hanging loosely from his grip.

I hear him take a breath, clearly irritated by my rejection.

He drops the towel on the floor and reaches into the tub, grabbing me by the hips.

"Bobby!" I scream as he pulls me completely out of the tub, and throws me over his broad shoulder. The bubbles clinging to my skin soak his dark-colored shirt.

"Bobby! Have you lost your mind?" I yell, while he walks us into my room.

He throws me on the bed, and grabs his shirt pulling it over his head. His abs and toned chest in perfect view causes my clit to pulsate with such intensity I feel I might combust.

"You know you want it just as much as I do. Stop fighting it," he mutters, his voice husky.

"I don't," I protest softly, but it's a fucking lie.

He slowly leans down, his fists pressing into the mattress on each side of me. His eyes hooded and mouth parted.

"The way you look at me contradicts the lies leaving your mouth, Jessica," he whispers, his tone smooth and strong, filled with confidence.

I swallow slowly, and take a deep breath. The way my body hums for him, and the way my voice cracks when I tell him to leave, he might just be right.

"Maybe," I whisper, my eyes trailing down his chest. He scoffs, and leans up, a smile playing his beautiful face.

He unbuttons his jeans, and pulls them down, his black boxers revealing an impressive hard on. I lick my bottom lip as I stare at it. I want to devour that thing, but not now. He slides over my body, his weight on the mattress sinking me further into his hold. His dick caresses against my inner thigh, causing me to arch my back and pant. I want to tell him no, reject him, but my body is defying me on so many levels. It's a hopeless fight at this point.

He kisses my neck, his abrasive scruff against my skin leaving a delicious burn. His hands travel up my thighs, slowly making their way between my legs. He thumbs my clit softly, causing me to involuntarily thrust my hips upward. I feel a burn between my thighs, causing me to look up, finding Bobby a hair's length away from my sex with his face. He smirks, and winks before I can even protest, sucking my clit into his mouth. The warmth I reached in the tub returns with an overwhelming velocity. I thrash forward with the loudest moan that's ever left my body. I can't even describe the sensations rushing through my core and licking up my body; it's so intense.

"God, you're better than I imagined," Bobby mutters against me, making me shiver from the vibrations. I have never let Bobby do this to me. In fact, nobody has ever gone down on me before. I never felt that comfortable with someone or trusted them enough for them to dive into something so personal and intimate.

He pulls himself away, my body cooling from the loss of contact, and stands up tugging his boxers off his hips and to the floor.

"I want to eat you out all night, babe, but I have to have you now," he admits, making me smirk.

His cock stands erect, swollen, and ready for the taking. I love Bobby's dick. I've never seen anything quite like it. It angles upward just slightly, so when he fucks me, the head always hits my g-spot perfectly. Nothing I have ever had compares to his cock, the best orgasms of my life have come from him. There is no denying that Bobby knows his way around a woman's body, and his skill in-between the sheets is flawless.

He grabs a hold of my knees, his mouth trailing up my leg, nipping at my inner thigh, and then kissing the sting his bite leaves behind. I run my hands up my chest, tweaking my nipples, wanting more and now.

"God, you're beautiful when you feel yourself up," he growls. "Touch your pussy," Bobby demands, clutching his cock.

I slide my tongue along my bottom lip and lower my hands from my chest down over my stomach to my clit. I circle myself causing a burst of tingles to drum through me. My core clenches, craving Bobby's dick.

"That's it, baby," Bobby replies huskily, his hand sliding up and down his shaft as he sits back and watches. "Flip over," Bobby instructs, his hands pushing on my side. My eyes snap from their lustful haze and widen with fear, my body tensing.

"What?" I ask, frazzled.

"Get on all fours," he clarifies, his blue eyes at half-mast, heavy with want.

"Bobby, no," I answer nervously, lifting on my elbows to sit up.

"Trust me," he whispers, lowering himself and brushing his lips over my belly button. I turn my head away, my eyes landing on my closet. The closet that holds my past. I want to move forward, and Bobby is the only person in the world who I trust to help me do it.

I push off my elbows, and turn myself onto all fours, my body on full display for Bobby to see, for him to do what he wants. My body vibrates with tension, my heart picking up its pace. I close my eyes and see Travis flash before me. His angry eyes stare at me while I'm on my hands and knees trying to hold in my sobs as he paces the floor with a whip.

Bobby slides his hand over my ass cheek sensually, making me jump from my terrifying images. I look up and see myself in the mirror on the back of my dresser, Bobby sitting on his knees behind me. I didn't even realize he climbed on the bed; I was so lost in my nightmare.

He caresses my ass cheeks with both of his hands, his rough touch savoring the feel of my silky skin. He slides his hands around the apex of my thighs, until his thumb hits my clit. He circles his thumb, his fingers sliding back and forth softly over my opening. It feels good, but I am too wound up and too scared to let myself feel anything more. Bobby presses his hard chest to my back, his lips brushing against my ear.

"Why are you so tense? We haven't done anything yet?" he whispers softly into my ear.

"I'm scared," I whisper, my fingers gripping the comforter. It's hard for me to admit I am scared. I am a person with a strong will. Having endured the lowest level of hell and not once mentioning the fear I had to stampede through to get past it all, it takes a lot for me to voice my fears aloud.

"Of what?" he asks, sliding his hand up my stomach caressing my heavy breast. There are so many answers to that question, so many fears traveling through my mind, but there is only one word responsible for that domino effect.

"Of pain," I mutter, closing my eyes tightly.

Bobby brushes the hair from my face, and takes a deep breath.

"Don't fear the pain; fear the message behind it," he remarks, tucking the loose hair behind my ear. I open my eyes, and look at my reflection in the mirror across the room. Bobby staring back at me intently with a look of care written across his body as he cocoons me with his frame.

"Do you want to stop?" he asks, sincerely. I take my gaze from the mirror and turn my head looking over my shoulder. Bobby's eyes gazing at me with sincerity and not anger.

"No," I answer.

"Just tell me to stop if it gets to be too much," he whispers into the back of my hair. I nod, my breathing picking up. It reminds me of a safe word, only mine never worked with Travis. I would yell our safe word and he would go harder, and rougher.

Bobby's finger slides under my chin turning my head slightly, and presses his soft lips to mine, kissing them. My bottom lip slips between both of his, and like that, my body immediately ignites, arching into him.

The stereo, that I had forgot was on, plays "Animals" by Adam Levine. The sensation of Bobby's fingers traveling down my stomach, over my mound, and between my swollen lips, leaves me gasping in need.

He growls against my mouth as his cock presses into my ass demandingly.

"I have wanted you like this for so long, Jessica," he grinds out with a heavy breath.

"Then take me," I pant, lolling my head back.

"I plan to," he replies.

The head of his length presses against my opening, making me inhale quickly. He pushes himself into me, a loud moan escaping his mouth as he fills me to the base of his cock. It burns as I'm stretched; the position he's in, I experience his full length. He pulls back and thrusts forward, causing my arms to tremble from pleasure, making me nearly fall headfirst into the mattress.

"You feel so tight like this," he moans, his voice so raw I barely understand him.

I whimper in response, pushing myself against him, my body greedy and ready to erupt into oblivion. He thrusts himself in and out, lowering his body on top of mine, and his arms wrapping around my front, pulling me close. Breathing heavily into my ear, he kisses the top of my shoulder, his cock driving into me. He lifts his hard chest off my back as he plows his cock in and out, his hand sliding down my back, over my scars. My body tenses immediately. The artery in my neck pulses with severity as I close my eyes and my heartbeat picks up. Behind my eyelids, I see Travis appear in memory, his hand in my hair screaming at me viciously, his other hand tightly grasping my throat causing me to see black from the lack of oxygen.

"Don't go there, Jessica. Stay here with me," Bobby whispers into my ear, sensing where my mind has drifted off to. My eyes flutter open, breaking the dark memory. I nod, trying to shake the memories away, replacing them with Bobby in the here and now.

Closing my eyes as his hand barely brushes my side, causes my body to tense in fear.

"Don't close your eyes. Open them, let me see your beautiful eyes," he instructs softly. I open my eyes and look in the mirror. My hair is wet on the ends from dipping into the bathwater. With flushed cheeks, my mouth parts as Bobby takes me from behind. He hovers his chest over my back, grabbing me by the hips as he swirls his cock inside of me just right, making me moan loudly.

He moves so effortlessly, his rhythm flawless. The tattoos inked along his toned arms are stunning; I focus on their painted beauty as I see his muscles grow taut with each thrust. Bobby is at his best, in his element when he is delivering pleasure. Lowering himself on my back again, he slides a hand around my front to rest on my collarbone. The hairs on my neck rise, his hand too close to my neck for comfort, my fingers dig into the mattress.

"Breathe, Hummingbird, I would never hurt you," he whispers into my ear, driving his hips forward causing his cock to hit my g-spot hard. At the renewed sensation, I release the breath I didn't realize I was withholding.

"That's it, baby. See how good that feels. Hear only my voice, see only me," he mumbles into my neck, his cock brushing across my bundle of nerves as he pounds into me. I notice my body blossom with warmth, and my knees begin to tremble.

I look at Bobby in the mirror. He is looking back at me from over my shoulder, his eyes caring and sensitive. His jaw is clenched as he chases his release, his hair sticking to his forehead from the sweat building, and his eyes are heavy with desire, never looking away from me.

"What are you doing to me?" I moan, not meaning to ask the question as I push myself backwards to meet his thrust, so desperately wanting to climax.

"Showing you how to live," Bobby whispers, slowing his hips into a torturous rhythm.

My body erupts into ecstasy, everything happening in slow motion I tremble as a warmth climbs its way from my core outward, licking up my limbs. I hear nothing but Bobby's harsh breathing in my ear, and see nothing but his blue eyes staring back at me in the mirror. His length hitting me in all the right places, throws me into oblivion. My pussy clenches around him hard, and my arms give out, making the front of me fall onto the bed as I tumble into the most intense release of my life.

"Fuck!" Bobby roars, pumping his hips uncontrollably, climaxing seconds behind me.

After Bobby stills, I lower my aching legs slowly from kneeling to lying flat, his sweaty chest resting on my back while he pulses inside of me. His chest heaving against me as he pants for air. His eyes pinning me in the mirror across from us.

Suddenly, something snaps inside of me as I stare at him, his eyes looking back at me passionately. The way his stare grounds me as he takes me in, not speaking, not moving, just devouring everything that I am as my walls begin to crumble. I cannot describe the snap; can't figure out what it means, but I can feel it continuing to splinter inside of me as I stare at

Bobby's reflection in the mirror. This emotion rising inside my chest is a lot like the first time Bobby and I ever had sex. It's one which is glorious yet terrifying.

I turn my head quickly and look at the wall. A spindle of emotions circulating through me like a virus. Once more, I close my eyes and see Travis, but it's faint; it's not as dire as before. I open my eyes and see Bobby smiling at me. His hand reaches over and rubs my arms before pulling me toward him, my front to his front.

"You all right?" he whispers into the top of my head.

I breathe in his smell of coconuts and sweat. My eyes becoming heavy as I nod. Bobby just unraveled my world and everything I *thought* I knew.

Bobby

"MOM, I'M HOME!"

Jessica darts upward, covering her bare chest with her hands. Her hair sticks out everywhere as she looks at the door with wide eyes.

"Shit, shit, shit," she curses, falling from the bed. I stretch my arms upward, my muscles cramped from sleeping.

I look over and see Jessica racing around the room, pulling clothes from her dresser and closet. She pulls on some white panties, and a matching top, her face flushed in complete panic.

"Get dressed," she hisses quietly, running her hands through her hair, pulling it from her face.

I yawn and roll over, eyeing my clothes on the floor.

Jessica huffs and grabs my underwear and clothes, throwing them in my lap.

"Hurry!" she whispers harshly. I raise my eyebrow upward as I watch her race into the bathroom.

I pull my underwear on, and scratch at my chest, my belly rumbling with hunger.

"Mom?"

I turn around and see Addie staring at me with shocked eyes. She has gotten so big since the last time I saw her, and looks just like her mother. Round face, blonde hair, blue eyes.

"She's in the bathroom," I tell her, pulling my jeans on quickly.

"Oh, okay," she replies, looking at the bathroom door.

"You hungry?" I question.

"What?" she asks, looking at me as if I have lost my mind.

"Are you hungry?" I repeat.

She leans against the doorframe and crosses her arms, her eyes roaming my face in curiosity before forming a smirk.

"Actually, yeah," she admits. "Liz's family are vegans, so I didn't get much for breakfast," she responds, shrugging. She squints her eyes and tilts her head, looking at me intently.

"What?" I ask, nervous, wondering why she is staring at me like that.

"You look familiar," she answers, tapping her rounded chin with her small index finger.

"Addie!" Jessica chimes in surprise as she is walking out of the bathroom.

"Mom," Addie greets.

"Uh," Jessica looks between Addie and me nervously, her forehead wrinkling with worry lines. She's clearly displeased I'm talking to her daughter. "Addie, this is Bobby," she continues, her voice shaky.

Addie takes her gaze from her mom to me and smirks. "How about that food?" Addie suggests.

"Food?" Jessica questions, her voice a tone higher than before.

"Yeah, you know, the kind you eat," Addie smarts. I can't help but laugh. Addie is so much like her mother.

"I need to go shopping. We don't have enough to feed everyone," Jessica snaps, walking past us, and toward the living room.

"That's okay. I got it," I reply, grabbing my phone from the floor.

"What?" Jessica stops, and turns, her face angry. I text our newest prospect, and ask him to bring me some breakfast before tucking my phone in my pocket. Looking up, I notice Jessica press on the small of Addie's back, urging her out of the room. *Yep, I'm in trouble.*

"What did you just do?" she whispers, walking up to me.

I smirk, and shrug. "Nothing," I lie.

"You need to leave." Her eyes plead with me to go.

"Why?" I question, tilting my head to the side. She's always kept her daughter away from me and the club. I have asked her why before and she just smiles and changes the subject. Maybe now that we are being honest with each other, she will actually tell me.

"I'm," she pauses, and closes her eyes while sighing, "I'm trying to do right by my daughter, Bobby. I don't need someone in her life who is just going to walk out," she states, her tone unwavering. I get it; she doesn't introduce men to Addie who are not sticking it out for the long haul. My track record with women is as thick as a dictionary, but I don't ever plan on leaving Jessica's life.

I nod, and head over to the counter, opening up cabinets in

search for coffee, ignoring her.

"What's wrong, Mom?" Addie asks, sitting on a barstool. Her little nose scrunched up with concern.

"Yeah, what's wrong, Mom?" I mock, looking into another cabinet.

"Nothing, I'm sure Bobby has a lot to do today is all," she lies.

"Nope, I'm good," I respond, trying not to laugh. I haven't turned around to look at Jessica, but I know her lips will be pursed and her eyes will be stabbing me with daggers.

"See," Addie responds.

Jessica scoffs and pushes me out of the way, reaching into a cabinet I hadn't checked yet. She pulls out a coffee can. I lean back against the counter, cross my arms, and watch her throw a hissy fit, throwing the lid on the counter and snatching the coffee pot from its place. I roll my lips onto each other, trying not to burst out into a fitful laughter. She'd be angry if she knew I thought she was cute as hell pissed off.

Jessica leans over the sink to turn on the faucet, her breasts spilling from her tight top as she hovers over the empty sink. My dick throbs, wanting another round with her. She is the only woman I can have sex with and wake up even hornier than before. My dick is insatiable for Jessica, addicted even.

I have always wanted Jessica doggy style, wanted her entire body for my taking. Last night was more than I could have ever imagined. The noises she made when my cock hit places in her that it never had before, the way her body moved and responded to my touch and sounds; it was epic. Plus, I got a mirror to watch every look that crossed her face, and every bounce of her tits. I'm surprised I lasted as long as I did. I was ready to bust a nut as soon as I found her masturbating. I smirk at the thought. I bet she thinks twice before she ignores one of my texts again.

"Mom, someone is at the door," Addie remarks, breaking me from eye-fucking her mom. I didn't hear a knock.

"I'll get it," I announce, pulling from the counter. I open the door to find Kane holding two paper bags and a cardboard cup holder filled with drinks. His long dark hair sits past his broad shoulders, and he's wearing his cut labeled as a prospect. He's only in his prospect days and already gets more pussy than I do. He says it's because chicks dig his year-round tan. He's Native American and the girls eat that shit up.

"Here," he grumbles, pushing the paper bag to my chest and holding the cups out for me to grab. His bushy dark brows slanted inward with annoyance.

"Thanks, man," I reply, grabbing the crap from him.

"Who knew you had sexy men at your beck and call," Jessica smarts over my shoulder. I turn and scowl at her, Kane laughing in the doorway. I turn and kick the door shut, shaking my head at Jessica.

"You have a sexy man at your beck and call and refuse to use it to your advantage," I snipe, pushing the cups in the cup holder to her chest. She huffs and sets them on the counter, pulling one from its place. Addie positions herself on her knees on the stool and leans over, plucking a cup from the cardboard cup holder.

"You wanna see something cool?" I ask, grabbing a straw from the bag.

Addie's eyes light up as she watches me. I tap the end of the straw on the countertop, scrunching the paper that covers it. I pull the scrunched up paper resembling an accordion off the straw and set it on the counter. I take the straw, get a dab of liquid from the cup, and drop it in the middle of the paper, making it appear as if it's crawling.

"It's like a caterpillar," I say, smiling, dropping another drop onto the straw's wrapper making it grow again.

"That is cool," Addie laughs, grabbing a straw from the bag.

I look over and see Jessica eyeing me, the depth of her blue eyes soft and endearing as she watches me interact with her daughter.

"Who taught you that?" Jessica questions softly as she eyes Addie attempting to make her own caterpillar.

"My dad," I mumble. She nods and opens the paper bag, digging for food. She doesn't ask more. She never does when the conversation goes toward my parents. It goes against that crossing the line of simple and easy, to complicated.

Jessica and I eat in silence, listening to Addie talk about some boy she is crushing on. Jessica doesn't seem to approve of her puppy love, but I say she's young. She hasn't lived unless she has had her heart broken a few times.

I crumple up the paper bag and throw it in the trash, and head to the bedroom to put the rest of my clothes on.

"I think we need to distance ourselves from one another."

I pull my shirt over my head, the fabric brushing along my bottom lip as I groan loudly at Jessica's statement.

"Why is that?" I ask, fetching my boots to pull on.

"I think it's best. So we don't grow feelings for each other," she mumbles, chewing on the pad of her finger. I know Jessica wants nothing of love; she has told me that before.

"The idea of falling in love with someone, giving them your heart, the organ that keeps you alive, is suicide." She has said it repeatedly. Last night was more than emotional. I figured she would wake up freaking out, and my suspicion was correct.

I stand up after tying my bootlaces and stalk over to her, her hand wrapped around her body as she continues to nibble on her finger. I slide my hand under her chin and tilt it upward, making her look me in the eye.

"Are you growing feelings for me, Jessica?"

She begins to talk, but it comes out a stutter.

"Maybe I should have made the rule for you not to fall for me?" I interrupt, my voice low and rough. I saw the way she looked at me after we had sex. She looked at me with an entirely different vibe.

Jessica's eyes squint in anger as she grabs my finger under her chin, pushing it away from her.

"This is just a game to you," she hisses, her blue eyes vibrant with rage.

I smirk, and run my hands through my hair. "No, it's not a game to me. I just think you are being ridiculous," I continue, putting my hands in my pockets.

"Me protecting my daughter is not being ridiculous," she snaps, placing her hands on her hips.

"I have been around for years, Jessica. I haven't gone anywhere. Not when you pushed me away, and not anytime soon. So why don't you really say what this is about. Stop using Addie as an excuse. Stop protecting yourself," I respond, my tone coming off angry more than I intended it to.

"Excuse me!" she shrieks. *Oh, shit! Here comes the crazy.*

"I think you need to take a fucking chill pill. Stop over thinking things," I clip, grabbing my cut off the floor. I need to split before this goes south. Besides, I need to get to the club anyhow.

"I—" she breaks off when I shake my head, and lean in, kissing her forehead.

I walk into the kitchen and ruffle Addie's hair. She's sitting at the counter still eating.

"See ya around," I mutter. Addie turns her head and smiles as I walk toward the door and leave.

9

Jessica

WHAT THE HELL JUST HAPPENED? I SIT ON THE COUCH replaying everything that took place starting from yesterday. I saw the look in his eye last night when we were having sex, the feeling of his arms around my body as he comforted me, and the way he acted as if he was Addie's best friend this morning. I close my eyes and sigh. Maybe he is right. Maybe I am the one breaking the rules, or maybe I am just over thinking everything in general.

"He seems really nice," Addie remarks, sitting on the couch. I turn and look at her, trying to read if she is joking or not, but the smile on her face is proof she is completely smitten by Bobby.

There is no denying that Bobby and I have chemistry, but I won't allow Bobby to fall for me and lay claim to me. I won't be trapped like that again. But it doesn't make Bobby any less alluring or charming. Even with the flaws of danger lurking around him, I am completely powerless to the way my body ignites for him.

"He is nice," I reply. I lean over, giving her forehead a kiss and then walk over to the food sitting on the counter.

◆ ◆ ◆

I'm looking at a chart for one of my patients, trying to focus, but my mind keeps replaying me and Bobby in my bedroom, my mind flicking through the images of how he and Addie clicked so well yesterday. I close my eyes and shake my head, trying to get a grip of myself.

"Get an IV in her arm. She's dehydrated from the heat," I inform the nurse as I walk back to the desk. As things start heating up outside, people forget to hydrate themselves, causing an ER visit.

"Dr. Wren, you owe me a date, ya know," Shane interrupts, laying his clipboard on the counter. I remove my gaze from the chart on the wall and look at him. I knew this conversation was coming. I have been dodging him for days, and he knows it.

"Why, so I can end up in the paper again?" I snide, grabbing a patient's file from the rack on the counter.

"Oh, but you looked so good plastered on the front page. Why hide it?" he laughs. "I have to feed the gossip hunters something, so why not some hot doctor?"

"I don't think so," I respond, looking at him from the corner of my eye.

"How about if anyone takes your picture tonight, I will break their camera," he replies and I can't help but giggle. Shane doing anything violent is an image to behold.

"We made a deal," he informs, his face emotionless. Deal, my head swims around that word, making me think of Bobby. I need to distance myself from him. I can feel myself becoming vulnerable. I don't want to love; I can't love Bobby. I made the fucking rule of no falling in love.

"I don't know, Shane," I whisper, exasperated.

"It's just as friends," he shrugs, making me feel silly thinking Shane wants more. Maybe I really am over thinking things lately.

"My shift ends in an hour. We'll go then and I'm picking the place this time," he rambles, walking off down the hall.

"Tonight?" I shriek, surprised by the urgency. He chuckles, walking away.

I look back down at the desk and see Nurse Helga staring at me, her dark eyes wide.

"What?" I ask, curious as to why she's looking at me with hazy eyes like that.

"Do you know how many nurses have been after that fine ass?" she laughs, looking down the hall where Shane strides away. Helga runs her hand through her dark hair, bobbing her head up and down in appreciation of Shane's backside.

I slap the counter and laugh. "Who needs to be seen next, Helga?" I question, changing the subject.

Bobby

SITTING IN A LEATHER CHAIR IN THE MIDDLE OF THE ROOM, I watch the growing crowd in the Wicked Birds strip club as I listen to Trove Lo singing "Habits". I just happened to walk into the Devil's Dust at just the right moment, or wrong, depending on how you look at it. Bull ordered me to come here and make sure things didn't become hectic. Watching naked chicks hump a pole for a few hours, why not? I could find worse things to do with my time.

"Bobby baby, I've been waiting for you to call me back," Diamond says seductively, walking toward me in some black fuck-me heels along with a black laced corset. Her dark hair falls over her shoulders in perfect curls as her eyes trail up and down my body.

"Hey, there," I reply, sitting up straighter in my chair. Shit, I have been ignoring her calls, but only because I've been busy with Jessica.

"Where have you been?" she questions, kneeling on the floor between my legs.

"Been busy, is all," I respond, giving her hand that is sliding up my leg, a tender squeeze. The music suddenly fades and the DJ introduces the next dancers to appear on stage, Diamond being one of them.

"Well, I'm glad you are here now. I hope you enjoy the show, baby," she coos, standing up and walking away. I admire her fine ass, making me groan in response. Diamond is a beautiful girl. I'm kind of curious why I haven't tapped that yet. Actually, I know why I haven't tapped that. She's not Jessica, far from it. And Jessica is all I've had on my mind lately. I sigh. Somewhere along the way, I became pussy whipped.

Some commotion catches my attention over by one of the stages. I look over and find some fat guy leaning over the stage grabbing one of the girl's legs. She looks down, startled, trying to pull her leg from his grasp.

"Shit," I mutter, standing from my chair.

"Come on, baby, take those pesky bottoms off," the guy encourages, pulling on her leg harder.

"Let go," I order, giving him a tap on the shoulder. He barely turns his head in my direction, eyeing me from the corner of his eye.

"Fuck off, this doesn't concern you, punk," he grunts, curling his lips in anger, his hand still wrapped around her leg tightly.

"You are in my club, harassing one of my girls. It concerns me," I growl, pissed. I broaden my shoulders, ready to pummel the asshole for his tone of disrespect.

The guy looks back at the scared blonde who is stumbling, trying to keep her balance.

"Maybe if you made your cunts worth the entry fee—" I collide my fist in his face, not letting him finish his sentence. Calling her a cunt throws me over the edge of anger and into rage. You want your front teeth missing? Call a woman a cunt in front of me and see what the fuck happens.

He falls on his ass, taking the skinny blonde off the stage with him.

"Shit!" I yell, grabbing the half-naked woman before she nose-dives onto the floor.

I pull her up onto her feet and steady her.

"You all right, babe?" I ask concerned, looking her over for injuries.

"Yeah, I'm okay," she mutters out of breath, running her hands down her bare stomach.

"Go take a break," I demand, tugging her away from the stage.

As she walks away, I see the fat guy trying to stand up, shaking his head back and forth from where I hit him. His mouth bloody, dripping onto his greasy shirt.

I stride forward and grab him by the collar, pulling him close.

"Get out of my club, now," I hiss, my tone a promising threat.

"Fine, man," he answers, trying to pull from my hold. I let go and watch him stumble out of the club, holding his mouth.

"Damn, brother, you only took over for a couple hours and you manage to beat up a customer?" Tom Cat asks, watching the guy leave. I look over my shoulder, not realizing Tom was even here.

"He was damn near pulling one of the girls off the stage by her leg," I defend, pointing at the now empty stage.

"I'm going to go make sure she's not hurt," I continue, making my way back into the dressing room.

I may have lost my cool, not handling things in the most professional way. But one thing my father taught me is to treat women with respect. I love women, and to see one hurt from a fucking bastard getting his rocks off by treating them like shit, I can't handle it. I've witnessed my dad punch a guy's teeth out for slapping an underage girl's ass at a gas station before. The memory still makes me smirk. My dad was a badass when he wanted to be.

I push open the red door covered in a gold design, and walk right into the ladies' dressing room. There are a bunch of vanities on both sides of the room. Small tables with huge back mirrors attached are outlined in light bulbs, along with chatty women sitting at them. I walk past a bunch of them, their tits hanging out, and some spraying perfume on them. At the back of the room, I spot the girl who was being harassed and go to her.

"You sure you're all right?" I ask, stopping a few feet from her station.

"Yeah, I'm fine," she responds, standing up. She has on a white thong and lacy top. It's sexy. I didn't notice it before from all the commotion.

"What happened?" Diamond asks, walking up to us.

"He rescued me from some scumbag trying to pull me off the stage," the blonde informs, rolling her eyes.

"You saved Sugar?" Diamond asks, her eyes raised in praise. "I mean I saw some commotion from my stage, but I didn't know it was that bad."

I shrug. "I guess I saved Sugar," I laugh nervously, running my hand along my neck.

"I think Bobby deserves a treat," Diamond suggests scandalously as her hand slides up my chest.

"Ooh, that is a great idea," Sugar agrees, her voice like silk as she walks behind me, running her hand over my shoulder.

The thought of two strippers fucking me is appealing, but regardless of what Jessica thinks, I am not about to give up on her. Sleeping with these two girls would make feel like I'm cheating, and my mother raised me better than that.

"I can't ladies. I'm on the clock," I laugh, my heart thudding against my chest in complete panic that I am turning down a threesome.

"Aww, baby," Diamond purrs.

"Darn, that would have been fun," Sugar adds, walking away.

"My shift is over. Wanna take me to get something to eat?" Diamond suggests.

I look down and see her honey-colored eyes peering up at me. I feel like shit ignoring her calls the last few days.

"Yeah, I can do that. Where you wanna eat?" I ask, running my hand over my chin, my eyes having a hard time not darting to the naked redhead walking by.

"Mexican, anywhere Mexican," she informs. "I know just the place," she continues, pointing at me as she walks to her mirror.

I smirk and nod.

Jessica

I SIT ACROSS FROM SHANE, A BOWL OF CHIPS SEPARATING US AND some Spanish music playing in the background. Luckily, no photographers have shown up yet.

"You look different," Shane remarks, popping a chip into his mouth and crunching down on it loudly.

"I do?" I question, grabbing a chip from the bowl as well.

"Yeah, less stressed. You been working less?" he asks, chomping on another chip and staring at me.

"No, about the same," I respond, taking a bite.

Shane nods, and looks off.

I pull my phone out and check it, making sure I haven't missed any calls over the music. I am on call tonight, so I have to be alert.

"You seeing anyone?" Shane continues, his eyes staring at me intently.

I open my mouth to answer, but shut it quickly not sure how to answer that. I am not with anyone, but with this deal Bobby and I have, I am not really available either. Then again, I don't want a relationship either, so maybe telling Shane I am with someone will have him back off a little bit.

My skin rises with a sudden chill, and the room takes on a sudden charge causing goose bumps to race up my arms. I look around the restaurant curious what has my body reacting the way it does and spot Bobby. He has his blond hair blown everywhere from riding on his bike, a snug gray shirt on, and that cut of his on top.

As his eyes survey the tables, they catch mine. My heart stammers in panic, the air zapped from my lungs. *Why is he here?* I quickly look away and see Shane, bobbing his head to the music, my eyes widening in awareness. *Is he going to beat up Shane?*

I release a breath I wasn't aware I was holding, and risk a glimpse at Bobby. I see a short woman step up next to him, her arm hooked around his waist intimately. She is wearing a short black dress and the tallest black heels I have seen on a woman. She's not afraid to show some skin that's for sure.

Shane turns in his seat, looking at what has me in a trance and spots Bobby.

"You know them?" he asks, popping another chip into his mouth.

"Eh, I know him," I nervously remark. Wondering if I should tell Shane to run for his life. Bobby and I have dated other people along the years we have been seeing each other, but we have never seen one another on a date the entire time.

Bobby and the girl walk our way, his blue eyes piercing me as he approaches. As my body temperature rises, I think of all the things that could go wrong in the next thirty seconds.

"Jessica, what are you doing here?" Bobby's tone unsettles me as he looks between Shane and me.

"Shane, this is Bobby. Bobby, this is Shane," I introduce, gesturing my hand between both men, and ignoring his question.

"Shane," Shane greets, holding his hand out. Bobby eyes it, before finally clasping it in a handshake.

"Bobby," he responds gravely.

"Hi, I'm Diamond," the dark-skinned girl adds, stepping up to shake my hand. I reach out and shake her hand. She is beautiful, stunning actually. I notice body glitter glisten off her chest from the light above our table, and her perfume wafts toward me as she shakes my hand. She eyes me with disgust, as if I just crawled out from under the table. I give her a death glare right back. Wouldn't be the first time one of Bobby's tarts gave me that look. When I do attend a club party, girls could throw knives from their eyes the way they look at me.

A waiter comes up and scoots a table right next to mine and Shane's, catching our attention. Apparently, the hostess thinks we are all here together. *Shit!*

"Um," Shane interjects, trying to look around Bobby to correct the hostess for the error.

"Ooh, a double date," Diamond claps eagerly and sits right next to me.

"Date, huh? Is this a date, Jessica?" Bobby asks, sitting across from me, his eyebrows raised mischievously. I'd tell him yes, and to shove it up his ass if I didn't fear for Shane's life. There is no way Shane would survive a fight against Bobby

"Actually it is. She took me to a coffee shop when I let her pick our first date. So I got to pick this time, for a real date," Shane explains, taking a sip of his beer.

I smile a tightlipped smile, my stomach suddenly not hungry.

"Is that right?" Bobby muses. "Funny, Jessica has never mentioned you," Bobby lies, his eyebrows inward as he looks at me. I take a deep breath, and prepare myself for a pissing contest.

"Yeah, she is kind of a private person," Shane continues, smiling brightly at me, talking as if we are close.

"She's not very private with me. In fact, she was rather open to me last night," Bobby continues, his tone earnest, making my cheeks flush with warmth from embarrassment. My hands grab a menu, seeking some kind of distraction.

"What's good here?" I ask, trying to change the subject.

"Good. I am glad she has someone she can open up with," Shane mentions, completely oblivious to what Bobby is indicating.

"Oh, man, I am the most open person I know," Diamond adds, smiling cheerily at Bobby. Bobby doesn't even look at her, making Diamond sit back in her chair with a look of displeasure on her face.

I swallow the lump in my throat and set the menu down, my aversion not working. This is too much. I'm not sure if I want to laugh, or bolt for the door. I take a deep breath trying to gain some self-control.

"Bobby is not much to open up to," I respond, trailing my eyes downward to Bobby's crotch, implying he has a small dick even though I *know* it's not true, but playing Bobby's game against him is something I can't resist. "But he gets an A for effort," I continue, eyeing Bobby wolfishly. Bobby smirks, knowing the game I'm playing. The look of the cat that is about to eat the canary playing across his face.

"Funny, I didn't hear you complaining last night," Bobby smarts, making my smile fade quickly. The table goes quiet, Diamond and Shane finally noticing the actual conversation.

"I'm going to go to the bathroom," I inform, my body sweating nervously from Bobby's confession. I scoot my chair back, and head toward the restrooms quickly. Maybe there is a window in there and I can just shimmy out and run like the wind. I snort at the image of me trying to fit my ass through a window in a restaurant bathroom, trying to escape a bad date.

As soon as my hand hits the bathroom handle, I'm pulled back, turned around, and my back is slammed against the door. My eyes land on two angry blue irises, belonging to Bobby.

"An A for effort?" he asks, a grin crossing his face. He grabs both of my wrists, plows them above my head, and spreads my legs open with his knee. "How about I show you how hard I strive for excellence," he grits, grinding his knee right into my clit. My body flames with desire and my head falls back against the door. We're in public. This thought thrills as much as it horrifies me.

Bobby slides his nose up the side of my neck, leaving a blazing trail of need behind. This is so wrong. It's not right doing this right here, but it feels so amazingly good.

"Go ahead and deny that our bodies are undeniably made for each other," he whispers into my ear, tugging my earlobe with his sharp teeth. My body arches into his on impulse, and I bite my bottom lip trying to keep from whimpering.

"I-I..." I stutter, not wanting to do this in a restaurant. "I can't do this here," I mutter, out of breath.

"I told you. When you're mine, you're mine, and right now, you're mine," he mutters against my lips, tugging my bottom lip that was pulled between my teeth with his. He slides his hands down my abdomen and under the waistband of my scrubs. My body trembles with passion, and my breathing becomes labored.

"Why are you here with him?" he whispers into my ear, his hands slipping under my panties.

"Why are you here with her?" I question, my core vibrating with excitement as Bobby's fingers brush against my clit.

"Just as friends, baby," he whispers against my ear, his fingers pressing hard against my clit making me moan.

"He's nothing but a friend," I whimper.

"You're mine, remember?" Bobby growls, pushing a finger into my heat, causing my head to fall back against the door, and sigh from Bobby finally giving my body what it craves, him.

"Ahem."

Bobby and I turn and find a little old lady waiting to get into the bathroom that Bobby and I currently block. She is clutching her purse tightly, her eyes darting anywhere but at us.

Bobby pulls from me hesitantly. His eyes promising me that this isn't over, his smirk giving off one delicious dimple. Just as he pulls away, his phone rings. He pulls it from his pocket and answers it as he walks away.

"Sorry," I whisper to the lady, pulling away from the door. I straighten my shirt down, and try to get a hold of myself before walking back out to the table.

Walking back, Shane eyes me awkwardly, his face twisted instead of beaming with cheer like usual. As soon as I sit down, my phone beeps with a notification.

"Shit," I curse.

"Getting called in?" Shane asks, his tone holding a solemn energy.

"Yeah," I reply.

"Hey, Diamond, I'm sorry but I have to go, too," Bobby states, giving her a kiss on the cheek. I stop in my tracks and watch as she lights up. My stomach knots from watching him kiss her. I'm jealous. Bobby looks up at me, his eyes unwavering.

"All right, well I guess the date is over," Shane interjects, breaking my eye contact from Bobby.

"Yeah, I have to leave, sorry," I mutter. I stand from my seat and walk out of the restaurant quickly, not wanting to see anymore of Bobby and Diamond.

I start down the sidewalk but am gripped by the arm and stopped short.

"Do you really have to go?" Bobby asks.

"Yeah, I was called in," I reply, looking over at the buildings.

"Do you really have to go?" I ask, fiddling with my phone.

"No, but I can see you don't like me with Diamond," he

admits. My eyes dart to his and relief spins my head to the point I feel dizzy.

I shrug, trying to play it off like I don't care. But the pain in my chest from seeing them together would beg to differ.

"No more dates for either of us while we are doing this? Even if it's just friend-dates," he suggests, digging his hands in his pockets.

I lick my bottom lip and nod. I don't know what is going on with me but I can't see him with another tart. He leans in and gives my mouth an earth-shattering kiss. I place my hands against his chest as he drinks me in, feeling his heart drumming against his chest in a violent rhythm. Feeling the lines we set for each other fading into something more, I wonder if he's just as scared as I am.

His soft mouth devouring mine is intoxicating. Possessive lips taking mine under the night's sky encourage me to sink into him. He grabs the back of my head, and deepens the kiss as if I'm the only one on the sidewalk. At this moment, I couldn't care less who walks past.

"I'll see you around, babe." Bobby kisses my forehead and walks away, leaving me gasping for breath and in a complete haze.

I stride around the corner. The hospital is just a block away so I decide to walk. My mind is in a complete jumble. I don't know what I am feeling or what I am thinking. I just know that I was jealous over Bobby for the first time ever, and I hate the feeling. It burns and feels like my chest is sinking all at the same time. I have seen girls climb all over Bobby, and him all over them, but not once have I cared as much as I did tonight. I need to try harder at distancing myself, but to do that, I'd need to move across the world.

10
Bobby

I SIT AT THE WOODEN TABLE IN THE CHAPEL OF THE CLUB, WAIT-ing for some of the brothers to show up after leaving the restaurant, Shadow called and told me to get my ass to the club fast. Lip got into some shit and we needed to gather quickly.

My fingers tap against the wood grain as I think about seeing Jessica with that doctor guy. It made me angry when he rubbed it in my face about how close he and Jessica were. I considered throwing Jessica on the table and fucking her right in front of him.

"You're here," Bull observes, walking in with a cigarette hanging out of his mouth. His dark hair slicked back, he pulls his leather cut onto his shoulders comfortably.

"Yup," I reply, still tapping the tabletop. A bunch of the guys come in after Bull, and sit down in their usual spots. I look over and see Lip holding his arm which is patched up with white gauze, his face holding a shadow of pain. Speckles of blood cover his clothes and face, causing me to eye him skeptically. "What happened to you?" I question, staring at the red blood seeping through the gauze.

"Bullet grazed me," Lip croaks, his voice scratchy.

"Sounds like a fucking mess to me. Why don't you explain?" Shadow insists, sitting near the head of the table. I turn and look at Shadow, curious at what the hell he is going on about. Shadow looks nervous as he runs his hands back and forth through his black hair. This can't be good.

"I was headed to Greg's Pizza and I took the back way. I stopped to light a cigarette and saw an exchange between some SUVs down an alleyway. I stood there for a second to get a better look at what was going on. Some men spotted me, and instantly started shooting at me, so I fired back," Lip explains, his eyebrows raised as he speaks.

"Why did they just start shooting?" I ask, shrugging. They had to be up to no good to draw their weapons and fire.

"I wondered the same thing at first," he informs. "I ran around a building to reload my gun when a man was being guided from the building toward a black car. When he went around his side of the car to get in, he spotted me and pulled his weapon, but I was faster. I shot him and ran," Lip rambles anxiously, shaking his head.

"Why did you run?" Shadow questions gravely. I nod, wondering why in the fuck he would run. We don't run. We aren't pussies.

Lip looks up from staring at the wooden table, his eyes holding a sense of grief as he looks at Shadow.

"Because," he mumbles, "it was Augustus," Lip continues, his eyes never leaving Shadow.

I stand immediately, my chair falling against the floor from the force. "You fucking shot Augustus?" I holler, my heart thudding against my ribcage. My hands become clammy, and the scar cutting into my abdomen flares with pain, a reminder of how Augustus nearly killed me.

"Yeah, it was either me or him. When he went down, his men ran toward him, and I made a break for it," he confirms, looking downward. I sense there is more to the story he is not telling me, his eyes avoiding everyone at the table.

"What are you not telling us?" I mutter.

He looks up and sighs. "It may be nothing, but as I was running away, I ran right into Doc," he explains, shaking his head as if he is sorry. All the breath rushes out of my lungs from the thought of Augustus's men seeing Lip with Jessica.

"How did that happen?" Bull asks, putting his cigarette out in an ashtray.

"I just ran, man. I was only a few blocks from the hospital, and when I was running, I slammed right into her. She was concerned with my arm, but I yelled for her to let me go, to get the fuck away from me," Lip nearly shrieks, his tone pleading for me to understand he did what he could to get her to go away.

"Were you followed, did anyone see you two talking?" I ask, placing my fists on the table, and closing my eyes trying to keep calm. Jessica could be in danger if anyone saw them conversing with each other.

"I'm not sure," Lip replies, his tone solemn. I rub my face, and exhale slowly. My fists clenching and unclenching, wanting to punch Lip in the fucking face for putting Jessica in such a position. I finally feel like Jessica and I are making progress, and this could ruin all that. Proving to her that my lifestyle is too much for her and her daughter.

"If anything happens to her, I will fucking kill you, do you understand?" I seethe, my teeth clenched so hard they may fucking shatter. Lip flinches from my threat, the rest of the guys at the table silent as I stare a brother down with deadly promise.

I've made sure the entire time I have known Jessica, that I never put her in danger. Then a brother goes and throws her into the most dangerous situation this club has had to endure. Augustus is a savage and doesn't care who he tears apart to make a point.

"Bobby, that's enough. Sit down so we can figure this shit out!" Bull hollers, snapping me from my haze of anger.

"This is not good. As soon as Augustus gets the chance, he is going to ID you and order his men after us," Old Guy motions from the back, taking my nerves a notch higher.

"Why did he shoot at you?" Bull asks, his tone exasperated as he looks at the wall confused. "I thought we were on good terms."

"Because he was doing something he didn't want us knowing about. He saw Lip with his cut and tried to take him out, before he could get back here and tell us." Shadow's jaw ticks in anger.

"I bet that is exactly it," I add. Augustus is the worst person to be in business with. To get his point across to our club last time, he tried to run down every one of our ol' ladies, killing one in the process. He has everyone in his pocket, making him one of the biggest kingpins on the west side. His reputation wasn't built on trust, but rather in blood and fear. If anyone saw Lip with Jessica, they could come after her. There is no way she would survive their tactics in getting her to talk, but there is no way I would let that ever happen. Augustus needs to go, and today.

"Shit, I need to call Jessica and warn her," I grumble,

pushing away from the table.

Jessica

I LOOK AT MY PHONE IN DISBELIEF AS THE NURSES CLOSE UP THE patient on the operating table. Augustus to be exact. I turn to get a better look at him, his long black hair pulled into a blue cap. His face blemished with age and pockmarks from acne across his cheeks. He was just rushed in for a bullet wound to the chest. Working the ER, I worked on him instantly. If I had known who he was, I would have taken my time digging that bullet out.

Bobby just called, concerned I might have been seen with Lip who was running after shooting Augustus. I was rounding the corner after leaving the restaurant and Lip slammed into me, nearly knocking me on my ass. He was holding his arm, blood rushing down his elbow at a fast pace. I was concerned, but he pushed me away and told me to fuck off. I didn't know he was in trouble, or that he might have been followed at the time. I just thought he was being a dickhead. I wasn't seen with him though. When I got to the hospital doors, Augustus was being rushed into the ER at the same time. I helped wheel Augustus in, his men right next to me. If they had seen me, they could have easily grabbed me, thrown me into the back of their car, and tortured me for information on the club.

Trying to control my mind, I close my eyes and inhale deeply. This guy killed a good woman of the Devil's Dust, nearly killed Bobby, and now might have the opportunity to finally kill Bobby and the rest of the club. I saved a monster, a plague about to wipe everyone I know out. Strings of memories flare in my mind, images of Bobby wheeled into the hospital when Augustus shot him years back. I thought Bobby was dead when he arrived at the ER. The things I said I would do differently if Bobby would just pull through never happened. I made empty promises of being a better person, living more openly, spending more time with Bobby, and accepting the club as family. All were forgotten over the years. But now, it seems my lies are paying their dues, and the ultimate fate of the club and Bobby's life might resume its deadly timeline.

I just stamped the death certificate of the club, and someone I care about more than I am willing to admit.

Bobby

I EYE THE FLUORESCENT-LIT HALL, THE SMELL OF ANTISEPTIC strong as I take in everything. I left my leather cut at the club, and pulled on a dark blue hoody, the hood concealing my face. I pull the hood down over my face lower, making sure I'm not seen as I sit in a chair directly across from the hall. I see where Augustus's room is; there are two bulky men standing guard, their heads wrapped up in a green bandanna, indicating they are men of Augustus. All men who work for him wear green. I told the brothers I was coming to the hospital to just check on Jessica, but now I'm here, I can't walk away from Augustus until I know he's dead. He is too much of a liability. If he wakes up and tells them who shot him, he could order a hit on the entire club.

I adjust my pistol in my waistband as I eye the hall under the hood of my sweater. I can't go in there until the men on guard leave or fall asleep. I don't need any unwanted attention with a confrontation.

I don't know what the hell I'm going to do when I get in there. I know he is going against the club's deal. He runs drugs on our side of town, and we run guns on his side. He is doing something against us; otherwise, why would he have tried to kill Lip.

Jessica ensured me Lip wasn't followed and nobody saw her with him, but I don't want to chance it. Augustus dies today, even if I have to sit here all night.

"Sir, have you been seen--?

I don't look up at the person questioning me, not wanting them to see my face. I keep my head down and nod. She pats my arm and walks off, leaving me to stare down the hall. I see Jessica walk toward the room, her blonde hair is pulled up high, and she's wearing blue scrubs. She talks to one of the guards outside of Augustus's room and a bolt of adrenaline shoots up my spine causing me to go deathly stiff. My hands twitch in fear of what they could do to her if they figured out who she was affiliated with.

They nod and she walks into the room, writing something on a clipboard. After five minutes, one of the guards leaves the door, walking down the hall. I slowly stand and take a step forward. I may have to take my chance with one guy. There is no way they are going to leave the door completely unguarded.

I see Jessica walk out of the room and give the guy still standing outside the door a pat on the shoulder sympathetically, before she walks down the long corridor. I notice her tuck something away in her pants pocket, looking over her shoulder nervously. I stop in my steps and raise an eyebrow at her unease. White lights begin to flash along the hall as a computer at the nurses' desk beeps like crazy. I take my eyes from the desk and look back down the hall at Jessica walking away quickly.

What the fuck did she just do?

Jessica

I WALK TO MY LOCKER, GRAB MY BAG, STUFF MY THINGS IN IT, and slam the door shut. My heart is thudding against my chest in mere panic as evidence that I just killed a man sits in my pocket. The blood in my body is racing so hard, trying to keep up with my beating heart. My vision wobbles with clarity. I. Just. Killed. A. Man. I inhale sharply at the thought. A sob racks from my mouth, and my hands tremble as I pull the drawstrings to my bag together. I lean my clammy forehead against the cool locker door, breathing in and out slowly, trying to steady my heart rate. I filled a syringe with adrenaline, and pumped it into Augustus's arm, giving him a heart attack. I don't know what I was thinking. All I could think about was Augustus killing Bobby. I pull away from the locker and shake my twitching hands, gaining some control. After a few moments of calming myself, I walk out of the dressing room. I have to get out of here. I can't be here in the state of panic I'm in.

"Dr. Wren, you gotta do something," one of the men I helped wheel in Augustus pleads as I walk past the room holding his dead boss. My head pounds with instant remorse as the man begs for me to save his mentor, but I know what I did will not only save Bobby and the club, but any other person that crosses paths with the likes of such a kingpin.

I give a tightlipped smile and rub his arm.

"I'm sorry. I did everything I could," I respond, my voice soft and low to hide the tremble of fear crackling through. The guy pulls away, runs his hand over his chin, and shakes his head.

"I'm sorry," I apologize again, my tone in the stern voice I use with everyone when they have lost someone close.

I continue to make my way toward the exit, my back wet from a nervous sweat, and my hands shaking uncontrollably.

"Dr. Wren," Nurse Helga calls, stopping me feet from the exit. I still and close my eyes before turning with a bright smile on my face.

"I need you to delegate this patient's care. I'm not sure if we should seek surgery, or send them to pediatrics and let them decide," she rambles, flipping through a patient's chart, her lips smacking together as she reads it over. Shit, the reason I was called in, I forgot with everything that happened with Augustus.

I walk to the desk and she hands me the chart. Looking it over, it's nothing serious, and looks like the patient will be handled better on pediatrics floor.

"Send them to pediatrics," I mumble, pushing the chart on the counter.

"Will do. See you tomorrow," Nurse Helga calls out, sitting down at the desk and lifting the phone to call pediatrics. I lift my hand and wave, and walk toward the exit, not faltering in my steps. I try to slow my steps as I head toward my Jeep, but I can't help but pick up the pace. My heart is slamming against my chest with every beat, my lungs burning, trying to keep up with my sporadic breathing. I have to get home. I have to get rid of the evidence.

I can tell nobody about this.

◆ ◆ ◆

I walk up the steps to my apartment, my hands still shaky, and my eyes filling with tears at the thought of actually killing someone on purpose. I'm a doctor. I save people not kill them.

I grab the keys in my pocket, my hand bumping the evidence in my pants. I close my eyes, and shake my head, fishing my keys the rest of the way out. As I look up, I see someone leaning against my apartment door, their legs crossed out in front of them. I stop as I eye the person. They are wearing a dark-colored hoody, the hood pulled over their face as they look down. Is it one of Augustus's men? I take a step back, and my shaking hands give out from fear. The keys in my hand fall, making a loud noise as they hit the ground.

Shit.

I look up from my keys now laying on the floor and see Bobby looking at me from under his hood.

"Bobby," I whimper, tears filling my eyes in relief. I try to hold myself together. I don't want him to know I just killed Augustus. I don't want anyone to know.

He pushes himself off my door and strides toward me quickly. I lean down and pick my keys up, closing my eyes tightly to push the tears away, trying to mask my emotions with a fake smile.

Bobby grabs my face, both of his large hands cupping my cheeks firmly. My watery eyes look directly at his wide blue ones. His eyebrows raise upward, and his nostrils flare from the hard breaths leaving his nose.

"What did you do?" His voice is shaky, but stern.

"I…" He knows. He knows I did something to Augustus. "I killed Augustus," I whisper, tears begin spilling from my eyes. I lower my head, cursing myself for just spitting out a confession I swore not to tell anyone.

Bobby inhales sharply as his hands press on my cheeks

harder. "Why would you do that?" he whispers in disbelief.

"For you," I mutter, a tear falling against my lips as I stare into two blue orbs belonging to this man I've grown fond of.

Just as I think he is about to yell at me, he smashes his lips to mine. I grab his wrists, kissing him back. My top lip sitting comfortably between his. He nibbles at my mouth as his thumbs caress my cheeks. This kiss, it's not like any other kiss Bobby and I have ever had with one another. This kiss is desperate; it's gut wrenchingly desperate.

"You stupid, stupid woman," Bobby mumbles against my lips, his tone emotional.

He grabs me under the thighs and turns, walking us to my door, his lips never leaving mine. He grabs the keys from my hand, letting us in. As soon as we are in and the door is shut, he plows me against the back of it, sliding one of his hands up my top, kneading my breast. I take my hands from the back of his neck and pull my shirt my head, exposing myself in my pink bra. He pulls me close, smothering his face in my breast, and leaving a hint of my perfume on his face. He pulls us away from the door, stumbling against the couch in the middle of the room, knocking a lamp over in the process. He lowers us to the floor, his hands unbuckling his leather belt, eager to push his pants down. His cock is hard and swollen to the point it looks painful. I lick my lips at the curve his cock displays, my pussy aching to have it inside me. I slide my hands up his shirt, my fingers gliding against his defined muscles. He lowers himself on top of me, my fingers sliding down his chest to his scar; the scar Augustus caused. Bobby looks between us, eyeing my fingers caressing his scar before looking at me. His eyes strong and intent as he looks at me with a passion deeper than yesterday. I wrap my hands around his neck, and pull his lips back to mine. His mouth desperately taking mine into a breathtaking embrace. He pulls away, brushing his lips along my cheek as he sits up on his knees.

"I'm going to fuck you, Jessica," he whispers against my face, stroking his cock.

"Please," I moan, arching my back off the floor, grabbing his shirt by the hem, and pulling it up over his head.

◆ ◆ ◆

Bobby fucked me on the floor of my apartment like we were each other's cure to the screwed-up world we live in. Our hands grabbed onto anything they could for friction and we clawed at each other's shoulders from the immense pleasure, leaving marks all over one another. Not to mention we both have rug burns on our knees, elbows, and hips. I was positioned on top of Bobby, underneath, and even beside him. The entire time I was lost in Bobby, his hard breathing in my ear, the noises he made when he came inside me. They reached something deep inside of me, breaking the suppressed emotion I have tried to deny for so long. The smell of coconuts and leather emanating off Bobby was a comfort to my fear; it was my serenity and made terror obliterate into bliss and pure pleasure.

When I closed my eyes, all I thought about was Bobby, and when I opened them, all I saw was Bobby. Travis wasn't even an ash in the inferno of raw emotion on the floor of my apartment. The torment of Travis, the fear of living for today, or the terror of yesterday was gone.

"Jessica," Bobby whispers into my ear from behind me, his arms pulling my body into the curve of his.

"Yeah?" I whisper half asleep, my body and mind incapacitated from just having the most vigorous sex ever.

"You know, I would have loved taking you to a coffee shop," he breathes out, brushing against the shell of my ear. My eyes open as I think about how much Shane complained about me taking us to a coffee shop.

"I've never gotten to take you anywhere, take you on a proper date." Bobby's hands run up and down my side as he speaks.

I turn my head just slightly, listening to him talk.

"I want to take you on a date, Jessica," he whispers against my neck, brushing his tattooed knuckles on my cheek.

"Bobby," I interject.

"Just let me take you on one," he interrupts. One date. It reminds me of our first time, how he just wanted to take me on one ride. That night was the night I noticed myself becoming attached to Bobby. I was more than frightened by the feelings toward him. I was brutally terrified. I clench my eyes and sigh. It's Bobby; he'll probably take me to a BBQ, arcade place, or something for the club anyways. Harmless. But it wouldn't matter where Bobby took me. I would enjoy it, and there lies the problem: I enjoy being with him.

"Okay," I mutter mindlessly.

"Yeah?" he replies, lifting himself up from the floor to see my face, seemingly shocked by my lack of rejection.

"Just one. I don't want to ruin what we have. Your life and mine are too different, too complex for us to mix, Bobby," I mutter, adjusting my head on the small couch pillow that holds both mine and Bobby's head.

"I hate to tell you this, but both of our lives are unconventional Jessica. That doesn't mean our being together would be a bad thing," he mumbles into the back of my neck, his breath tickling me.

I breathe deeply as his hands slide along the scars of my

back tenderly, but my body doesn't tense and my mind doesn't flicker with distressed memories of what was. I smile, the feeling of Bobby's fingers caressing my imperfection welcoming instead of suffocating. "Yeah. Maybe," I whisper, closing my eyes to sleep. I knew this would happen and that both of us would break our own rules. The plan to distance ourselves going in the opposite direction. It was inevitable with the overwhelming hold we have on each other. It scares me that I may lose the only person in this world who could take what is left of my heart and burn it.

◆ ◆ ◆

Waking up this morning, my body's sore from the abuse Bobby so deliciously delivered last night. My hand swipes the hair from my face, a note sticking to my arm hitting me in the cheek. I pull the blue post-it note from my arm and look it over.

Be back — Sex God

"Sex God?" I laugh.

I stretch my arms and gaze around the room, finding my clothes slung all over the floor and the lamp knocked over. It got pretty wild last night. I walk to the bedroom and find some gym shorts and a white tank top, and put them on. I don't want Addie to come in and see me naked. That would be an awkward conversation.

I am tying up my hair into a ponytail and the front door opens. Bobby walks in with a bag in his hand and a cup holder in the other with a couple of cups.

"Just for you," he remarks, handing me a cup. I smile and take it, the sides of it warm against my palm. I hold it to my nose and inhale.

"Mmm. Coffee," I respond, grateful.

Bobby smiles, revealing two sexy dimples in his cheeks and sets the bag down on the counter. He digs in his pocket and pulls his cell phone out that's vibrating.

"Shit, I need to get to the club," he whispers, stuffing it back in his pocket. He peers up under his thick lashes, and braces himself against the counter with both hands gripping the sides.

"Where's the evidence?" he asks gravely. My mouth suddenly dries and my throat constricts at his question.

"Why?" I ask, turning to dig into the bag of food.

"So I can get rid of it, babe," he responds, his tone as if I should know that.

"You are not taking it to the club, Bobby," I smart. "I don't want them to know anything about what I did," I clip, pulling out a breakfast sandwich. Bobby scoffs, and walks around the counter, crossing his arms, scowling at me.

"And why is that exactly?" he asks, clearly offended.

Turning to face him, I sigh. His blond hair is still a mess from last night, and his clothes are wrinkled from lying inside out on the floor. He still looks sexy though, even with a disproving look written on his face. The club has had a few instances where people have come in claiming to be a part of the MC, only to find out they were enemies of the club, causing a shit storm in their wake, and lives to be taken in the process. I can't take the chance there's still a rat in the pack who hasn't been weeded out.

"Truth?" I ask, running my tongue along my bottom lip nervously.

"Please," he mutters.

"Your club has a bad track record. How many people have come in and said they were loyal and turned out not to be who you thought they were? The last thing I need is word getting out I offed the biggest drug lord in California," I explain, my tone serious. Bobby nods his head in understanding, his hand rubbing the stubble on his chin, making a scratchy noise against his palm.

"I understand that so I won't say anything to the club," he replies, surprising me. "Unless it needs to be brought to light," he continues hesitantly, causing me to groan in response.

"All right," I mutter. I know going against his club would make him one of those people who betray the brotherhood, so asking him not to say anything unless he has to will have to do.

"So where is the evidence?" he asks, shrugging.

"It's in my pocket," I reply, pointing to my pants sitting by the door.

Bobby walks over to my wrinkled pants, carefully sliding his hands into the pocket, pulling the capped syringe out.

"I'll make sure no one finds this," he mutters, sticking it into his pocket.

He looks down and sees my scrub bottoms with my pink underwear tangled in between them. Looking at me, he grins. He reaches down, grabs my panties, and sticks them in his jeans pocket.

"Drop them, buddy. Those are my expensive panties." I point my finger at him. He smiles and stands up, ignoring me.

"I'll see you tomorrow for that date," he adds, giving me a wink before opening the door, locking it, and leaving.

My eyes widen and my heart sinks. Shit, I forgot about the date.

I sigh heavily and sit down on the stool, sipping my coffee, my mind running wild with what has happened in the last twenty-four hours.

I hear the front door handle wiggle, making me look over at

it warily.

"Addie?" I question loudly. The handle stops, making me lift an eyebrow. I slide off the stool and walk toward the door. I push up on my toes to look out the peephole, but I don't see anything but Bree's door across from me. I unlock the door and open it, finding nobody there. I look down the hall and spot muddy footmarks staining the carpet from my door to the stairs. I look inside my apartment curious if Bobby brought mud in on the bottom of his shoes, but there is not a trace of it on my apartment floor. I look back at the shoe prints in the hallway and realize the shoe print is too small to be Bobby's. My heart stammers. Someone was trying to get into my apartment. Were they waiting for Bobby to leave? I slam the door shut and lock it quickly. My heartbeat picking up rhythm in my chest. Could it be one of Augustus's men?

"Mom?" I yelp and turn around quickly, finding Addie rubbing her eyes trying to wake up, wearing her Hello Kitty pajamas.

"Hun, I thought you were at Bree's," I reply, clutching my chest in panic. She nearly gave me a heart attack.

"I came over late last night to sleep. Bree is in my room sleeping on her laptop's keyboard," Addie laughs. Bree is a studying fool. It's not the first time she has fallen asleep at her laptop and drooled on her keyboard.

I give a half laugh, my frayed nerves keeping me from seeing the full humor in the situation.

"What happened in here last night?" Addie raises a brow, looking around the aftermath of mine and Bobby's exhilarating sex session. Thank God, Addie is a sound sleeper, and I pray Bree had her headphones on.

"Hungry?" I ask, pointing toward the counter containing the bag Bobby brought, avoiding her question.

Addie nods and runs to the counter, pulling the bag open eagerly. I lean against the back of the door, and chew on my fingernails nervously, watching Addie dig the food items out of the bag.

Killing Augustus was a stupid, stupid move. More dangerous than anything I've ever done. What the hell was I thinking? Where did the courage and brass come from?

"Hey, look, extra straws to make caterpillars with," Addie yells excitedly, holding a handful of straws.

My eyes widen, and my mouth parts at the sincere gesture; Bobby thought of my daughter.

◆ ◆ ◆

Walking into work today, my nerves are on edge. I should have called in, but that would look suspicious, I never call in. There is no evidence that I had anything to do with Augustus's death, no reason for anyone to suspect foul play, but if it had and they did an autopsy, a surge of adrenaline in Augustus's bloodwork could come back to me. I take a deep breath and climb out of my Jeep. The sky fills with gray clouds and there's lightning in the distance. I run toward the entry as rain begins to fall against my skin.

"Good afternoon, Dr. Wren," Nurse Helga yells from the desk.

"Afternoon," I reply, heading to the dressing room.

I walk in the room and find my locker door dented and yanked open, my stuff scattered all over the floor.

"What the hell?" I whisper, my palms sweating anxiously. Someone broke into my locker and rummaged through everything in it.

"Oh, man, it looks like you have been stolen from," Nurse

Helga gasps from behind me. I turn to face her, my cheeks turning red. I know I wasn't stolen from. Someone was searching for something, possibly a syringe with my fingerprints on it.

"You want me to call security, babe?" Helga questions. She places her hand on my shoulder making me jump.

"What?" I ask. I was so consumed of what I was looking at I tuned her out. "No, it's fine," I reply, grabbing papers and scrubs off the floor.

"All right, well, I came in here to tell you we're backed up and need you out here quickly," she explains, walking back to the door.

"Yeah, okay. I'll be out in a minute," I mutter, exasperated. I should call Bobby, tell him about the mud prints, and now this, but that will make him tell the club what I did, and I don't want that. Whoever was here didn't find what they were looking for obviously. So hopefully, nothing else will occur.

I clean up and splash some cold water on my face, my nerves taking over my entire body. I am a sweaty mess. I wipe the beaded sweat already forming on my forehead and walk out of the dressing room.

"Dr. Wren," Shane greets, nearly running into me as I exit. His tone is formal and unfriendly.

"Shane," I respond, tilting my head to the side, curious why he's acting the way he is. "Are you okay?" I ask.

"Yes, fine," he remarks, writing on the clipboard in his hands. He gives me a fake smile before walking off. I sigh and let my head fall against the door. With the date we went on, and the way Bobby got into a pissing match with him, I don't blame Shane for giving me the cold shoulder.

"Shane!" I yell, running down the hall. "Shane, I'm sorry," I confront, catching up to him. He stops and tucks the clipboard under his arm.

"I'm sorry about yesterday," I continue.

Shane exhales a tired breath, pinching the bridge of his nose.

"Look, Jessica, you are a great doctor and an incredibly talented woman, but you are not available, no matter what you may think. The way that guy was staring at you last night, the way you were looking back at him..." he scoffs. "Do me a favor, the rest of the male population a favor, and tell the next poor son of a bitch who comes your way that you are seeing someone upfront—"

"It's not a relationship. I mean...Bobby and I..." I struggle to find the words, not sure what we are exactly. Shane huffs, licking his lips as he squints his eyes, glaring at me.

"I'm just going off what I saw last night. Considering how defensive he got right off the bat, I'd say you are taken, whether you choose to see it that way or not," Shane remarks, shaking his head. "I thought the guy was going to break my neck just by looking at me, Jessica," Shane complains. I roll my lips onto one another, and look down the hall. I was afraid Bobby might kill Shane too, so what do I even say to that?

"Are you fucking him?" My head snaps in Shane's direction, my mouth gaped open in shock.

"What?" I ask, my cheeks fuming with heat.

"Are you fucking him? Because you both came back from the bathroom pretty flushed in the face," Shane states, his tone calm and collected.

"I..." I struggle to answer, nervous at how forward he's being.

"Yeah, that's what I thought," Shane responds, giving a half laugh before turning to walk off. I clench my jaw, my hands squeezing tightly. Anger bubbling to the surface at his crude tone.

"Hey, Shane." He turns, his smile arrogant.

"I tried to warn you I didn't want to go on a date with you, that I don't date pussies. Next time a woman says that to you, you might take the hint," I smart, my eyes narrow in anger. "And you're right. That guy probably would have snapped your neck. Alphas like Bobby tend to take out the weaker of the pack." His face falls, its color turning a ghostly white. I smile before turning and walking off.

11
Bobby

"SO HE DIED OF A HEART ATTACK?" LIP QUESTIONS, SITTING beside me at the chapel's table. He looks like shit. His eyes are bloodshot with dark bags under them, and his bandage on his arm needs changing.

"Yeah, that's what Jessica told me," I explain, interlocking my fingers and resting my hands on the table. I hate not telling the club everything I know; it goes against everything I believe in. But Jessica asked me not to, scared for her safety if someone sided with Augustus under the table. I feel like shit not trusting my brotherhood like I know I should, but if I'm being honest, our club has had some shady motherfuckers waltz up in here in the past.

"Well, that worked out for everyone then," Bull laughs, lighting a cigarette. I nod and give a tight-lipped smile.

I look over and see Shadow eyeing me suspiciously, one

eyebrow raised.

Shit.

I look away and tap my fingers against the tabletop. With Shadow and I growing up together, we know the look and tone of one another when we are bullshitting. He knows I'm bullshitting right now. Hopefully, that VP patch doesn't give him a big head. There was a time I stood up for him against the club when he and Dani got into some shit. He took a bullet for dating the president's daughter and I was there by his side. He better have my back now.

"We got some wind that the Howlerz were buying guns from Augustus. I think we'll take us a little ride," Bull remarks, eyeing the smoke from his cigarette climbing toward the ceiling. The Howlerz are a small MC here in town. They usually buy guns and sometimes the occasional pot from us, reselling the pot and cutting us in on the payment. As a small club, they pay up front with cash, so we don't mind them around our territory, 'til now. Them buying from someone else while on our turf is humiliating. It was different when they used our merchandise and we got a cut, but dealing with someone else, we just get fucked in the end. We lose business and our street credibility with having another MC competing so close to home.

"I'm game," Lip adds, pulling his pistol from his waistband. I cock my eyebrow at him.

"Got some anger issues there, Lip?" I ask, laughing.

"That asshole Augustus shot me. For what? To deal with these asswipes?" he yells, pointing toward his arm.

"Let's ride, boys," Shadow hollers, standing up.

Everyone gets up from their chairs, beginning to leave. I stand up, my chair sticking to the hardwood floor, making me kick it back so it will move.

Just as I reach the doorway, a hand clasps on my shoulder, squeezing with force.

"So what really happened?" Shadow growls in my ear from behind, his voice low making sure nobody can hear him.

"I don't know what you mean," I reply, turning my head to look at him fully.

Shadow huffs, knowing I'm lying.

"Try again," he demands, squeezing my shoulder, trying to intimidate me. I flex my muscles under his grip, dissipating the pain. He is strong; I give him that, but I have been working the weights here lately and can easily take his ass. I reach with my other arm and grab his arm, quickly twist it behind his back, and push him on the table. He starts laughing as I twist his arm harder.

"I get it. I get it," Shadow yells, his tone of laughter gone. I pull away and run my hand through my hair, watching Shadow closely in case he tries to retaliate.

"I said nothing happened, so nothing happened," I repeat, my voice serious.

"I think you're protecting Doc, and I understand that. Just don't let it get the club in deep shit in the end, brother," Shadow replies, stretching his arm that I twisted behind his back.

"I had your back when you met Dani, when shit went fucking downhill quick around here. Don't let that VP patch get to your head, brother," I confront.

"What the fuck did you say to me?" Shadow's head wrinkles in anger.

"You heard me. I didn't know half the shit that was going on between you and Dani, yet I took a damn bullet for it. I love Dani like a sister and would do it all over again, don't get me wrong. But standing there telling me what is going to happen after everything I've done for you, ain't flying," I shake my head, my jaw clenched. Shadow's face softens as he nods.

"You're right. I just don't want anyone to get hurt or worse," he admits.

"They won't," I respond.

Shadow walks over to me and slaps my back.

"I got your back, brother."

I nod and head toward the door, declaring this conversation over.

Rain falls, slapping me in the face as we ride toward the Howlerz. Lip rides past me, coming in behind Shadow and Bull. He better chill out, or he is going to get more than a graze from a bullet. He is out for blood, angry he ran like a bitch from Augustus, but I don't blame him. He was out numbered and didn't stand a chance. He was smart running.

We pull up to a little storefront that has the Howlerz logo printed on the glass in brown and white. That is how you know they haven't been around long. No club with a record would throw their club colors on the front of a building. Not only does it attract law enforcement, but enemies as well.

I back my bike into a parking spot and cut the motor. Thunder erupts in the sky as the rain comes down harder. Bull gets off his bike, puts his helmet on the handlebars, and walks to the front door, opening it and walking in uninvited.

I follow in and shake my head back and forth, throwing off the rain droplets clinging to my hair.

"Well, well, well," Bull chants, eyeing the shitty-looking club. I've seen crack houses in better shape than this place.

There's a torn-up leather couch sitting in the center of the club, a stripper pole in the corner with a cougar dancing around it, and what I think is supposed to be a bar on the opposite side of the room. It's small and made of brown tile, with hand built shelves holding cheap whiskey.

"What are you doing here?" one of the men asks, pulling himself off the ripped-up couch. He strides forward, his patch reading Leo as he glares at Bull.

"Where's Bain?" Bull asks, resting his hand on his gun in his holster. Warning the fucker that if he tries anything, he will not hesitate to shoot him. Bain is the president of this poor establishment, and the one who has to explain his actions of crossing us.

"I don't know," Leo snaps, tilting his chin upward defensively.

"Maybe the Howlerz should trade your worthless ass in for a hot maid. This place is a dump," I insult, kicking a loose floorboard with my boot.

"You insulting our colors, man?" Leo grits, pointing his dirty finger in my direction. The worst thing a brother could do is insult another club's patch, or colors. Did I just do that? Kind of.

"All right now, just find us Bain so we can be on our way," Bull intervenes, pushing Leo in the chest, causing him to back up.

"What can I do for you, Bull?" I look around Leo and see Bain. He is about a foot shorter than me, with dark hair and one streak of gray sweeping right through the front. But he is buff as shit, and from what I hear, he practices that karate shit.

"I heard you're doing business with someone else under the table. Is that true?" Bull asks, tilting his head to the side. A cute little blonde girl walks up behind Bain, tying the front of her blouse into a knot. She looks up, brushing her hair from her face and winks seductively at me. I smile and wink back.

"It wasn't anything personal, Bull. He was just cheaper," Bain explains, snapping his fingers at some young guy sitting behind the shitty bar. The guy bends down and brings out a dusty beer bottle, opening it with his teeth, and handing it to Bain.

"I thought we had an understanding. You buy from us, cut us in on profit, and you can stay in my territory," Bull reminds him as he plucks a cigarette from his pack.

"I don't remember signing anything," Bain smarts arrogantly. Laughing as if the joke is on us, causing the rest of his men to laugh along with him. I start to laugh along, Bull and Shadow as well. I stop laughing and reach down, grabbing my pistol from its holster, aiming it right at Bain, Shadow and Bull doing the same.

The Howlerz stop laughing immediately, their faces pale.

"What's wrong? Something not funny?" Bull asks, tilting his head to the side condescendingly, making me laugh.

The blonde woman licks her lips, eyeing me as I aim a weapon at the man she just came out of the back room with.

"Look, man, let's just sit down and get some shit in writing. That's all," Bain remarks, giving a half laugh. A fire rings out, making the blonde jump and scream. The cougar dry humping the pole runs off into one of the doors behind her wailing.

Leo looks down at his leg, blood seeping through his jeans.

"I like to sign in blood," Shadow clips, aiming his weapon back at Bain.

"You fucking shot me!" Leo shrieks, eyeing his leg like it might fall off.

I aim my gun at another of the men sitting at the bar.

"Should we negotiate terms? Sign some more? 'Cause I have plenty of bullets," I laugh.

"No, that's enough. We won't go anywhere else. You made your point," Bain yells, placing his arms up in the air. He is clearly outnumbered; he's smart to give in so easily.

"Good," Bull remarks, placing his gun in his holster.

"If only signing the paperwork to a new bike were this easy," I laugh, placing my gun in my holster.

"Don't make me come back here," Bull threatens the Howlerz.

We turn to leave, Shadow eyeing Bain as we exit just to make sure nobody tries to be stupid.

◆ ◆ ◆

Back at the club, we park our bikes and head towards the club house.

"That chick was totally giving you fuck-me eyes," Lip states, walking next to me.

"Yeah, she was," Tom Cat laughs, striding up beside me, limping from the road rash on his leg.

"How's the leg?" I question, ignoring their observation about the woman flirting with me.

"Eh, it's pretty nasty looking." Tom looks down at his leg and shrugs.

"I'm surprised you didn't try and take her home. What's up with you?" Lip questions, flicking his tongue ring with his tongue, his brows furrowed down in confusion. He's right. I would have grabbed that blonde and took her with me any other day. Just to piss Bain off.

"Got my mind in other places," I reply, shrugging.

It's not a lie. Jessica agreeing to go on this date with me has me fucking nervous as hell.

"Like what?" Lip questions.

"I'm taking Jessica out tonight," I inform shortly.

"Nuh uh." Lip stops, looking at me like I'm crazy. His eyes squinting and mouth parted as he stares me down, looking for any sign of joking.

I stop and smirk like a schoolboy who's taking the hot chick to prom, and his buddies just figured it out.

"You are?" Lip laughs, patting me on the back.

"This whole time I thought you were just fucking crazy when telling stories about being with Doc. You were actually telling the truth," he continues, shaking his head as he rambles.

I scowl at his confession and open the club doors, ending the conversation; otherwise, I might kick his ass for calling me crazy.

My mouth drops open and my eyes widen. The whiskey along the bar is along the floor shattered. The couch is over turned, along with stools and chairs, and the TV above the bar is busted in.

"Shit," Bull whispers, eyeing the mayhem. Shadow grasps my shoulder and leans in.

"Could this be blowback from what you're keeping from the club?" Shadow questions. I look around the room; the damage is minimal. Surely, Augustus's men didn't do this for a warning of war; it's not their style.

"I don't know, man," I reply, running my hand through my hair anxiously.

12
Bobby

I SLIDE MY HAND OVER MY CHEEKS, WONDERING IF I SHOULD shave before picking up Jessica. The scruff has grown just a bit past stubble.

"Nah," I whisper, dropping my hands to my side.

My hands are sweating and my heart is palpating. I'm nervous and think I may throw the fuck up. I comb my hair back with a brush and look in the mirror. "Fuck that," I whisper, running my hands back and forth messing it up. I look like a tool with combed hair. "Screw it," I mutter, turning away from the mirror. Feeling warm, I roll my sleeves up to my elbows. I decided to dress up, wearing a black button-up shirt, and blue jeans that don't have holes in them. This is my idea of dressing nicely. I close my eyes, trying to steady my nerves as I adjust the last cuff on my sleeve. Jessica has come a long way, emotionally and mentally. A darkness that once consumed her, now unveiling its hold and letting that light of hers escape vibrantly. I think this whole ordeal has changed both of us. The connection that I once felt is deeper. When I'm with her, my chest literally fucking constricts to the point of painful from the rush I get, but the feeling is intoxicating. I'm alive. When we're separated, I don't feel anything but dysfunctional.

I shake my head at the thought. It explains a lot. All the girls I've slept with over the years, they were all there trying to fill a void that Jessica planted in my soul. There are a million reasons why I should have let Jessica walk out of my life, a million rejections when I should have taken the hint, but I just didn't care. I stayed and kept pushing because of how I felt when we were together.

I walk toward the main room, contemplating grabbing a beer to calm my thoughts when I spot Cherry and Dani sitting on a couple of stools at the bar. Dani's sipping on a beer and Cherry's sliding her hand on a leather cut laying on the bar top. The place is cleaned up; the ol' ladies doing most of the cleaning, while me and the guys argued about who was going to replace the TV. We all pitched in, in the end.

"Holy shit, you look stunning, Bobby," Cherry chimes, eye-fucking me from top to bottom. I stop and look myself up and down.

"I clean up okay, I guess." I grab the beer from Dani, taking a large sip.

"You're nervous," Dani observes, smiling.

"What? No, I'm not. It's just like any other date," I remark, taking a bigger gulp.

"Uh huh. You might want to wipe that fountain of sweat off your forehead before you see her then," Dani laughs, pointing at my face. I groan and wipe my forehead with the back of my hand.

Dani stands, a look of concern etching across her wrinkled forehead.

"You going to be all right?" she mutters, pulling me to the side of the bar away from Cherry.

"I'm a fucking wreck," I admit.

"Bobby Whitfield, nervous about a female. That has to be a first. If only Shadow were here," Dani smarts. I smirk and run my hands through my hair.

I love Jessica. Admitting that to myself has a rush of adrenaline spike through my chest. A string of excitement and fear mixing to form one coherent thought; I'm over my fucking head.

"Jessica is different. She has always been different," I admit.

"I know that. I am just glad you are finally admitting it." Dani places her hands on her hips, her eyes narrowed. Man, how the tables have turned. It used to be me giving Dani a hard time about her and Shadow; now she's riding my back about Jessica.

"What's that?" I ask, gesturing toward the cut on the counter, changing the subject. It looks new, and as far as I know, the boys and I haven't discussed patching any new brothers in, so it must be out for another reason.

Cherry turns, her face serious as she runs her hands over the leather cut.

"A birdy told me you were going on a date with Doc," Cherry informs, picking the cut up.

"Would this birdy be a little shit with a lip ring?" I laugh, referring to her ol' man Lip. She laughs and holds the cut up, the back of it reading Property of Bobby, with the club's colors under it.

"What the fuck is that?" I ask, my tone serious as my eyes widen.

"We all know you want Doc to be your ol' lady. We've heard the way you talk about her. Seen the way you look at her," Cherry laughs, but I'm not laughing. In fact, I feel like I can't fucking breathe in this shirt.

"We want to make her family just as much as you do," Dani remarks softly, standing up from her stool.

"I don't think—"

"Don't try and deny it, Bobby," Cherry interrupts me. I puff my cheeks out as I exhale, my sweating escalating with the turn in conversation.

Cherry slams the cut to my chest and stands from the stool.

"It's been how many years, Bobby? How much longer are you going to deny that you don't want to be with her?" Dani questions, her tone sincere. I look at her and see her caring green eyes pleading for me to break my walls. I run my hand through my hair and exhale slowly. There has always been something about Jessica, always something about her.

"I never said I didn't want Jessica. Ever. She had her way of doing things, and I had my own. It just seemed right not to throw things into complicated before," I respond, folding the cut in my hands.

"You seem to be talking past tense there," Dani observes. I suck my bottom lip in and nod.

"Yeah. Well, things have changed," I mutter.

"It's time to make her a part of the family permanently," Cherry continues, smiling.

I am not going to lie, the thought of seeing this on Jessica has my dick twitching with excitement. I can see her wearing this, and only this in my bed.

I sigh loudly and sling the cut over my shoulder. I grab my keys to my new blue Chevy and head toward the garage, leaving the girls to resume their evil plotting of my love life.

"Good luck!" Dani yells.

I stuff the cut under the truck seat, afraid if Jessica sees it, she will run for the hills. I start the engine, the truck shifting from side to side with every press of the accelerator. I slowly pull out of the garage and head toward the highway. Being on my bike so often, it feels weird riding in an enclosed vehicle.

I leave the radio off as I head to Jessica's, mulling over the boundaries I've crossed in the last week or so.

"Fuck," I mutter, knowing this could be bad. Tonight could either go really well, or destroy Jessica and me.

Parking outside Jessica's house, I climb out of my truck. Reaching for the security gate, it opens, the lock still broken. I angrily slam the gate shut and walk inside the building in search of the landlord. Assuming he is the first apartment right when you walk in, I slam my fists on the door repeatedly.

The door swings open and the pudgy excuse for a man walks out. A remote in his hand, and he's wearing a stained white shirt that's too short to cover his gut. His eyes widen and his mouth gapes open when he sees me.

"The gate, it's still broken, why?" I question, my hand pointing toward the gate.

"I called about it and they said they would get out here as soon as they could, man," Dudley explains, his voice shaky.

"Get it fixed, and quick," I threaten.

I walk up to Jessica's apartment and knock on the door, my temples throbbing from the rush of blood racing to my head from nervousness. The door opens slowly and my breath catches. She is wearing a white dress that falls just before her knees. The fabric resting against her tan thighs. Following her long legs down to her high heels, I have to adjust my dick and look up. Her blonde hair is down and curled at the ends and her face is glowing. Her pink lips lift into a smile, revealing two drop-dead sexy dimples.

"Fuck, you're beautiful," I whisper, making her laugh. My heart slamming against my chest as I check her out.

"Subtlety never was your strong point," she remarks, her cheeks turning a dark shade of red.

"Subtle? I'm thinking of saying screw the date and taking you back into that apartment and fucking you in that dress you look so hot," I reply, closing my gaping mouth shut, and smiling wolfishly.

She laughs and walks out, shutting the door and locking it.

"Where is Addie?" I question.

"Staying at Bree's for the night," she answers, pointing to the door across from us.

"So I get you for the whole night?" I ask, lifting my eyebrows up and down suggestively.

"Like you need the whole night," she mocks, walking down the hall.

"Touché," I remark.

My eyes instantly find her tight ass. My hands involuntarily clench in on themselves, wanting to squeeze it.

"Where are you taking me?" Her comment makes my eyes snap up from her ass to her face.

"What?" I ask, confused.

"Hey, eyes up here, buddy." She motions her fingers toward her face.

"I ain't making any promises," I reply honestly, making her shake her head.

I walk her out to my truck and she stops suddenly, her eyes scanning over the blue Chevy.

"This yours?" she asks surprised, her hand gliding along the hood.

"Yup, just got it," I inform.

"Well, I was wondering how I was going to ride on the back of your bike in this," she adds, biting her bottom lip.

I laugh and open the door so she can climb in.

She steps inside of the cab, her dress riding up right under her ass cheeks as she climbs in. Not able to take it anymore, I reach over and squeeze her ass before she sits on the seat. She turns her head and glares at me, making me laugh mischievously.

I shut her door and jog around the other side of the truck to get in.

"Wow, this is really nice," Jessica admires, running her hand along the dashboard in appreciation.

"Thanks," I respond, turning the key. I push my foot onto the accelerator, causing the motor to roar. I look over at Jessica and lift my eyebrows with every push of the gas pedal, making her laugh.

"Boys and their toys," Jessica chuckles, shaking her head.

I slam the truck into gear, and floor it, making the tires screech against the asphalt. Jessica grabs onto my arm and the door, and giggles hysterically.

The night is warm and noisy with nature calling as we drive toward the ocean with the windows down. Looking over and seeing Jessica watch the night fly by her with her hair blowing in the wind, I can't help but grin. She is so incredibly beautiful. Every time we are together, I'm more convinced we should be together. I pull up to the graveled parking lot, only a couple of old fishing trucks parked. Looking out past the few vehicles, there's a bunch of docks holding boats.

I hurry out of the truck and head toward Jessica's side, helping her out. The salty smell of the ocean is strong and the hostile waves crashing against docks are loud. I look up at the sky, hoping the storm will hold off long enough for us to enjoy the night.

"You brought me to the beach?" she questions, looking out toward the ocean.

"No," I reply, grabbing her hand and guiding us toward the smell of salt, and the waves of the ocean.

We wander down cemented steps and onto a wooden dock. We pass a couple of small fishing boats, and other watercrafts. I turn to the right, pulling us toward another dock with bigger and faster looking boats.

"Umm, Bobby?" Jessica mutters as we pass boat after boat.

"This one," I whisper, pulling us down the dock toward a red and white speedboat. I step onto the boat, and reach for Jessica's hand, helping her step over from the dock.

"You, um, know how to drive this thing?" she asks nervously, eyeing the boat.

"Yeah, I know how to drive this thing," I laugh. "My father taught me how to drive a boat. Once you learn, you never forget it."

"Is this your boat?" Jessica asks, walking further onto the boat.

"Kinda, I'm renting it," I answer, stepping around her. The boat is big from standing on the dock, shadowing over the dock and other boats nearby, but once you are on it, it's actually kind of fucking small. The back of it holds an inboard motor, taking up most of the boat. Past the motor, there is a row of red and white leather seats along the back, while in front of that is the captain's chair with a passenger chair next to it. I walk up to the bow, admiring the triangle of red and white cushions completing the shape.

"It'll do," I whisper, stepping back.

Jessica saunters up to the triangle of cushions, looking over the rim of the boat before plopping down belly first on the pillows, kicking off her high heels. I chuckle, untying the boat from the dock. She looks at ease and seems to be enjoying herself. I was afraid she would defy me the entire date, making this a nightmare. I position myself in the captain's chair and search for the keys.

Finding them located in a cubby under the steering wheel, I start the ignition. The boat vibrates as the motor rumbles through the night air.

"Hold on," I warn, pulling the boat away from the dock. Once we are off and on our way, I push the throttle forward, letting the boat rip through the tide. Jessica squeals as we fly through the night, the sound of her laughter is one I haven't heard before. Sure, she's laughed, but to see her like this, hear the depths of her laughter...it's new and I can't help the cocky smile displayed on my face that I brought it out of her. I drive until we are far enough out that nobody can see or hear us, and turn the motor off.

"Oh my," Jessica gasps. I crawl out from behind the wheel and stagger toward her. The waves the boat caused splash along the side of the watercraft, jolting it back and forth making it hard to walk as we sway harshly.

"The stars are so bright out here," Jessica murmurs, looking up at the night's sky. I crawl up next to her and flip over, looking up at the stars.

"Wow," I mutter.

"I bet you get laid every time you take a woman out here," Jessica laughs, her eyes wide as she stares upward. My brows furrow, and I swallow the sudden lump in my throat rising from her statement.

Jessica turns from looking at the stars and sits up on her elbows.

"What's wrong?" she asks softly.

I sit up and climb off the cushions, the conversation heading somewhere I wasn't expecting. I run my hands through my hair, and find the stereo. I flip the plastic cover protecting the stereo and turn it on. "Painted On My Heart" by Cult is playing. I haven't heard this song in forever. I turn the volume up, and flip the cover back down.

"What did I say?" Jessica continues.

"Nothing," I lie, wanting her to drop it.

I blow out a steady breath and return to the cushions, laying on my back and facing the stars. Stars I saw many times as a kid, I just forgot how vibrant they looked over the years. Jessica rolls on her side, her dress shifting up to her hips, revealing a dainty blue triangle between her thighs. I reach down, and slide my finger along the top of the elastic of her panties. Jessica looks down, her eyes becoming heavy with lust as I sweep my finger down further grazing her clit. She lifts her thigh, inviting me in.

I roll over on top of her, spread her legs with my knee and dip my hand down, gliding my finger in-between her wetness. I press my lips to hers, kissing her cherry-glossed lips and don't hold back. She parts my mouth with her tongue, flicking her tongue against mine. I grab both sides of her face, my thumb circling the apples of her cheeks as I look at her, her blonde hair splayed around her like a halo, the flushing of her cheeks sexy. She reaches forward and unbuttons my shirt, one button at a time, her eyes at half-mast staring at me intently the whole time. I slip my hand between her back and the cushion finding the zipper to her dress. I pull it down, the snug fit of the dress loosening along her frame. I trail my finger along the dress's straps clinging to her shoulders and glide them down her arms slowly, my lips kissing behind the trailing fabric.

Her firm breasts sitting in blue cups greet me; enticing me. I dart my tongue between the valley of her chest, before giving the side of her tit a bite. She arches her back and moans loudly, her fingers tangling in my hair. Once on my knees, I pull my shirt off as Jessica sits up and runs her hands over my abs, her lips brushing against my belly button. She unbuckles my belt and pulls my pants down my hips. I kick them off along with my boots as she fingers the waist of my boxers and slowly yanks them down, my dick springing free.

I run my hand through her hair as she looks up from under her lashes.

She grasps my cock. I hiss with surprise at her demanding this control. She leans forward and flicks my dick with the tip of her tongue, triggering my legs to tremble from anticipation, my dick sprouting a bead of semen. Licking the dew from my dick, her actions seem to be in slow motion. The moon lights up her skin and her blue eyes look up at me desperately. It's an image I program in my mind forever; she looks innocent, yet completely erotic.

Snapping me from my daze, she encloses her mouth around the head of my cock causing my world as I know it to explode. Bliss, it feels like pure undeniable bliss. The sensation of her warm mouth sucking my cock is remarkable. I dreamed of the day she would suck my dick, longed for the day she licked cum from the head of my cock. She bobs her head all the way down my shaft; I don't hold back my groan as my head falls back looking up at the stars.

As much as I want to blow my load in her sweet mouth, have the taste of me on her tongue, I want her body. I close my eyes and pull out of her mouth.

"Jesus, that was," I huff, looking for the words to explain the feeling. She smiles, and lies back on the cushions, satisfied with herself. She knows I have been wanting that forever. "Oh, no, you don't. Get back over here," I pant, grabbing her by the hips, pulling her back to me. I flip her over on her stomach, and rip her panties to shreds. My lips curve into a smirk as my dick pulses with the urge to come. I notice she has two little dimples right above her ass and they are fucking cute as hell.

Gliding my hand between her legs, I skim them along the opening to her pussy, finding her wet and ready for my cock. She lifts her ass into the air and mewls from my soft touch.

I rub the wetness glistening on my fingers on the head of my dick and guide myself between her legs. Finding her pussy instantly, I thrust deeply, my balls squeezing from the sensation of having her wrapped around me.

Her head flings back, causing her hair to spread across her shoulders, a curtain of blonde. I caress my hand up and down her spine as I slowly drive in and out of her. Her pussy pulses around my cock and her knees tremble against the cushions as she takes my length.

I lean down and grasp her by the shoulders, pulling her off her hands and up against my chest. I wrap one of my arms around her tits, the nipples pressed tightly against my forearm, and slide my other arm along her abdomen as I piston my hips.

Her moans vibrate through her chest against my arm, making my dick tighten. She turns her head slightly, looking at me, her breath in short spurts as I continue thrusting. Reaching up, Jessica wraps her arm behind my neck, never taking her eyes off me. The look she gives me, the way it penetrates my soul, it's like I am the only person she sees, that nothing makes sense but the two of us wrapped around each other.

My hands glide along her curves, taking in every scar,

every freckle, and perfection of her body. "You're so fucking beautiful," I whisper into her ear. She leans her head on my shoulder, and moans as I continue to drive my cock into her.

I bend slightly and kiss her lips. It dawns on me while we kiss that I am not fucking Jessica, not having sex with her, but making love.

Wetness coats my cock as she constricts along my shaft.

"Bobby," she whispers, warning me she's close. Hearing my name on her lips causes my dick to squeeze, and my balls to obliterate with warmth.

"Bobby!" Jessica yells into the air, her body climaxing. Her nails dig into my neck and her legs widen more as she releases, allowing my dick to hit the back of her. We fall over onto the cushions, my body lying on top of hers as I pump my hips back and forth slowly.

I groan loudly into the side of her neck, the pressure spreading up my shaft and triggering me to come inside of her. After we both still, the high of sensation faltering, I fall next to her, both of us panting, taking any oxygen into our lungs that we can get.

"Looks like I am sucker for a boat and stars too," she laughs, still panting. I roll off her and look up at the sky.

"I haven't brought anyone out here," I admit, making her laugh fade. "My dad used to take me out all the time. When I was younger, we would fish at night. He told me one time that he got my mother to finally agree to be more than friends by taking her out on his boat." I pause, remembering how he was always preaching to me about how to love a woman. He had such high expectations; I never felt like I would be able to deliver what a woman deserved. "My dad told me to take a woman out at night on a boat, but not just any woman. One that meant something to me." I turn to look at her, her face lax and her blue eyes focused on me, not giving anything away.

I turn my head and look back up at the sky.

"Your dad sounds like he was a good man," Jessica murmurs, ignoring the fact that I chose to take her out on a boat.

"Yeah, something like that," I laugh half-heartedly. My father was actually kind of a brute behind my mother's back, but a gentleman in front of her. I learned everything I know about women from my dad. He was a ladies' man back in his day before he met my mom.

"Was he in the Devil's Dust?" Jessica questions, rolling on her back to look up at the stars. My eyes trail along her naked frame, the moonlight glistening off the sweat beaded between her tits.

"No, he was a firefighter," I tell her.

"What about your mother?" Jessica continues to ask.

"My mother was the type of woman to always help the community, churches, schools, you name it. She was a saint," I reply, thinking about my mother and how much of a kind woman she was. "My parents were great. I got into trouble growing up based purely on liking trouble. I don't have some crazy reason or fucked-up past to justify why I am the way I am, or why I like to cause havoc at times. I just enjoyed it mostly, well, I enjoy it still," I laugh, making Jessica giggles.

"Whenever I got thrown in jail or juvie as a kid, my dad would pick me up and take me home when I was allowed out. When I walked in the door, my mom would smack me in the back of the head and give me a plate of warm food. They never paid my bail or pleaded for early release; they made me do the time for my crime, but they never judged me. They were just there for me as I paid the price for liking trouble," I inform, smiling from the memories.

"They sound great, Bobby. I'm sorry you lost them," Jessica

whispers.

"Yeah, me too," I mumble. Thunder sounds from clouds further at sea, moving toward us. The wind picking up as it heads in our direction.

"What about your parents?" I ask. Jessica sighs, pulling her hair out from her neck.

"My dad is the kind of guy who knows everything and everyone; has connections everywhere. His main goal in life is to be successful, and will do nothing less than exceed what is expected of him," she informs, her lips pursed.

"He sounds like a tool," I reply honestly.

"He is," she laughs.

"Your mom?" I question, wondering if she is the bitch to go with the tool.

"She is actually pretty cool when she wants to be. She's the only one I talk to anymore," she whispers, frowning. I knew she only talked to her mom, but she's never said why she doesn't speak to her dad.

"Why is that?"

Jessica inhales a deep breath, and shakes her head. "For one, I am not a brain surgeon like my father wanted me to be, and I am not married to some bigwig who's living life in the limelight so he can be praised for his outstanding parental guidance," she explains. "I am not what he wants in a daughter, and to be honest, he is not what I want in a father," she continues, shrugging.

"He knew I was living in hell with Travis, but he looked the other away. All he wanted was to be on the board of Travis's family's hospital," Jessica mutters, making my head whip in her direction.

"You want me to beat his ass?" I ask seriously. Jessica's frown turns into a fit of laughter, relaxing my frown and joining in.

"I think I'm good," she whispers, gazing up at the clouded sky that suddenly strikes with lightning.

"We better get this back to the dock," I suggest, grabbing my shirt from behind her head. I pull my button-up shirt on but leave it unbuttoned. Grabbing my jeans and boxers, I pull them on as Jessica dresses. I lean over and kiss her forehead as I head to the steering wheel.

Driving back to the dock, I watch Jessica. She's sitting up at the front, watching the waves, her hair blowing in the wind.

I park the boat and place the key back where I found it. Climbing off and securing it to a dock post, I reach for Jessica's hand, helping her off.

"That was amazing, Bobby. I can't believe you rented a boat," Jessica remarks, admiring the craft swaying back and forth in the waves.

"Get the fuck away from my boat before I call the cops!"

Jessica and I both look toward the shore, finding an older man raising a fist and running on the dock toward us pissed.

"Um, Bobby," Jessica starts, turning to eye me warily.

"Okay, so maybe I didn't rent the boat. Run!" I yell, pressing on the small of her back. Jessica grabs her shoes and runs laughing. With the older guy gaining on us, I grab Jessica by the waist and throw her over my shoulder, running with her slung over my shoulder. We run all the way up the wooden dock and onto the beach laughing the whole time. Out of breath, I stop, and lower Jessica who is red in the face from giggling so hard.

"Oh, my God, that was so much fun," Jessica pants, eyeing the dock to see if the old man is coming.

My hands on her hips, I pull her ass toward the front of me. Watching the horizon ignite with lightning, I place my chin on her head, still chuckling at getting caught for joyriding. Any other girl would have been pissed I stole a boat, but Jessica loved it, and loved getting caught.

"I love you," I whisper into her head. I feel Jessica stiffen under my hold, and turn slowly, causing me to release her. My heart beats violently against my ribcage, realizing what I just said.

"I mean, I—"

"No, you said you love me," Jessica reaffirms, her eyes widening with surprise.

I inhale and swallow the lump in my throat. Why deny it?

"I did say it. I do love you," I whisper, looking down at the sand beneath her bare feet.

"You said you wouldn't. You promised," Jessica murmurs, her voice cracking with emotion and edged with anger.

"I've loved you since the day you and Addie walked into my life, Jessica. I just didn't realize it 'til recently. I wouldn't allow myself to believe that I fell in love before now. I know there are a dozen reasons why we shouldn't be together, but I don't fucking care," I tell her, my tone gaining hostility at the thought of her pushing me away. Again.

"NO!" Jessica yells, pushing at my chest angry. I turn my head and take a breath at her reaction. "I will not be trapped in another relationship. I won't be with another dangerous man!" Jessica screams loudly.

I snap my head toward her and clench my jaw. "You killed a man, Jessica. You are just as dangerous as I am!" I yell angrily, making her even angrier. "And you love me," I mutter, my eyes furrowed inward as I stare her down.

"No I—" she pauses and inhales quickly. "No, I don't," she whispers, her voice wavering.

"Yes, you do," I press, my tone serious.

Jessica shakes her head, tears running down her face. "It

doesn't matter if I do or not. We can't be together because of the club's fucking rules, Bobby," Jessica protests.

"Bullshit," I mumble, rubbing my hands together and looking out at the ocean's waves turning hostile from the storm.

"What?" she turns back to me with vicious eyes.

"Bullshit, Jessica," I repeat. "When are you going to stop with the shit excuses and admit you're just afraid of being hurt, of having your heart broken?" I yell, my voice echoing through the night. Jessica sucks in a sudden breath, her nostrils flaring at my confrontation. "Admit it!" I roar, pointing at her.

"I am! I am afraid of loving you, Bobby. You're a player, a manipulator who likes to live life on the edge. How long after being with me are you going to get bored and walk out on me and Addie?" Jessica sobs, tears running down her face, one hand tangled in her hair in dismay.

"I wouldn't do that. I'm not Travis!" Jessica winces when she hears her ex-husband's name leave my mouth. Jessica gives a half laugh, breaking the sudden shock written on her face.

"You said so yourself, Bobby, you can't commit. Look at us. We can't even go on a date without fighting," she continues, wiping the tears from her face. I turn, running my hand on the back of my neck irritated.

I did say that. We've both said a lot of things along the years, defending why we shouldn't be together. But they were just excuses, lies. In reality, I'm just as afraid of being hurt as she is; scared I can't deliver what she needs from me. I thought maybe Jessica was breaking through the fear that caged her, but it looks like she isn't any more free than she was when I met her. Travis will always be a part of her, terrorizing her, keeping her from opening up to me fully.

"Yeah, we fight, everyone fights. I tell you when you're

being a bitch, and you tell me when I'm being a dick," I mutter. Jessica's eyes widen before squinting back to anger.

Lightning strikes just above us as the clouds sprinkle cold rain.

"Take me home, Bobby," Jessica demands, turning and walking up the cement steps, back to the truck. The anger racing through me makes my face flush with heat, my jaw clenched to the point it aches.

"What the fuck ever. You're crazy, you know that?" I growl, having enough of the denial that racks through every word leaving Jessica's mouth.

She turns back and glares at me. Her lips parted in disbelief as she stomps back down the steps.

"Fuck you, Bobby!" she yells, pushing me in the chest with the hand carrying one of her heels.

"Move," I snap, pushing her hand away and stalking past her.

Still standing on the last step, I hear her gasp as I make my way up. I have never talked to Jessica like this, never treated her anything less than what she deserved. 'Til now. I'm fucking pissed and my chest burns with hurt. I laid it all out there and told her how I feel, hell, how I've felt since day one thinking she might finally see that what we have can triumph fear. Our love is an unclear path, but it's filled with possibilities. As the fear in our relationship lies on a previously traveled path, it imprints its painful memories to heart.

13

Jessica

TENSION CLOUDS THE RIDE BACK TO MY APARTMENT. I AM AS FAR on my side of the truck as I can get, leaving a wide amount of space between us as I look out the window. I had one rule. One. *Don't fall in love.* I've made sure not to allow myself to fall in love with Bobby since the day I met him. I've kept boundaries and rules, but I got stupid and played with fire.

The truck stops and Bobby shuts the engine off. He looks over at me and sighs heavily. "Jessica," Bobby mutters, his voice exasperated.

I open the door, and get out, slamming it shut behind me. The rain plasters my face as I make my way to the security gate. The raindrops mixing with my tears create a cocktail of misery. The tires of Bobby's truck squeal when they bite the asphalt for traction as he speeds off. My heart sinks and guilt riddles up my spine with all that has transpired. What did I do? Why did I deny it? Why am I so scared?

I don't even bother to try and enter my code in the security gate; I know it's not fixed and will open without it. Once inside, I head to my apartment. I stop in front of Bree's door and hear music and laughter. I'll let Addie stay over there for the night; I need some time to myself. As I pull my key out of my purse and stick it into the handle, the door pushes open without me even unlocking it. I cock my head to the side and eye it. I notice black scuffmarks along the door jamb and my heart leaps into my throat. I lightly push the door open. My apartment is trashed. The couch is overturned and the kitchen cabinets are all open with boxed food thrown all over the floor. I take a step in to get a better look at the disaster. The lamp is on the floor, the bulb flickering, emanating an eerie glow

Chest burning from the violent beat of my heart, it thrusts against my ribcage as I eye the devastation that is my apartment. This can't be good. This is *not* good. I turn to leave, but the door is pushed closed stopping me where I stand. As the door shuts, a shadow moves from the wall. I take a step back, trying to identify the figure who was hiding behind my door.

"I wondered when you would show back up." An arctic chill travels up my back at his voice. I can't place it, but it brings fear to the surface.

The shadow steps away from the wall and into the flickering light. My vision wavers, everything around the person blurs from fear. All I hear is the rush of blood swimming in my head and my heartbeat drumming in my ears.

"Grant?" I whisper, utterly terrified of the man standing before me, my voice echoing in my head as my upper lip sheets with a coat of sweat. Struck in the grip of fear, my body stiffens and my eyes widen. Lungs blazing with the urgency to resume breathing, I take a painful breath.

It's Grant, Travis's brother. To the untrained eye, it would be easy to confuse Grant with Travis; they look almost identical. But Grant is not nearly as distinguished. Grant's features slack where Travis's were sharp and squared off. Grant's blond hair is combed back, a stray in the front curled down onto his forehead. Bloodshot eyes sunk in with dark circles stare back at me. His frame is thin, but the muscles on his arms speak of his strength. He squints his eyes, his eyebrows slicing inward maliciously.

"Hello, Jessica," he hisses, his tone sharp and his voice slicing up my back with alarm.

I stumble over a picture frame on the floor and fall against the kitchen island. "What are you doing here?" I ask nervously.

"Oh, you know, the usual. I was in the neighborhood, wanted to stop by and see my sister-in-law who killed my brother, and is now taking all his money," he remarks condescendingly. The hairs on my neck stand as I regain my footing and stand straight. Grant was always quiet and distant when I saw him while I was with Travis, leaving him unpredictable.

"I don't know what you're talking about," I say, my voice growing in strength.

He stomps forward, making my body shrink onto a stool sitting in front of the island. He reminds me so much of Travis; all I can do in response is tremble with fear.

Gnashing his teeth, eyes angry and defined, he scowls at me in pure hatred. He grabs me by the throat and pulls me off the stool, my heels falling from my feet as he lifts me from the floor.

"You know exactly what I am talking about. My father told me Travis's death was finalized, and that his will goes to you and that kid," he grits, his fingers digging into my skin painfully, but not enough to limit my breathing. I close my eyes. Grant looking like his brother is bringing back memories.

"You will do as I say if you want to breathe another day, Jessica." Travis's voice echoes in my head. Even though it's Grant's fingers around my neck, all I feel, all I hear is Travis.

"Do you know the life I have lived because of you?" he asks, disgust evident in his voice. The roughness of his tone breaks me from my familiar stirring, making me open my eyes. "My parents resigned their positions from the board of the hospital and have spent every dime they have on finding Travis. Leaving me on the streets," he says, eerily calm.

I know he was not one to follow the family's footsteps in medicine, but why would he live on the streets? It makes no sense that his parents would do that to him. I try to shift my body hoping to touch the floor with my feet to relieve the pressure he has around my throat. I'm able to pull slightly, allowing the tips of my toes to hold some of my weight, letting a rush of fresh air sweep into my lungs.

"Where's the money?" Grant asks, his voice eerily calm despite his hand clamped around my throat.

"What money?" I choke out, scratching at his arms to let me go, my toes aching from all the weight they're holding. My eyes find Grant's that are dilated, and more bloodshot than I thought. I look at his arm and notice track marks. Little beady, black ink spots strike up his arm. He's a drug addict. His parents throwing him on the street, they aren't supporting his drug habit, and with him on my doorstep demanding money means one thing. He wants the money from Travis's will.

"What?" Grant growls, frustrated. I open my mouth to try to speak but only scratching noises come out. He lets go of me, allowing me to fall to the floor. I cough, trying to get all the oxygen I can into my lungs.

"I don't have it," I grunt, pulling myself up using the stool.

He turns quickly and backhands me. Staggering back, I somehow remain on my feet, my ears ringing loudly from the contact. I clutch my smarting cheek, heat and pain claiming the delicate flesh as I glare at Grant.

"Look, we can do this the easy way or the hard way." He turns and smiles a Cheshire grin. Holding his arm up, my eyes land on his hand clutching the collar Travis used to put on me; the one in my shoebox in my closet. My eyes widen and my lungs seize to breathe as I see it.

"What's wrong? Bring back old memories?" he taunts, stepping toward me, unbuckling it. "Travis told me the things he would do to you in this, brag about it even," Grant continues, he reaches forward, and slides his fingers along my neck where the collar would imprison me.

"Please, no," I cry, trying to pull away, but he grabs me by the hair violently. I pull my hand back slapping him across the face as hard as I can. Immediate anger flashes in his eyes as my palm burns from the harsh contact. He thrusts his arm forward to grab hold of me, but I quickly side step him, running around the island in search of anything to protect myself.

"Unless you want to bring pain upon yourself, you will get over here and do as I say," Grant speaks slowly, his voice reminding me of Travis. In fact, Travis spoke those exact words to me before. My body wants to obey out of fear, the scars on my back a reminder of what would happen if I wouldn't do as I was told. Fighting the urge, I close my eyes. Bobby instantly appears behind my eyelids, his blue eyes looking at me with longing.

My hair is yanked back, my eyes snapping open. Before I can react, my face is placed against the counter with force. The cool vinyl is fixed around my neck, and I hear it lock into place. My eyes well up with tears as my past rears its ugly head.

Everything I have ever tried to forget is happening all over again. In sheer terror, I hyperventilate, my body shivering and struggling to breathe. Once more, I close my eyes, remembering Bobby holding me along my neck as he brought me to pleasure. I exhale a shaky breath as I replace all the painful memories with moments filled of pleasure, calming myself in the process. The look in Bobby's eyes as he held me. Every sexual encounter I had with him. Every look Bobby ever showcased, now clear as day. Bobby has always loved me and I love him. He was right. I'm just afraid of being hurt; I've been trying to protect myself.

"Don't fear the pain; fear the message behind it," I mutter. Grant growls in frustration as he grabs my hair with both hands bashing my head into the counter once more, this time knocking me into complete darkness.

Bobby

I STOP HALFWAY DOWN THE STREET AND PULL THE CUT OUT from under the seat. I clench my hands into the leather, my teeth gritting with anger. If I leave, Jessica won't call me for weeks, possibly ever. She will do everything in her power to ignore me and purposely distance herself from me. I fucked this up. I should have never said anything. I should have never allowed myself to get to this point. But I did, and what I said to her was true. I throw the cut onto the seat next to me and turn the wheel. I stomp on the pedal and drift into a complete circle, heading back to Jessica's. I can't let her get away, and I can't give up that easy.

Driving into the parking lot, a red minivan flies out, running over the sidewalk, and nearly clipping the bed of my truck.

"What the fuck, man?" I yell out the window of my door. The guy in the van slowly turns his head, his eyes menacing and lip curled as he stares at me behind the driver's side window. He looks familiar, but I can't place where I know him from. Then again, I come across a lot of fuckers who look menacing, being a part of the Devil's Dust and all. I park my truck and run up the stairs to Jessica's apartment. As I get closer to her door, I notice it's open, and there is blood spotting the floor. I slowly push it open and see the apartment's trashed, resembling the club's break in.

"Jessica!" I yell, running into the apartment. I race into Jessica's room, bathroom, and Addie's room, but I don't find her. I close my eyes trying to think, trying to calm my racing thoughts. That guy in the van popping in my mind, the way he was driving that minivan like he stole the fucking thing. The way he looked familiar. He had to have had something to do with this.

I look across the hall, and run toward the apartment door placed adjacent to Jessica's apartment. Jessica told me her babysitter lives right across from her. Maybe she is over there. Maybe the sitter heard something.

I pound on the door rapidly, not faltering until it is swung open.

A black-haired college-aged woman opens the door, her hair in pigtails and thick glasses on her face. "What the hell?" she snaps, eyeing me pissed off.

"Is Jessica in there with you?" I question, looking over her shoulder.

"No, she went on a date," the girl replies, looking at me suspiciously.

"Bobby!" Addie hollers excitedly from the couch.

"Hey Hun. You both stay in here. Lock the door. Don't come out of here, do you understand me?" I yell, pointing at the babysitter. Her eyes widen, fear written on her face. "Do you understand?" I roar, slapping my hand against the doorframe trying to get her attention.

"Yes," she peeps, her eyes filling with tears. I turn and run down the stairs.

I jump in my truck and race in the direction the van went, hoping I can catch up to it.

Jessica

MY FACE BURNS AND STINGS WHERE MY FOREHEAD WAS slammed into the counter. I try to open my eyes, the muscles in my lids resisting. I notice the worn out seat beneath my arms, and the hum of a motor around me. I'm in a vehicle. Sitting up slowly, my head swims with a fog. My eyes land on the blond in the front and it all becomes clear. Grant. The van swerves, throwing me into the side of the window with a loud thump. Grant looks in the rearview mirror, his eyes locking with mine.

"I will shoot you in the head if you try anything," Grant threatens, tapping the steering wheel with the barrel of a gun. I nod in understanding, and sit back in the seat. I can barely breathe with the fear rushing through my chest. The thought of dying today is too much to bear. I don't have what he wants. I never went and met with the lawyer to finish the last of the details.

"I don't have the money, Grant. I haven't signed the papers yet," I tell him, trying to make him understand I don't have anything to give him. My hands tremble with terror, causing me to fidget with them.

"Bullshit," he scoffs, running his hand under his sniffling nose. He looks in the mirror and furrows his brows in anger. His eyes make me wince in my seat. He's fucking crazy. No matter what I say, he won't care. He has Travis's blood in him making him a part of the sadistic gene pool.

"You better get it by tonight then, or I will kill you. I'm not playing games," he yells, clearly agitated.

"Where are you taking me?" I ask, looking out the windows, trying to get an idea if there's a way to escape or scream for someone to hear me.

"When I came here, I watched you. Saw you hanging with that biker guy, so I followed him. Which led to a motorcycle club. That is when I pieced it all together," he replies, ignoring my question. "You killed my brother, you had some gang kill my blood, and you're the reason my parents told me to go to hell, that if I were more like Travis, they wouldn't feel so worthless as parents. You, it's *your* fault!" he screams, shaking the steering wheel in a fit.

I look down at the floor, the gravity of the situation becoming clear. Grant is going to kill me tonight. Even if my luck pays out and he doesn't kill me, if I manage to pay him and he lets me live, he thinks I had Travis killed. He'll run back to his parents playing the good son, telling them what happened. The authorities will take the club down and I'll never see Bobby again. I close my eyes tightly, Bobby's words of how I was just scared to love seeping through my mind. How I use excuse after excuse of why I couldn't be with him. He was right. I'm just scared of loving him, scared he will get tired of me, just like Travis did. But he's not Travis. He was never Travis.

I blow out a steady breath, contemplating the thought of the authorities taking me to jail, taking Addie from me. I lived cautiously all these years, never doing anything to bring attention to myself, trying to stay away from danger the best I could, and for what? The very past I was running from to come and show me I wasted my life in fear and pain. I have to do something. I can't go out like this. I can't let this happen. Looking up, I watch Grant ranting about how much of a bitch I am. He's distracted. Lifting myself off the seat, I dig my bare feet into the floor for leverage. I mentally prepare myself for what I'm about to do, knowing it could kill me.

On a slow exhale, I push myself forward, flinging myself into Grant's lap. Hands grasping the gritty steering wheel, I jerk it to the side so the van whips to the side violently. Tires screech loudly as we become airborne, the motor sounding with a loud hum as we take flight. Everything slows while in midair. Fast-food bags and plastic bottles toss around as we tilt. Releasing a breath, I blink; time resumes its fast pace. The van slams to the ground. Everything that was in the air, falling down with it.

Violently, I'm jostled to the ceiling and then to the floor over and over as we flip down a hill before finally, my body strikes to a sudden rest. Every part of me aches and my neck throbs from the harsh whiplash. I cough and wheeze trying to pull air into my lungs.

Eyes firmly closed, my face winces from little wet droplets hitting my cheeks. Prizing my eyes open, I discover I'm outside the van. I was thrown out at some point. I slowly roll over, looking for the van. I find it just a couple feet from me. It's hissing and smoking, crinkled like an old soda can slammed up against a large boulder.

A loud creaking noise draws my attention to the opening

door; it's barely hanging on its hinges. Adrenaline races through my heart when Grant falls out of the door, coughing and groaning. I turn and start trying to crawl away. My body is tense and sore from the wreck, making it hard to move.

"Oh, no, you don't," Grant laughs. I whimper in an attempt to move faster.

Forcing my achy body to cooperate, I push onto my knees trying to stand and run, but one of my ankles is pulled back, slamming my chest back on the ground. I turn and find Grant's bloody hand latched onto my leg. His head is bleeding profusely, drenching one side of his face in a thick red ooze. I grab at the grass, trying to pull myself from his grip when I notice a black crowbar feet away, no doubt fallen out of the van. Survival. The word slams into my mind. It's my only choice if I'm to survive. I look back at Grant who is laughing at my weak attempt to escape, the vinyl collar restraining my neck, reminding me I'm still wearing it. I grit my teeth and bite my lip. *I can do this.* I flip over on my back, sending a shockwave of pain shooting through my bruised body, and use my other leg to slam it into Grant's balls. He instantly lets go of my ankle and I surge forward, seizing the cold steel with one of my hands.

"Bitch!" Grant curses angrily. I look behind me just as Grant grabs my arm, flipping me over to look at him. As he pulls me, I swing the crowbar, slamming it against the side of his head. The sound of metal and bone makes a chilling sound. He stills and his eyes roll in the back of his head as he lets go of my arm, falling to the ground. A sob racks from my mouth as I pull away from him, watching his head bleed out from the gash the crowbar inflicted.

Knowing it's either him or me, I regain my focus and try to subdue my sobs as I crawl on my knees over to him. Pulling the crowbar over my head with shaky hands, tears blur my vision. I take a deep breath and slam it down on his head again. His face that resembles Travis's looks back up at me. All the pain he caused me, the way he talked to Addie. The first time he physically hurt Addie all reel in my mind like a horror movie. The pain. Torture. Belittling. All fogging my head in a haze of uncontrollable anger.

I scream loudly as I thrash it down onto his skull again. I lift my tired arms to hit him in the head one more time, but can't muster the strength. I can no longer feel my hands, my limbs in general. Everything is numb. My instinct to survive is the only thing I can feel; it's pounding in my brain so hard I can barely see straight.

"You can't hurt us anymore," I sob quietly, falling onto my hands, panting.

Tires screeching at the top of the hill catch my attention. I freeze wondering if I should run and hide, but know I have no choice but to remain. My body is shutting down.

"Jessica!" Bobby's voice is a balm to the chaos around me. I look toward his voice and watch in relief as he runs down the hill.

"Bobby!" I cry, my body releasing its tension.

He sprints all the way down the hill. His unbuttoned black shirt flapping against him.

Ignoring my frozen limbs, I clamber to a stand and stumble toward him, the crowbar still in my hand.

Bobby smashes into me painfully, wrapping both arms around my frame, and tucking my head into the crook of his neck.

"Bobby, I love you," I cry, holding my bloody hands out to the side, nuzzling my face into him more. Bobby pulls me closer, resting his nose just above my ear.

"You were right. I was just scared. I am scared," I mumble into his shirt.

"I love you, too, Jessica," he whispers.

He pulls away looking me over warily. Glancing down at myself, my white dress is splattered with specks of blood, my hands covered in back splatter from hitting Grant with the crowbar. I look like a psychopath.

"Fuck," Bobby whispers, running his hand along my bicep. I turn and look at what he is staring at. My eyes catching my upper arm with a shard of glass sticking out of it.

"Don't pull it out. It will bleed worse," I warn. I can't even feel it, so I know it's bad.

He reaches down my arm and grasps the crowbar still in my hand, taking it. He rounds me and squats near Grant.

"He's Travis's brother," I quietly say, stepping up beside him.

"That's why he looks familiar. You did a number on him, Jessica," Bobby remarks. He reaches forward, and rolls Grant over, applying his hands to Grant's neck looking for a pulse. "He's definitely dead," Bobby informs, dropping the crowbar to the ground.

"I had to do it. He pieced together I hired the club to kill Travis," I explain, defending my actions. Bobby shrugs, glancing at me.

"I would have killed him for nearly hitting my truck," he adds seriously. "I think you had a pretty good reason to do what you did." Bobby stands up, and walks over to me, tucking his arm behind my head.

"What the fuck is this?" Bobby whispers, his fingers pulling at the collar still wrapped around my neck.

"It was Travis's. Grant put it on me," I mutter, trying to take it off anxiously. I know with Bobby here I'm safe, but the idea of being a prisoner in this collar is suffocating.

Bobby curses under his breath and turns me, his hands sliding over my shoulders to the clasp on the back of the collar. It makes a loud noise as he unbuckles it, the clicking noise resembling a locking mechanism on a cage. Goosebumps rise all over my body as a heavy breath leaves my mouth. I turn around, my eyes glazed with emotion, finding Bobby eyeing the collar with anger.

"I'll make sure nothing ever hurts you again, Jessica," Bobby promises, pulling his arm back as far as he can and throwing the collar deep into the distance; it quickly merges into the darkness of the night.

Sirens suddenly catch my attention at the top of the hill, along with tires screeching to a halt.

"Oh, shit, what do we do?" I ask nervously, eyeing Bobby in fear.

"Freeze!" A cop screams, pointing a gun in our direction.

14
Bobby

"SHIT," I WHISPER.

The scrawny cop tripping down the hill I recognize as Skeeter. He's as dirty as they come. He used to be paid for his scum ways by the club, but he got greedy wanting more under the table than he deserved. When he didn't comply, he tried to blackmail us. So we flipped it around on him, making him look like a fucking fool to the police force. He has been out for us ever since.

"Jessica, this is all me," I mumble, causing her to turn and eye me with confusion. "Don't tell that cop a fucking thing except Grant kidnapped you. When I found you, he attacked me, and I reacted. That's it," I inform her.

If the hospital gets record of her killing someone whether it is self-defense or not, her career will be over. I watch her body tremble with fear, her dress and body covered in blood. Blood.

Shit, I don't have near enough on me to convince anyone I did this. I look up the large hill and see Skeeter and another cop trailing down it slowly, focusing on their steps rather than me.

I lean down and grab the crowbar, and slam it into Grant's lifeless body, causing blood to splatter all over my hands and clothes.

"Get on the ground, Bobby!" Skeeter yells, just feet away from me now. I run my hand up and down the crowbar quickly, trying to erase any prints Jessica might have left behind. "Get on the ground!" Skeeter repeats, pointing his gun and flashlight right in my face.

I hold my hands out as I slowly kneel, the crowbar still in my hand.

"You too, get on the ground," Skeeter shouts at Jessica. Jessica drops to the ground and puts her hands above her head. I smirk. Jessica looks good as an outlaw.

"Leave her alone," I encourage as I lower myself to the ground fully.

"Shut up!" Skeeter shrieks, kicking me hard in the shoulder, making me hiss.

"That was uncalled for, don't ya think?" I grumble, staring up at Skeeter who walks over to Jessica. Another cop finally makes it down the hill and strides to me, huffing and puffing out of breath.

"I called it in. More are on the way," the fat bastard wheezes.

"Yeah, okay. Thanks, Bow," Skeeter replies, eyeing Grant's body.

"He's got a weapon," Bow informs Skeeter.

Skeeter looks over at me and scowls. "Drop it to your side, Bobby. Don't try anything stupid or I'll shoot you where you're lying," Skeeter threatens, pointing his gun at me.

I slowly pull my arm out to my side and drop the crowbar to the ground.

Bow straddles me and zip ties my wrists together, panting the whole time.

"Do you have any other weapons on you?" Bow wheezes above me.

"No," I mumble, my chin resting on the damp ground.

I look over and see Skeeter grab Jessica's elbows lifting her off the ground. He slides his hands down her sides a little too slow for my liking.

"You got any weapons on you?" he questions in her ear, his eyes staring at me as he asks her. He knows what he is doing. He's trying to get a rise out of me.

"No," Jessica replies softly.

He leans down and slides his hands between her legs, going a little too far up, causing Jessica to flinch.

"Hey!" I holler, pulling against the fat cop holding me.

"Get off me," Jessica mumbles, pulling away from Skeeter. Skeeter frowns, his porn-stache twitching above his lips. He purposely grabs Jessica's arm where her injury is, making her cry in pain.

"You don't have the power here, sweetheart. I do," Skeeter grunts, licking his lips as he eyes her. He jolts her by the arm and pushes her forward, causing her to fall to the ground.

Jessica pulls herself onto her knees, trying to get up as Skeeter pushes his boot into her back forcing her back onto the ground. My nostrils flare with rage and my hands clench with the impulse to violently give Skeeter an ass whooping for mistreating my girl.

"You wouldn't be resisting arrest, would you?" Skeeter taunts her, causing me to snap.

I growl loudly as I pull away from the cop holding me. I rip my wrists in opposite directions, the zip ties cutting into my wrists until finally snapping. The cop behind me yells a warning to Skeeter as I stride toward him, my wrists burning from the cuts the zip ties left behind.

Skeeter looks up from staring at Jessica, a smirk turning into a sudden grimace. I pull my fist back and slam it into Skeeter's jaw, dropping him to the ground.

Jessica looks up, her blue eyes pinning me with praise as a smile creeps up her round cheeks.

Her face quickly frowns, her eyes widening. She reaches her arm out, her lips parting to speak. But before she can get a word out, there's a severe slam against my upper back. I turn and see two police officers raising their hands, banters gripped tightly in their palms. Bow thrashes it against the back of my knees, causing me to collapse. Within seconds, they fly on me, cuffing my wrists. Skeeter stands, holding his jaw. His eyes squint with anger, and he pulls out his nightstick. His eyes hooded with a violent promise that I am going to pay for my actions.

"No!" Jessica screams.

"Look away," I mouth to her, knowing this is going to be ugly. Jessica nods, tears flowing down her cheeks.

"It was worth it," I laugh as she turns her head, a chuckle escaping her sob.

Jessica

Two Weeks Later

"**BOBBY TOOK RESPONSIBILITY FOR EVERYTHING. HE TOLD THE**

cops he killed Grant in self-defense after finding Grant had taken Jessica against her will. Having Jessica as a witness, and the fact that Bobby's record goes to show he doesn't shy away from confrontation, the police didn't argue when arresting him. From what our lawyer says, Bobby is in deep shit for dislocating Skeeter's jaw, and in return Skeeter is trying to botch the self-defense plea against Grant, causing the authorities to second-guess the statement and Jessica's statement," Bull informs, smoking a cigarette.

"That means they will be going over the evidence with a fine-toothed comb," Hawk sputters from the back of the table, scratching the beard on his chin.

"Nah, Skeeter is a fucking moron. I'm sure he half-assed the evidence," Shadow encourages, making me feel a little hopeful.

I sigh, running my hands over my face. My bloodstream runs with inflamed rage at the thought of Bobby sitting in jail because of me. After the club's lawyer arrived at the police station and confirmed I was a victim in the whole charade, and further explained how I got blood on myself trying to break up Bobby attacking Grant, I was let go. But to be honest, after Bobby hit Skeeter, the police didn't question me much. They wanted Bobby to go down in flames for attacking one of their own. They don't really seem to care about my involvement.

"He's looking at doing some time, babe," Bull continues, looking right at me with grief in his eyes, his words making my heart sink.

"That fucker Skeeter is a weasel," Lip grunts, shaking his head.

"He baited Bobby," I inform. Reaching over, I swipe the cigarette out of Bull's fingers and take a large drag. Bull lifts an eyebrow at me shocked as I exhale.

"I'm stressed out," I remark, taking another puff. I have

been known to have a cig here and there, and have smoked the occasional joint with Bobby as well. I'm no saint.

"You get visitation with him?" Lip asks, flicking his lip ring with the tip of his tongue.

"Yeah, I am heading over there now before I have to pick Addie up," I add, putting the cigarette out in an ashtray. Bobby has been in county jail for two weeks and it's killing me. I can't wait to see him.

"Go see him. Give him our love, darlin'," Bull instructs, standing from his seat at the head of the table.

"Will do," I remark.

◆ ◆ ◆

I sit on a yellow plastic chair on one side of double-sided glass. The lighting is dim, and it smells like piss in here. The white paint on the walls is chipped revealing the gray cement and the floor is missing tiles. I can only imagine what it looks like where Bobby is held. I sigh and shake my head. This is all my fault. Bobby shouldn't be in here because of me. Travis and Grant were my problem, and now Bobby is suffering behind bars. I smirk, Bobby. My knight in shining armor.

A giant metal door buzzes on the other side of the glass and Bobby walks out. My body sparks and my breathing hitches as I see him. I watch Bobby shuffle to a matching yellow plastic chair on the other side of the Plexiglas. He's wearing a blue jump suit, his hands handcuffed in front of him. His blond hair is messier than usual, and he looks pale from the lack of sun.

"You got ten minutes, inmate," an officer sneers, walking past our booth.

Bobby lifts the phone, using both of his cuffed hands, and puts it to his ear. His forehead has a square patch of gauze concealing an injury, his eyebrow stitched with beady little black string snaking in and out of it. Those cops beat the shit out of him that night. I turned my head like he told me to, but I'll never get the sound those nightsticks made when they plowed into Bobby's body out of my head.

His face sparks with longing when he sees me, brightening his eyes. "Hey, babe," he greets, with that wolfish smirk of his.

"Hey," I whisper, pushing to the edge of my seat, wanting to be closer to him.

"How are you?" he asks, looking at me through the glass.

"All right I guess." I shrug.

He nods, biting his lip.

"You?" I ask, brushing my hair off my shoulder.

"Eh, jail hasn't changed. Shit food, good drugs," he laughs. Revealing two dimples that remind me just how much I miss him. It also reminds me of how much of a bitch I was when we were last together.

"I'm going to get you out of here," I inform, looking up from under my lashes.

Bobby smiles and nods, his eyes wrinkling on the sides as he focuses on me. "I know you will," he responds.

"Time's up," an officer remarks, standing behind Bobby.

"That wasn't ten minutes!" I yell through the glass at the fat cop. The cop smiles arrogantly, reaches over, and grabs the phone out of Bobby's hand, slamming it on the hook.

Bobby gives me a wink before standing. The guard pushes Bobby in the back making him walk, and the steel door buzzes before it opens and takes Bobby out of my sight.

I hang the phone up, slouching back in my chair and sigh. I don't know how to get Bobby out of here. I'm not a lawyer. I don't know a credible lawyer and I don't have those kinds of connections. My eyes widen at the thought. Connections. My parents. The only way Bobby is getting out of here is if I talk to my parents. The connections they have might work in Bobby's favor. The last door of my troubled past I'll have to pass through.

"Fuck," I grumble.

◆ ◆ ◆

I pull into the country club I usually meet my mother at and wait. I called her as soon as I got out from visiting Bobby yesterday, and asked her to meet me in the parking lot today. She of course was very concerned, considering we just met and shouldn't meet again until next month.

Fingers knock against the glass on my door, making me jump from my thoughts.

"Jessica, is everything okay?" my mother asks as I roll the window down.

"Get in," I demand, eyeing my frazzled mother. You can tell she jumped in her car and drove straight here. She has on sweat pants and jacket. No big poufy hair or gigantic hat you could see from afar.

She nods and walks around my Jeep.

"What is going on? Is Addie okay?" she questions before she even climbs into my Jeep.

"Yeah, she is fine," I reply, turning in my seat to face her.

"Have you heard anything from Travis's family?" I ask, resting my hands on my steering wheel.

"No, they don't talk to us since they backed out of the board of the hospital," she informs, shaking her head. I close my eyes and swallow. My tongue sticking to the roof of my mouth like sand paper. I'm not sure how much detail I should give her about what happened with Grant, but I need to disclose some information if I'm going to get any help.

"Grant came to see me," I finally spill, making her gasp in reaction.

"He suggested I had something to do with Travis's disappearance and wanted the money from the will I was to receive," I start. My mother turns in her seat, clutching her chest.

"He kidnapped me and threatened to kill me if I didn't give him the money," I pause, deliberating if I should tell her I killed him. Will she ever look at me the same if she knew I had another's soul staining my hands? "I did what I had to do," I whisper, not giving her the gritty details. She tilts her head to the side, clearly wanting me to explain, but I choose to ignore it. "Because of that, someone I care about is taking the wrap for me. He is looking at a long time in jail if I don't do something, Mom." My eyes fill with tears.

"He?" my mother asks, taking her hand down from her chest, and reaching over to grasp mine in comfort. I nod, wiping the tears that have escaped and splashed on my cheeks.

"Who is he, this sudden hero of yours?" my mother asks, her tone heartfelt. I laugh, thinking of Bobby as a hero. But when I think about it, he has been my hero since I met him.

"He has been there for me and Addie since day one. I have done everything in my power to keep him away though. Not ready for the idea of falling in love, depending on another and getting hurt more than I could possibly bear." I close my eyes just thinking of the wasted years, and I shake my head as I fiddle with my fingers nervously. "The way he lives his life, I'm not sure I can be what he needs me to be," I admit.

"You're not making any sense, Jessica. What do you mean his way of life?" my mother asks, her face twisted in confusion.

I laugh nervously. "He's a part of a motorcycle club," I

meekly respond.

My mother starts to laugh uncontrollably, her hand resting on her mouth as she tries to restrain her fit of giggles.

I raise an eyebrow at her. Her reaction disturbingly different to what I was expecting.

After she contains herself, she looks away from the window and looks at me, her face bright and cheery. "You poor thing. You take after your momma more than I thought," she mutters, smiling big.

"What do you mean?" I question with a shrug.

"Before I met your daddy, I was in love something bad with another man. A love you only see in the movies, and he happened to be a *biker*," my mother emphasizes the word biker. "He did some illegal things, and I would ride on the back of that sexy bike of his while he did it. His dad was a biker too, but didn't think Leo was quipped to be a biker, so Leo went out of his way to prove his dad that he was the man for the job." She closes her eyes and shakes her head like she's remembering it in vivid detail in her mind. "He had tattoos and long hair. He was almost too much to look at. Man we were wild," she laughs, opening her eyes.

"What happened?" I ask, shaking my head in confusion. Where is this mysterious biker guy?

"My dad, much like yours, didn't approve. Forbid me to see Leo again. When I didn't abide by his rules, we moved in the middle of the night and I never saw my love again," my mother says, her words grave as she remembers.

Mom whips her head in my direction, as if the thought of missing the man she fell in love with fluttered away. "I love your father. I do, but I loved Leo, too." She turns her head, her cheeks turning red. "Leo made me fall in love with him. He was relentless. Always chasing me, saying the most outrageous things," she continues, laughing. I smirk. He sounds just like Bobby.

She reaches over and grasps my hand, her bright eyes staring at me. "Don't fight it, Jessica. Don't fight your feelings if you truly care for this man of yours." She gives my hand a firm squeeze. I take a sudden breath and nod.

"Me and daddy will take care of this," she continues, letting go of my sweating hand.

"But dad..." I begin, knowing my dad will not want anything to do with Bobby if he saw the tattooed outlaw he is.

My mother scoffs.

"When you were with Travis, I was not the most attentive mother. I didn't know just how severe it was, Jessica. Your father told me to butt out, let it be, and I did. I have regretted that choice every day since you left. Your daddy just recently had a heart attack and is seeing things in a different light lately. He will do what I ask I am sure, but if he doesn't, I will be leaving him," she informs seriously. I remember when mom told me he had a heart attack; she said he was different. I didn't know he completely changed his outlook on life though.

"You are our daughter," she continues. "It's in our nature to fuck up along the line of parenting, but when we get the opportunity to correct our wrong doings, we should, and this is one of those times. With age comes wisdom," my mother adds, smiling.

Without thinking, I fling myself into her, hugging her. She tenses, hesitating before wrapping her hands around me. The woman before me has transformed into a mother I had never dared to imagine.

"You just said the word fuck," I laugh into her shoulder.

"You have to come to Thanksgiving though, and bring this biker hero, along with Addie," she whispers against my ear, completely ignoring my observation of her swearing, making me laugh.

"Mom, I don't know," I start, knowing there are so many bad memories in Nevada, and the idea of my dad meeting Bobby is already making my palms sweat.

"Baby, from what I understand, there is nothing left in Nevada that can hurt you," she laughs. I shrug and give a crooked smile, not confirming or denying that notion.

"Yeah, but dad—"

"Despite your father's actions, Jessica, he misses you and Addie. He will come around if he wants his daughter back in his life," she interrupts, her lips pursed with determination.

"All right, we'll come," I say, exasperated.

15

Jessica

IT'S BEEN TWO DAYS SINCE I SAW MY MOTHER, AND I'M GROWING
more and more anxious by the hour. She assured me these
things take time and that there were plans in the works for
getting Bobby out of jail.

"Did you brush your teeth?" I ask Addie who walks to her
room from the bathroom, getting ready for bed.

"Yup, love you, Mom," she yells, shutting her bedroom door.

"Love you, too," I mumble, knowing she can't hear me.

I sit up, looking over the now clean apartment. I'm so
thankful that some of the guys from the club helped clean it up
after Grant trashed it. I head into my room and flop on my bed.
Glancing toward my closet, I spot the repacked shoebox. My
eyes furrow inward. That box needs to go. There is no reason
to suffer in a turmoil of fear anymore. Decision made, one
which has my heart leaping into my chest, I stand, snatching
the box from the shelf. I check on Addie in her room, finding
her snuggled in bed and already dozing off. I shut the door and

head to the kitchen drawer. After grabbing a lighter out of one of the drawers, I make my way to the front door.

I run down the stairs and out the back lobby door to the community grill. I throw the shoebox on the charred rack and set it alight. I watch it burn. The smell of freedom and the sound of my fears crackle as the flame claims the entire box. Not many people would understand why I kept this box. Why I would keep something I was trying to move on from. To me it was simple. It fed my fear. Every day I saw it, it reminded me why I needed to tread lightly, make careful decisions that would protect Addie and me. It was a daily reminder that being lonely wasn't such a bad thing considering how much pain I was in before. Only in the last few weeks, I realized I lived in more fear trying to make sure I never relived what I had been through, than the fear I had endured when I was living that nightmare.

Safe, protected, secure. These are words, but nothing more. Their meaning a cloak of reality. It's impossible to be fully in control of your well-being. Life reminds us we're human; we just often choose to ignore it. I'm trying to survive this fucked-up world, and I finally refuse to sit back and allow the savage beast of fear to dictate my life.

When I killed Grant, a burden of fear that divided me from Bobby was finally obliterated. Maybe it was the near-death experience, Bobby telling me he loved me, or maybe it was when Bobby took that collar off me and threw it into the devouring darkness. Whatever it was, all I know is I am in love with Bobby, and of course, it hurts. It hurts to come to terms with the notion, and not have him here with me to tell him over and over again.

After the box is nothing but ash and a couple of charred rings, I turn and run back inside. Leaving my past to dwindle in the summer breeze.

◆ ◆ ◆

I sit at the club waiting for Bull to tell us the fate of Bobby's future. My mother called this morning and said she spoke to as many people as she could in their circle. They had caught a break. Apparently, my dad actually pulled a bullet out of the chief of police in Nevada two months ago and is repaying the favor to my father by contacting the chief of police here, who will pull some strings for Bobby. Several hours later, Bull called with the verdict from the lawyer.

Bull scratches his head of dark hair, before resting his arms on the table sighing heavily. His hesitance makes me nervous.

"Bobby is getting off with self-defense with Grant, but due to his history and assaulting Skeeter, he is serving three months in jail, then released on probation after that," Bull informs the table. "He's lucky, someone is looking out for him; that's for sure," Bull adds, looking directly at me.

"Lucky fucker," Lip clips, smiling. I laugh, grateful it's months and not years in jail. I can do three months. I can't do three years. I'd go insane missing him, and knowing he was behind bars because of me would kill me.

The guys start hooting and hollering over the news as I get up, and walk out of the room. I smile and laugh, relieved Bobby will be out soon.

Bright, hot sun beats down at me when I leave the club-house; sweat beads and trickles down my back. A familiar motor roaring draws my attention across the courtyard.

Bobby's blue truck pulls into the parking lot, the loud motor vibrating off the club as Shadow drives it into the garage, turning the engine off. He climbs out at the same time Dani is getting out of the passenger side.

"It's nice, but I like your mustang better, babe," Dani flatters Shadow, rounding the back of the truck.

"Hey, Doc," Shadow greets, sliding his hand along the bed of Bobby's truck.

"Hey," I reply, eyeing Bobby's truck. The last time I saw it was when it was wrapped up in caution tape at the crime scene.

"It was released from evidence this morning," Shadow answers my unasked question. I walk around him and open the truck door, the smell of Bobby greeting me. I see Bobby's cut sitting on the seat, and I reach over and grab it, lifting it to my face. But it doesn't smell like Bobby; it smells of fresh leather. I unfold the cut and notice the back of it says Property of Bobby. I gasp and eye it. Was this meant for me?

"He was going to ask you to be his ol' lady," Dani says, now standing beside me.

I look at her, her green eyes vibrant with excitement, before looking back at the cut.

"It's a privilege, ya know. Taking that cut makes you our family, and we do anything for family," she smiles, trailing her finger along the patches stitched into the leather.

"But if you take that cut, you are Bobby's. Don't put that jacket on, Doc, if you're second-guessing that," Shadow instructs, his tone serious. I look at Dani to see if he is joking.

She nods at his words. "True, but I'm pretty sure you're already Bobby's anyway. You're just not wearing the property patch yet," she smiles, making me laugh. She's right. I was Bobby's the day he laid eyes on me. He even said that himself. Whether I wear this cut or not, it wouldn't stop him from claiming me as his. It would just make him happy to show his world I'm his woman.

Bobby

I GET OUT IN A MONTH. I HAVE BEEN COUNTING THE DAY LEADING up to three fucking months. Jessica's visited a couple of times, and I've received letters that smell of her, but it's not enough. I've jacked off so many times since being in here; I don't remember what a real pussy feels like anymore.

"Is that a fight?" Yuki asks, walking up to the gilded bars that contain us like we're animals. Yuki is a short fucker, with tattoos snaking up his neck. He hasn't been half bad as a cellmate.

We watch Geo and Sandler wrestle in their cell across from us. They're always arguing, bitching at each other. It can be good entertainment, but it's fucking annoying in the middle of the night. That is what we do for a majority of our time in here: watch others fuck up and fight over petty crap. So far, I haven't had any run-ins with anyone, but that's because I'm in the county jail and not prison. Most of the people who would want to fuck with me are in prison, not in county.

Sandler lands on his back when Geo flips him over. Giving Geo the advantage, he climbs on Sandler and punches him hard in the face. Both Yuki and I both wince with that one.

"Bet?" Yuki suggests. You want things in here, the best way to get them is by winning bets. That's how the trade of the world is in here. I've scored a lot of shit winning bets. I should go to Vegas when I get out; try my luck with actual cash instead of cigarette, playboy, and pills.

I eye Geo, deliberating his pros and cons. He's huge, like a sumo wrestler, his fat making him strong, but his large size makes him slow. Sandler is tall and skinny, making him an easy target, but he has muscle in his arms, and he's quick. If he's quick enough, he could win easily.

"Yeah, I got two packs of cigs that Sandler wins," I bet.

"Oh, dumb move, brother," Yuki laughs, clearly happy with gambling on Geo.

Sandler wraps his arms around Geo and pulls him downward, wrapping his legs around Geo's upper body. Geo stands up, slamming into the back of the wall and falling on his back, giving Sandler his opportunity. Sandler grabs Geo by his head and bashes it into the concrete floor, causing Geo to go limp.

"Pay up, bitch," I remark arrogantly, holding my hand out for payment.

"Fuck, I didn't see that coming," Yuki mutters, shaking his head.

"Break it up!" a guard yells, banging his nightstick against the bars.

"Fucking pigs," Yuki curses, turning back to his bunk.

"Four more weeks," I grumble, pushing away from the steel bars.

Jessica

I LAY ON MY SURFBOARD AND STARE UP AT THE BRIGHT BLUE sky, the sun casting heat on my sweaty body as the waves slowly take me back to shore. One more week and Bobby will be home. Hell, I feel like I'm in prison too. All I want is to touch the scruff on his face, run my hands through his blond hair, and hear the nonsense from his cocky mouth. Never having Bobby not there for me before is hard. It was easier to walk away from him before as I knew he would always be there when I needed him. Having him in jail, however, and away from me 24/7 is torture. I'm going insane.

To admit I have given love a second chance, to put myself out there deliberately, knowing fate could terminate my scarred barrier of strength, causes me to take a sudden breath, shock riddling through my core. I don't know if I'm stupid to allow myself to become so vulnerable, or if I'm simply along for the ride. My impending future now out of my control.

In the last three months, I have accepted the club as family and taken Addie to meet everyone. I can still see Bull and Shadow's stunned face when I pulled up to the club, Addie riding with me in my Jeep.

"Bull, Shadow, this is Addie, my daughter," I explained, *running my hand down Addie's long blonde hair.*

Bull's eyes were so wide, his eyebrows nearly met his hairline. Shadow just stared at her with his mouth apart in awe. They were both shocked I had brought Addie to them. I thought I was protecting her, keeping our distance, but really I was keeping a family that would go to the end of the earth for her, at arm's length because of my own selfish fears.

"Nice to meet you," Addie said sweetly, holding her hand out to shake. Her white sundress flapped in the wind as she looked up at the two burly men.

"Well, hello there, darlin'," Bull greeted, shaking her hand. He squatted down, getting eye level with Addie and beamed one of the most sincere smiles I have seen on Bull.

"Hi," Shadow responded, shaking Addie's hand. His face was tense, looking between Addie and me like he couldn't believe I'd actually brought Addie to the club.

"My have you grown," Bull muttered, eyeing Addie intently. Addie smiled and swayed back and forth as both Shadow and Bull stared at her.

A wave pushes me with force, forcing me to open my eyes from the memory and cling to the sides of my board.

I was surprised with Addie's confidence when she met Bull and Shadow. I thought she would be nervous meeting a bunch of rugged bikers, but actually, Bull and Shadow seemed more nervous than she did.

Every one of the ol' ladies took to Addie quickly, going on and on about how much she looked like me, and if I'm not mistaken, I think Dani's son, Zane, already has a crush on her. Thank goodness, their age gap will never let that go any further than a crush. Dani encouraged me to bring Addie by her dance studio for ballet, and of course, Addie was more than willing to take her up on that offer.

I sit up on my board lazily and see I'm only feet from the shore. Members of the club are standing around and talking, some of them around the grill cooking and laughing. This is the first get together I brought Addie to, and so far she seems to be loving it.

Wading out of the water, I tuck my board under my arm, and head along the beach to the group.

"I can give you something to ride, hot momma." I look over my shoulder and spot a pack of guys with their surfboards staring at me hungrily. Their bodies are tanned beyond healthy, and their hair is bleached from the sun and ocean.

"Keep talking and your mother is going to be riding to your funeral," I sass, shifting my board under my arm, glaring at them. They stop laughing, looking at me as if I've clearly lost my mind. To be honest, I have. Waiting for Bobby to get out has been torture all on its own.

"You heard her. Now get steppin'," Lip orders, throwing his tattooed arm around my neck.

The bunch of surfers grumble under their breath and head

for the parking lot.

"I think I had that covered," I laugh.

"Yeah, I know you did. I just wanted to make sure you didn't go nuts. Bobby has told me you can be crazy," Lip informs seriously.

"He said that?" I question, pulling back and trying to act offended. But I can't mask the smile creeping on my face; it sounds just like something Bobby would say about me.

Lip laughs, and runs his hand up his chest. His pierced nipple catching my eye. Damn that looks like it hurt; it's making my nipple ache just by looking at it, and not in a good way.

"I think Dani said dinner is ready. If you want to scoop up Addie and Zane from their intense sandcastle building and then grab a plate," he informs, tugging on my neck with the crook of his arm.

I walk over to Cherry, Zane, and Addie, all building a huge sandcastle. Cherry is wearing a skimpy yellow bikini and is covered in sand from head to toe. Addie and Zane don't look much better with all the sand that is covering them as well.

Crap. That sand is going to be a nightmare to get out of Addie's hair.

"Hey, let's go grab something to eat and take a break," I suggest, holding my hand out to Addie.

"Oh, come on, Mom, we're almost done," Addie whines, filling a bucket with sand.

Zane stands up from sitting on his knees and points at me, "No, no!" he yells, making me laugh.

"Seriously, five more minutes. This is the sandcastle of all sandcastles," Cherry begs, a green bucket in her hand filled with sand. I can't help but giggle at her desperate plea to play in the sand with the kids. It reminds me of something Bobby would do.

"Jesus, Cherry, really?" Lip laughs, shaking his head.

"Hey, this is kick-ass, buddy," Cherry says seriously, scratching a circle around the castle with both of her hands, imitating a moat.

"You sure you don't want to run, Doc, because now's your chance," Lip laughs, crossing his arms, a toothpick sticking out of his mouth.

"You're a good girl, now, but you stick around, who knows what you'll become," he continues, eyeing Cherry.

I smirk, grabbing the toothpick out of his mouth.

"I wasn't that much of a good girl to begin with anyway," I respond, sticking the toothpick at the very top of the castle.

"Oh man, that was the perfect touch, Doc!" Cherry yells, standing up to eye the tooth pick.

"I don't even know what to say," Lip laughs, walking the other way.

Bobby

"YOU'RE GETTING OUT TODAY, BROTHER," YUKI OBSERVES, looking at the calendar on the wall.

"Yep," I reply.

"You guys get some yard time. Let's go!" a guard hollers, his voice echoing throughout the cell. I lower my feet from the sink, and pull myself up from reclining on the bottom bunk.

The guard eyes me as I walk past him.

Yuki hands me a cig and I take it; tapping it against my palm.

"What will you not miss the most about jail?" Yuki asks, scratching the back of his neck, making small talk.

"No more shitty food, and no more yard work," I laugh, placing a cigarette between my teeth to light.

"Five more months and I'm out," Yuki replies, leaning up against the fence. Yuki got caught dealing drugs, landing him in here. His dumbass sold weed right to an undercover cop. Lucky for him, it's his first offense and he's got a hell of a lawyer.

"So what are you going to do when you get out?" Yuki asks, interlocking his fingers into the fence and looking out.

"Fuck my girl," I reply quickly, making Yuki laugh. That is the one thing I miss for sure, sex. Over the last three months, I have wondered if Jessica reverted to her fears and old ways, and has run home locking herself behind closed doors. Sure, I have letters and talk to her on the phone here and there, but that don't mean shit. Time apart changes people. I have seen enough inmates raging through the jailhouse 'cause their wife or girlfriend got tired of waiting for them and fucked the neighbor, or family talked them into finding a better man.

After seeing it daily in here the last three months, I can admit; I'm fucking nervous.

"What are you going to do when you get out?" I ask, taking a drag of my cigarette.

"Back to dealing," he mutters, exasperated.

"Seriously?" I question. Why the fuck would he do that? He's not a top-notch dealer. He's not in a gang or brotherhood so I'm confused why he would go back to slinging shitty drugs just to land up back in here.

"Money is too good to walk away from," he responds, shrugging. "My mother is in a nursing home, my wife is diabetic. Those bills don't pay themselves, man," Yuki continues.

"Bobby, let's go," Officer Smith yells from the door.

"That's me," I mumble, exhaling smoke.

I give Yuki a slap on the back and hand him my half-smoked cigarette.

"See you on the other side, man," Yuki smiles, giving my back a slap.

I head toward the locked door that leads me out of this hellhole, passing pissed-off guards along the way. Impatiently, I lean against the door waiting for one of them to unlock it.

I get my civilian clothes back, along with my leather cut. I instantly shrug it on, the feeling of its worn leather comforting on my back.

"See you soon, Bobby," Officer Smith mutters, knowing I'll be back. I probably will.

"Keep my bunk warm," I reply, walking toward the locked door.

It buzzes and I push it open. Closing my eyes, I inhale the satisfying smell of freedom, so much sweeter on this side of the fence, and the sun hotter from this side of the jailhouse.

"Bobby!" My eyes jump open. Waiting for me is my crew, who are all sitting at the end of the parking lot. Motorcycles, from one end to the other, and my blue Chevy parked beside them all. I smile and jog toward them, ready to get the fuck away from here as quickly as I can. The truck door opens and Jessica flies out, running toward me. Spotting her, I run faster.

She plows into me, her lips smashing onto mine aggressively. I grab her by the hips and pick her up, and her legs wrap around my waist. My hands clenching her back, pulling her closer to me. The smell of her, the feel of her, fucking pure bliss. I grasp her back harder and feel leather under my palms. I pull back, and look her over, noticing she's wearing a leather cut.

"You're wearing my property patch," I whisper in disbelief.

"I am," she responds, smiling. I smirk, and narrow my eyebrows at her.

"You know that means you're mine. Forever now," I growl, leaning in and nipping her bottom lip.

"Yeah, I think I was yours from the beginning," she laughs.

"Yeah, you were," I agree. "I need five minutes alone with you, wearing nothing but this," I whisper to Jessica, the idea of her in nothing but a leather cut hardens my dick painfully.

"Just five minutes?" she asks, tilting her head to the side.

"What can I say? I've been locked up, baby. Five minutes is over achieving."

Epilogue

Jessica

I SIT AT THE BAR WATCHING **ADDIE PLAY WITH ZANE.**
"He is such a ladies' man," Shadow remarks, handing me a beer. I laugh, seeing Zane blush as he laughs at Addie's silly faces.

"Just like his Uncle Bobby," Bobby insists, stretching his arms above his head nonchalantly, making his shirt ride up revealing his tattooed abs.

"Yeah, something like that," Shadow chuckles, lifting his beer to his lips.

I walk in the kitchen to get a plate of food for Addie, before all the burley men eat it all.

"Your daughter is beautiful," Cherry compliments, cutting up meat from behind the kitchen counter. She has her strawberry-colored hair pulled up into a sloppy ponytail, and is wearing a green shiny top I can just barely see over the counter.

"Thank you," I reply, taking a paper plate off the counter. "Do you need any help in here?" I ask, watching her manhandle a slab of meat with a butcher knife.

"Oh, no, I got it," she replies, looking up at me with a big smile.

"Addie can be a handful, but I suppose most kids are," I state, digging some fruit from a bowl.

"Don't I know it," Cherry laughs, wiping her forehead with the back of her hand.

"You have any kids?" I ask, grabbing some chips from a bag.

"Uh," she begins nervously, her cheeks flushing a bright red. Cherry looks up at me her eyes widening and her face in a sudden panic. "Would Addie like some ice cream? Dani bought a whole bunch of ice cream, and if the kids don't eat it, Shadow will." She turns to open the freezer door quickly to avoid my question.

Plucking out a giant tub of chocolate ice cream, she drops it on the counter. She looks at me and smiles, making me question if there was a sense of panic before or if I imagined it.

I nod, not taking my eyes off her, curious what made her react the way she did. Like she didn't even realize what she had said or something.

I take a plate to Addie and Zane, and sit on a stool watching Lip, Bobby, and Shadow laughing about something.

Bobby looks up, his eyes holding mine. He smiles, pats Shadow on the back, and walks toward me. Once before me, he grasps me by the hips and draws me in close, his mouth tickling the shell of my ear.

"I wanna fuck you," he whispers, making my panties instantly dampen.

I bite my bottom lip and eye Addie and Zane making food art.

"She's fine," he mutters, pushing me backwards. My head falls back and I laugh hysterically while I'm herded down the hall.

I turn around and seize him by the shirt, dragging him along until I reach his room. I kick the door open and pull us both in.

Bobby slams the door shut and grasps me by the ass cheeks, lifting me up. He presses his lips to mine, taking my mouth forcefully. Our bodies tangled in an embrace slam against the door before we stumble onto the dresser, knocking everything on top of it onto the floor. My legs tremble with anticipation, a fire spreading wildly in between them.

I clutch the hem of my shirt and lift it, my leather cut falling to the floor with it. Wasting no time, Bobby dashes his head forward, kissing along my chest, his hands squeezing my breasts possessively hard.

I moan as his hands dart around my back undoing my silky bra. The sound escaping my mouth sounds more animalistic than human. The silk falls from my breasts, releasing the weight of them.

He slides his rough hands up my thighs, across my abdomen, over the peaks of my breast, and along my arms, pinning them above my head. He scrapes his teeth along the bud of my nipple, creating a spark to come alive, which plasters my skin with goose bumps. He sucks my nipple into his mouth, his tongue swirling around it, before slowly releasing the wet nub. I fall into the moment and the sensations he's giving me, silently pleading for him to take me already.

He pulls back, releasing my arms, and removes his shirt, revealing his chest outlined perfectly with muscle. I can't help but run my hands over his pecs, before scratching my nails down over his abs causing him to hiss. My hands fondle the button on his jeans while his hands undo my shorts.

As soon as his pants are free, I shove them down his toned thighs, using my feet to kick his boxers the rest of the way. He yanks my pants down to my ankles and softly pulls my panties down my hips.

He slides his fingers between my legs and inside my sensitive heat. Desire ignites inside me at his touch. My head falls back from the overwhelming connection. I place my feet on the edge of the dresser and widen my legs, encouraging him to go deeper.

"Someone's excited," Bobby pants, spreading my wetness around my clit. I clench my teeth and nod as the sensual feeling of pleasure builds around his dexterous hand.

Bobby places both of his hands on my knees and stills, drawing my eyes to his. He smiles at me, before lowering his head between my thighs. My body trembles as Bobby flicks his tongue against my clit, his fingers teasing my opening.

"Oh, my God," I pant, lost in the moment.

Bobby sucks my clit into his mouth as his fingers slowly enter me. My pussy grips around his fingers, chasing that realm of pleasure I so desperately need.

A blossoming warmth spreads in my lower half, causing my toes to curl around the edge of the dresser. Just as I think I can't take anymore, stars burst behind my eyelids. Bobby's warm tongue lowers, licking me, nibbling, and taking my climax hungrily.

Bobby lifts from between my legs, his mouth glistening, and grabs me by the hips, pulling my ass to the edge of the dresser. My body still coming down from my climax, all I can do is comply in a daze.

In one swift move, he impales me with his length, my body

panting in response. His blue vivid eyes pin me. Silently speaking to me as he places his hand on my back and lifts me, turning me until my back slams against the wall. My arms wrap around his neck as he holds one of my legs, pulling them upward to where it's resting on his shoulders, while the other leg wraps around his waist tightly.

He thrusts his hips forward making me whimper from the depth his dick is taking.

"Oh, fuck yeah," Bobby mutters, closing his eyes.

He pistons his hips. The curve of his dick hitting me is heavenly. I run my hand through his hair, glancing at the strands that are sticking to his forehead from the beads of sweat formed. His eyes flutter open, holding me as he fucks me against the wall. His mouth parts and his forehead creases. His hold on my hips strengthens, and his pace becomes erratic with need. His dick pulses, warning me he is about to come.

"Bobby," I pant, and with that Bobby closes his eyes tightly and comes. Grunting along the side of my neck, and the sensation of him gripping onto me like I'm his next breath sends me falling over the edge seconds later. Pleasure driving up my legs and igniting in my core is too much to contain. I don't hold back the loud moan which escapes as my body's still wrapped around his tightly.

Bobby holds us in the same position and walks us to the bed, before falling on top of me.

Basking in the afterglow of our vigorous fuck, I will myself to move, not really wanting to. I'm more than content to stay in Bobby's arms. "I need to check on Addie," I mutter, pulling myself up from the bed.

"Zane really seems to like her," Bobby laughs.

"They have pretty much been inseparable the last three months," I tell him, grabbing my clothes off the floor and dressing.

"Hmm," Bobby responds, standing up, and finding his boxers to get dressed.

I walk out of the room, Bobby right beside me as we make our way back into the common area. Bobby leans over and kisses me passionately, before smacking my ass, and making his way back to the boys.

I take my seat in a metal chair and watch Bobby in his element around the other guys, while Addie and Zane play.

I know I have come a long way, but I also know I still have a ways to go. I have overcome my fear for the most part, and have learned to replace my painful memories.

I await the day Bobby can handcuff me to the bed, make me his, and give him that control. I loved being spanked and just losing control. That was before Travis took it to another level, scaring that realm of ecstasy for me. I would love to get back to that place again with Bobby. It will happen. I know it will eventually. It will just take time.

I turn and look at Addie, her care, and ease with Zane as he tries to tickle her. I bet Bobby would have beautiful babies. My eyes widen, surprised at the thought.

"Hey, babe, is it all right if I take Addie for a ride?" Bobby whispers into my ear from behind, making me jump.

"Uh," I hesitate. Trying to gather my thoughts from sex, babies, to Addie riding on a motorcycle.

"What were you just thinking?" he asks, brushing a hair behind my ear.

"Nothing," I answer quickly. "I don't know if Addie is ready for that," I reply nervously. I don't know if *I'm* ready for her to ride on a motorcycle.

"Mom, can I go for a ride on a motorcycle? Zane is going," Addie yells, running toward me.

"Yeah, she looks pretty nervous," Bobby remarks, laughing.

I roll my eyes, and laugh. "You go slowly, Bobby!" I demand, pointing my finger in his face.

"I will. I will," he chants, taking Addie's hand and striding toward the door.

"With my eyes closed the whole time," he jokes, making my heart sink with fear.

"Bobby!" I yell, standing up and following him outside. He stops suddenly, and rushes toward me, cupping both of my cheeks in his hands.

"Trust me, Hummingbird." I glare at him for using that nickname in public. He smiles knowingly and gives my lips a quick peck before pulling away.

I groan, and watch him walk away holding Addie's hand.

"I thought Lip was a handful. Girl, you're in for a wild ride with that one," Cherry laughs, walking up beside me.

I groan and shake my head. "Don't I know it," I mutter.

I watch Bobby put a helmet on Addie, and the way he shows so much care around her is enough to make any woman swoon. He straddles his motorcycle, helping her on behind him. Addie hugs his stomach, her face beaming with joy. Addie looks over and spots me, smiling on the spot and waves.

Bobby grabs his handlebars, kicks his bike off its kickstand, and looks toward me. His eyes catch mine as he smirks and he gives me a drop-dead sexy wink.

"You ain't living unless you're riding, right?" I ask, looking at Cherry. Something I have heard the guys say before. It never really made since before, but it does now.

She laughs and nods. "Right."

The future is unclear for Bobby and I, and God knows the next chapter for us is one that will be full of hardships and reasoning. But I don't care because we'll survive. We've faced the biggest fear that plagued us as a couple; the fear of falling. Nothing can stop us now.

The End-ish

THE DEVIL'S DUST #4

coming 2015

ACKNOWLEDGEMENTS

This book was so fun to write; probably one of my favorites. It was like having sex. It was so exhilarating while writing it, but now I feel I'm ready to hibernate for a couple of months to recharge.

The process of this book could not have reached the point of publishing without the help of my friends though. They helped me mold it, and smooth out edges to make it perfect.

I want to thank the readers first. This book would have never happened without you to begin with. The love you have for the Devil's Dust, and the support you have shown me is breathtaking.

I want to say a BIG THANK YOU to my beta readers. Every one of you have helped me so much in getting Bobby and Jessica to their perfection. Nisha, Keisha, Brie, Bel, Stephanie, and Amy. (Bel, you pushed me to the point I thought I would break, and I love you for it!)

My street team, I adore you guys. You've supported me every day since day one. My Readers Addict Group, thank you as well for the support in my work.

I have had so many blogs help me in the process of not just this book but all of my books. I want to thank you all so much. What you do takes a lot of time out of your daily lives and I appreciate the time you take out for my work.

Big thank you to Love Between The Sheets Blog for the cover reveal, it was amazing.

I can't thank Rock Stars Of Romance enough for hosting the

blitz and tour for The Fear That Divides Us. You were very patient with me and brilliant at what you do.

My author friends who have also helped me along the way, I fucking love you!

And of course my family, you are my backbone in this whole thing!

ALSO BY M.N. FORGY

What Doesn't Destroy Us
(The Devil's Dust #1)

The Scars That Define Us
(The Devil's Dust #2)

The Broken Pieces Of Us
(A Devil's Dust Novella)

The Fear That Divides Us
(The Devil's Dust #3)

Love That Defies Us
(A Devil's Dust Novella)

ABOUT THE AUTHOR

M.N. Forgy was raised in Missouri where she still lives with her family. She's a soccer mom by day and a saucy writer by night.

M.N. Forgy started writing at a young age but never took it seriously until years later, as a stay-at-home mom, she opened her laptop and started writing again. As a role model for her children, she felt she couldn't live with the "what if" anymore and finally took a chance on her character's story.

So, with her glass of wine in hand and a stray Barbie sharing her seat, she continues to create and please her fans.

STALK HER

Website:
www.mnforgy.com

Goodreads:
www.goodreads.com/author/show/8110729.M_N_Forgy

Facebook:
www.facebook.com/pages/M-N-Forgy/625362330873655

Twitter:
twitter.com/M_N_FORGY

Newsletter:
mnforgy.com/newsletter/

M.N. Forgy's Reader Addicts Group:
https://www.facebook.com/groups/480379925434507/